TWO SEEING EYE® DOGS TAKE MANHATTAN !

...a love story

by Lloyd Burlingame

Library of Congress Control Number: 2012908614

Publisher:
Guide Dog Adventures
New York, New York

Printed by:
CreateSpace LLC
Charleston, South Carolina

Burlingame, Lloyd
  Two Seeing Eye Dogs Take Manhattan! ...a love story

ISBN: 1-4774-4602-8

For Evan Rhodes,
the ever-generous, dog-loving
Prince of Minetta Lane

TWO SEEING EYE DOGS
TAKE MANHATTAN!
...a love story

Contents

PART III:
Kemp at Work and Hickory at Play: Viennas, Here We Come!
November 2006-November 2007

INTRODUCTION by Tony Walton

The pages that you are lucky enough to have in your hands (unless you happen to be using an e-reader) are, essentially, an entertaining love story about—and by—two remarkable Seeing Eye dogs, Hickory and Kemp, who mysteriously but triumphantly bring a happy ending to the catastrophically interrupted life of a remarkably gifted friend of mine.

In the fall of 1957, Lloyd Burlingame and I met at the offices of the stage designers union in New York, after passing their eye-wateringly stringent exam. Not long after, we each raised our right hands and, in the presence of union officials, swore "to be good brothers."

We were both passionately in the thrall of the theatre—"theatre critters" determined to somehow join the ranks of the very small and very tight circle of Broadway designers then shining brightly on the Great White Way.

Amazingly, that dream came true for both of us at almost the same time, and Lloyd, in a kind of designer's euphoria, spread his work in sets, costumes, and/or lighting design over a wide range of successful—even triumphant—productions on Broadway and in his beloved world of the Opera. He had fallen under the spell of Mozart at a very early age, and that inflamed passion carried him to what must have been the fulfillment of his most romantic dreams: the invitation to design a flock of masterpieces by the magical Amadeus.

Lloyd's hectic journey as an "officially approved" designer took him from Arlington, Virginia, to a Fulbright scholarship for study at La Scala, Milan. En route he delivered innumerable designs, in each of his three disciplines, at Carnegie Tech (now Carnegie Mellon University), the Arena Stage, and the Pittsburgh Playhouse. In the thick of all this, Lloyd—like myself—was invited to take a compulsory two-year "side-step" into the armed forces -- he into the Signal Corps, me into the Royal Air Force (mostly training in Canada as one of the more cheerfully inept pilots ever granted "wings").

By 1959, we were both busy Off-Broadway—Lloyd achieving his first favorable notice in the *New York Times*, for his designs for Jerome Kern's *Leave It to Jane*, which achieved a two-year run and brought much pleasure to many, myself included. My own overlapping Off-Broadway adventures were varied and fun, but none enjoyed a run like that hit of Lloyd's.

By the beginning of the '60s we had both realized our dreams of becoming Broadway designers. Lloyd with Lionel Bart's musical *Lock Up Your Daughters* and I with a one-night-stand (alas): *Once There was a Russian,* by acclaimed American playwright Sam Spewack. A decade later, my friend, too, experienced the vagaries of this world we shared, during the dementia of launching *Via Galactica.* Helmed by the ever-courageous Peter Hall, this became one of Broadway's mightier calamities—though Lloyd's interstellar design won him the appellation "lighting wizard" (courtesy of the *Washington Post*).

For another British Peter—that towering genius Peter Brook—Lloyd designed the brilliant lighting for the blinding-white, circus-themed *Midsummer Night's Dream. Live Design* magazine just rated this never-to-be-forgotten production FIRST among the "10 most memorable Broadway designs of the last 40 years"; the *New York Times* called it "the Shakespeare Production of the Century."

High on Lloyd's list of other favorites, he counts the young Brian Friel's triumphant arrival on Broadway with *Philadelphia, Here I Come!* Lloyd designed its scenery, costumes, and lighting, providing an ideally unified design for this tender, bitter-sweet comedy. This was the first of thirteen shows that he succeeded—unmatchably—in designing for the legendary "Devil of Broadway," David Merrick. Lloyd, remarkably, maintained an excellent relationship with this devil throughout all their adventures, and even lived to cheerfully "tell the tales."

I only worked for this satanic individual twice before sidling off into less-hellish employment, but Lloyd—as superb a diplomat as he was a designer—emerged unscathed. Another remarkable triumph he shared with Merrick and Peter Brook was Brook's stunningly original production of Peter Weiss's *Marat/Sade*.

At the pinnacle of his design career, in the '70s, NYU's (now Tisch) School of the Arts invited Lloyd to renew, restructure, and lead their Design Department. He accepted the position and in merely a year began revolutionizing their inert program, bringing in such teaching masters as his close friend the revered Oliver Smith— designer of such triumphant trifles as *My Fair Lady*, *West Side Story,* and *Hello, Dolly!*

Amazingly, in four short years the department built such a favorable national reputation that the great Jo Mielziner (Lloyd's first Broadway employer) declared it to be "the best design school in the country." For twenty-six years, Tisch—and its international reputation—continued to grow.

By this time Lloyd's standing, both at NYU and on Broadway, was such that I was entirely flabbergasted—and emotionally devastated—to learn that, at the peak of his powers, Lloyd had—with nearly no warning—been declared "legally blind." What worse catastrophe could befall a visual artist—and especially one in whose care were many oncoming generations of stage, TV, and film designers. I could conceive of only a total meltdown, had such a calamity befallen me or any other of our colleagues whose life's work depended on their sight. Lloyd must have had days when he came close to something similar; he certainly suffered a period of creative denial. But he pushed on. (I've personally seen such staggering fortitude equaled only once, by my "childhood sweetheart" Julie Andrews, when an inept medical procedure destroyed—heartbreakingly—her irreplaceable singing voice.) Heroically, Lloyd began to reinvent himself.

I am unable to fathom the depths of despair that my colleague and friend must have felt. As fate would have it, I was either in California or overseas on film work during Lloyd's discovery of this nightmare. So it was a while before I learned of his remarkable stoicism: With a powerful determination, he had embraced the new technological miracles that made it possible for him to re-educate himself in reading and writing. For a time, he stretched the last vestiges of his usable vision to create—on an ever-increasingly large scale—

such works of art as giant fabric collages, until, at last, he finally lost the ability to "make visual" the imagery of his dreams.

Lloyd's protean design career was over, his treasured role as teacher of design gradually turned over to his carefully chosen colleagues. Still, given his ability to deal with people, his organizational and administrative skills, and the support of his dean, he retained his position as Chair. Until his retirement age, the university gained from his continuing contributions as leader of the Design Department.

But neither a design career nor the actual teaching of design is a "job"; they are callings. To lose both was a blow of devastating proportions. And yet one more inescapable predicament remained: his adaptation to the mobility issue. Solving this led indirectly to writing this book. Following a walk during which—white cane in hand—he was cruelly directed into a thick stream of oncoming traffic, Lloyd learned about Seeing Eye dogs. He entered their training program at the famous guide dog school The Seeing Eye—and changed his life forever and for the better. In partnership with Hickory and then Kemp—two handsome yellow labrador retrievers—Lloyd grew undaunted by any challenge the Big City threw his way. No longer a biped, he became a *Lloydbrador*. Joined at the hip with his devoted partners, he has even been able to book a box at the Opera. With Hickory or Kemp resting—long-sufferingly—at his side, Lloyd once again revels in the magisterial music of his beloved Mozart.

With a Seeing Eye dog, there is a deep visceral connection which goes far beyond that of a pet and its owner. The tale of Lloyd's astonishing transformation—conveyed enchantingly by his fabulous, furry, four-pawed partners—is expressed with a combination of affection, patience, stoicism, deep-bonding, and determination. It moves from Lloyd's original passion for Art, Craft, and the wonders of the World of the Theatre—to a very different kind of love story that incorporates tenderness, deep inter-species understanding, profound around-the-clock affection, and an open-hearted embrace of "reality" in all its many mysteries.

Judging from the present mood of my old friend and colleague, Lloyd has never been happier or more engaged with life than he is today: He has moved from an acutely constricting darkness to the shimmering light of a renewed joy in living.

So read this book. You will be very glad you did.

. . . And long may Kemp's magnificent tail wave!

TWO SEEING EYE DOGS

TAKE MANHATTAN!

. . . a love story

PROLOGUE

"He's a Seeing Eye dog—not a pet—and he's allowed to enter any place."

We had just been stopped dead in our tracks at the door of the Village Diner.

"Get that damned dog out of here!" commanded the tall young man doing the stopping.

"We" were: My Partner, his eye-helper Charlie, and I, Hickory. I was shocked by our host's angry insult.

My Partner continued to protest: "Hickory is a guide dog," he explained in his Mr. Rogers nice-guy voice. (He was exceptionally polite, assuming that our "greeter" didn't know I had a right to be here.)

"I don't care *what* kind of dog he is; dogs are not allowed in this restaurant!"

I thought this rude man must himself be blind: could he not see my harness—or its sign stating, "Ignore working dog"? Or My Partner holding my harness handle as all people with Seeing Eye dogs do—and wearing dark glasses?

"You see, it's the law that guide dogs can go anywhere and everywhere with their visually challenged partners," soothed My Partner. He hoped not to make a scene on this, our first visit to a New York restaurant.

I was perplexed: This was our first day working together in my new hometown. We had been welcomed in the restaurants and coffee shops of Morristown, New Jersey, during our month-long training at The Seeing Eye guide dog school. What was this moron *thinking*? Would we be received in this way at every eatery? I had become used to the friendliest greetings from everyone and had entered the diner wagging my magnificent tail in anticipation. It drooped at this rejection.

"I don't know anything about any law but that one," the man snarled, pointing to a sign warning, "No Dogs Allowed." "Can't you see that sign? Now, get out."

"No, I can't see to read anything," My Partner calmly replied, "and that is why I travel with my excellent guide dog. Now, we would like to be seated, please."

"What is it about 'get out' you don't understand?"

Charlie took action: "I'm calling the cops. This is a violation of the Americans with Disabilities Act and this bastard ought to be arrested!"

"No, no," urged My Partner, "We're here for a nice lunch, not a fist fight."

"I'll call the police myself to have you thrown out, if you don't get moving," snapped our host.

I had taken quite a dislike to him and seriously considered a good, old-fashioned, sharp nip to his ankle—or at the very least a threatening growl. But I remembered my training: Barking, biting, and growling are all off-limits for us working dogs. Oh, how I wanted to pee on his shoe . . .

When Charlie asked to see the manager and was told that we were looking at him—we'd had enough. "Let's get out of here," said My Partner. "I know a better place to eat right down the street."

He gave the "outside" command and we left, my companions shaking their heads and my tail defiantly upright.

On the sidewalk, My Partner looked sad and a little confused. Until we'd met at The Seeing Eye, his only housemates had been cats—and they don't go out much. This kind of thing hadn't come up before. He wistfully mumbled, "I hope we have better luck at Cozy Soup and Burger," then commanded, "Hickory, forward." I led the way. As we walked two blocks downtown to try again, I became more and more angered by the way I'd been treated, and I was prepared to push back if we had any trouble. I didn't understand why My Partner had been such a wimp with that moron at the Village Diner. I wondered what my life would be like in New York. I was saddened to think that it might be much less dog-friendly than my time as a puppy in Princeton and as a dog-in-training in Morristown.

At the Cozy Soup, life began to improve. A very motherly woman welcomed us warmly. "What a handsome dog!" she exclaimed. "Oh, how I love you."

"He's a Seeing Eye dog. It's okay for him to go in restaurants, you know," My Partner ventured hesitantly.

"Of course it's okay. We love having guide dogs visit us," she replied. "Now, let's find you a table." That friendly greeting was a great relief and called for some serious tail wagging. My Partner gave the "follow" command and I trotted right after my new best friend, the happy hostess. This was more like it. She gave us a corner table that was just right for me—it protected my tail from rushing waiters and diners who weren't looking. I made myself comfortable underneath it—lying down at My Partner's left side, as I had been taught—and began my watch for falling crumbs. I checked the floor for any bits of breakfast that might not have been swept up. As he and Charlie sat down, My Partner warned, "Be careful. Hickory is known as 'the napkin thief of Morristown' and may well be on his way to earning the title, "Napkin thief of Greenwich Village."

That annoyed me a good deal; I was counting on snagging Charlie's napkin as soon as he wiped something interesting on it—like ketchup or burger juice. Charlie didn't help things either. He said he was well warned and would be "extra vigilant." (This morning was having too many ups and downs.)

Our waiter was a well-fed fellow (no one hid napkins from him) with a jolly Italian accent. He brought me, unasked, a large bowl of water. I thumped my mighty tail in thanks and slurped away. He returned, took the lunch orders of the bipeds, and asked if he could bring me anything to eat. "How about some nice ham? Would your dog like that?"

My tail was thumping faster. I *liked* this place! . . . But My Partner struck again. "Many thanks," he said. "But Hickory can't eat off the diet prescribed by his school, and also it's a bad idea to get him into the habit of being given food from the table. I really appreciate the offer though."

That refusal was downright cruel; no one consulted me. But I knew to bide my time. "Everything comes to him who waits" . . . I did.

My companions discussed the "access issue" at the Village Diner and considered how to deal with similar rejections in the future. I was more concerned with the *near* future: Charlie had ordered a cheeseburger deluxe and that promised a tasty napkin. I had nothing to do but go into "screen-saver mode": keep still and listen to the conversation. Charlie said we made a good team—he could tell how much My Partner thought of me as both guiding eyes and now constant companion. Because he had been My Partner's weekly eye helper for a year, Charlie had been around for all of the searching and training that brought us together. Now he said he would like to ask a question he had been wondering about. "Lloyd," he began (that's what bipeds call My Partner for short), "what exactly led you to switch from using your white cane to partnering with a Seeing Eye dog?"

I didn't know the answer, either, so my ears pricked up.

My Partner was an important Broadway stage designer and university teacher when he began to gradually lose almost all of his vision. That didn't stop him for a long time but, finally, last year, he retired. Having taken that big step, he felt free to admit the seriousness of his loss of vision to the world. And more importantly, he told Charlie, to himself. He eagerly took up the cane, feeling this would solve the mobility challenges of big-city living. He was sure that white cane would invite other pedestrians to offer some neighborly assistance. At first he traveled close to home, but gradually he ventured farther, sweeping his cane to more challenging locations.

What he said next shocked me more than being tossed out of the diner.

One bright summer day My Partner-to-be screwed up his courage. He tapped his way west from his home in Greenwich Village, heading for very dangerous crisscrossing intersection by St. Vincent's Hospital. Even for the fully sighted, this complex crossing is risky. For him, the risk had increased over the years as he slowly lost his vision.

My Partner walked down Seventh Avenue to the hospital at high noon. There he stood waiting to cross, his long white cane extended. He listened carefully to be sure he heard the traffic pattern correctly before crossing. Behind him, some men were talking—construction workers on their lunch break. One called out, "Hey blind man, it's okay to cross now."

Lloyd Burlingame

"Really? It's okay to cross?"

"Yeah, trust me, it's all clear!"

Leading with his cane, this trusting old professor stepped into the street . . . and a taxi horn blared in his ear! A strong hand jerked him back; the taxi swerved and sped past. On the curb the Old Prof shakily asked, "What was that all about?" The Good Samaritan who had rescued him replied, "That jerk was sending you out into traffic." Harsh, loud laughter rang out behind him. My Partner's trust in his fellow man died at that moment.

Now, in this friendly café, I wanted to stand up and comfort my Old Prof—nuzzle him and lick his face. But I was still on duty, so I had to leave the comforting to Charlie as My Partner continued his sad story. Feeling totally vulnerable, he said, like a turtle, he had pulled in his head and retreated into his protective shell. He had folded up his cane, stashed it away on the top shelf of a closet, stayed close to home, and lived like a hermit for months.

But he hadn't given up. Pondering his near-fatal crossing, it came to him that a Seeing Eye dog might protect its human partner and keep him out of moving traffic. Maybe—just maybe—a dog would be a trustworthy guide. But it turned out that my clan had betrayed him once too.

He'd been leery of us since he was only five—when a cocker spaniel had bitten him on the nose. (Not just bitten, but hung on for dear life!) Now, as he described this moment to Charlie, I saw My Partner's pain. *He* saw the image of his little-boy self standing up—the cocker he'd been petting still dangling from his bleeding nose. The Old Prof raised his hand to the right side of his adult nose, to feel the long scar that still shows. I was embarrassed for us canines, and I wondered how he ever got the courage to contact The Seeing Eye. He told Charlie about his doubts back then: Could he live and partner with one of us? Would a guide dog sense his nervousness? What if the dog disliked him? But he had realized that he had only two choices: to give the possibility of partnering with a dog the benefit of the doubt—or to accept the unhappy alternative of partnering more vulnerably with a cane. So he had investigated possible guide dog schools and talked with friends who lived and worked with canine partners. And he had decided to invite one of us into his life.

At lunch, hearing all of this for the first time, Charlie and I were both horrified—especially by what those bipeds had done. Now I knew why My Partner had hesitated at the St. Vincent's intersection yesterday, when Jeff from The Seeing Eye guide dog school had showed us how to cross. When the Old Prof and I had begun to form our partnership, back at the school, I had sensed how badly he wanted us to succeed as a team. Now I understood his nervousness and intensity then. And I truly understood how much our work together meant to him. I promised myself that I would be worthy of his special trust.

My mind—and nose—wandered back to Charlie's paper napkin. Before I had gotten lost in the Old Prof's story, I had been carefully watching the ripening of that tidbit, like a bird dog. Enriched with smudges of cheese, ketchup, burger juice, and salty grease from the French fries, it was ready for snatching. I deftly swiped it from his lap and ate it. Mighty tasty.

A moment later, Charlie said, "I've lost my napkin; it must have slipped to the floor." He leaned down to retrieve it, felt around his feet, and found my paw. I must say, he was pretty quick to blame me. "Well, I was warned, wasn't I?" he asked. "Next time I'll know better." Too bad he's such a quick learner.

***

I had begun my career of petty theft at the home of my puppy-raiser family, where the dad taught English literature at a boarding school. *His* response to my pick-napkining was literary—he called me "The Artful Dodger." That's a character in a book by one of his favorite writers, Mr. Dickens. It's about a boy named Oliver Twist. He lives in an orphanage and he's always hungry—like most of us retrievers from Labrador. I think I'm more like Oliver than Dodger. "Please, sir, can I have some more?" could be my motto, too.

16   Lloyd Burlingame

***

I worked in partnership with the Old Prof for the next eight years—a long time to be on duty 24/7, every day of the year, in stress-filled New York. Even loyal Seeing Eye dogs can't work forever—not even mighty Labs. When I started dreaming about my puppyhood in the country, I took that as a sign: Time to think about leaving my post in the city. When my retirement did come around, My Partner—My Best Friend—wanted to throw me a party. We invited thirty of my other closest biped friends and admirers, and I tried to imagine thank-you gifts for all of them. Finally I realized that I already had the perfect gift. Not long after moving to New York, I had noticed that the Old Prof was still writing in the daily journal he began in Morristown. If he could do it, why couldn't I? Now my own journal was full of eight years of memories, all typed up as we went along by my very own scribe: You Know Who. He and I selected and edited highlights from my Manhattan diary, to make a small book for my friends. Scattered among our adventures were nuggets of information about guide dog training and partnering. And answers to friends' and even strangers' questions, like: "Hey, Buddy, how do you see to pick up after your dog?" And, "Daddy, why does that doggy have a handle?"

We took the first draft to a nearby copy center and were helped there by a sympathetic young fellow from a country called Sri Lanka. The Old Prof and I appreciated his lively interest in our project. When we returned to check a sample copy, Ramesh shyly confessed, "I took the liberty of reading your manuscript at home last night. I enjoyed it very much."

I swished my mighty tail, and my pal smiled, "I'm glad you liked it."

"You are a good writer," said our friend.

"Oh, I can't take credit for that," My Partner replied modestly.

"If you didn't write this, then . . . who did?" Ramesh politely asked.

"Hickory, of course."

A long pause. "Your dog can *write*?!"

"Well, I do the actual typing; Hickory knows exactly what he wants written and dictates it to me."

"In English?"

"Yes, mostly in English," the Old Prof continued, straight-faced. "However, Hickory is from Labrador and occasionally uses words and vernacular expressions in Labradorean. I look these up in *Webster's Labradorean Dictionary*."

Smiling broadly, Ramesh leaned toward me over the counter: "Hickory, thank you for sharing your adventures."

I flashed my own bright smile—gleaming white teeth set off against black lips—and honored him with my famous propeller tail, circling supersonically.

Still smiling, Ramesh shook My Partner's hand, winked, and said, "You're a very fine scribe."

***

The party was—what is that word? Bitterandsweet. Everyone seemed very glad to receive the copies of my little book—*Hickory: Adventures of a Seeing Eye Dog in Manhattan*. But they all knew it was a thank-you *and* a good-bye. The Old Prof laughed and smiled, but he knew, too. That was the bitter. I started to think about staying. But, much as I had enjoyed the roller-coaster ride of big-city challenges, I longed more and more for the rural life. I dreamed of running free—out of harness in meadows like I did in Princeton, and romping with other unleashed dogs, like we all did at the puppy kennel. I had paid my dues by being a "good dog" in fancy restaurants, at formal ceremonies, gallery openings, and opera houses and concert halls. (Many of these were V-E-R-Y B-O-R-I-N-G. I sure hadn't known what I was in for, back in the summer of 1998 . . .)

PART ONE

Hickory: Adventures of One
Seeing Eye Dog in Manhattan

1998 - 2006

Lloyd Burlingame

THE EARLY YEARS: 1998 – 1999

*Guide Dog Hickory training at The Seeing Eye
with new partner, Lloyd Burlingame*

CHAPTER ONE

Getting Ready to Make It in New York, New York

Summer and Fall 1998

During that summer of '98, my unknown Partner-to-be was searching for a canine-friendly apartment in New York City. Across the Hudson River in New Jersey, I doggedly prepared to learn the guide dog trade. The intense basic training began with my being what the bipeds call "socialized"—living with a human family. By nature I was already "social" with my canine family and friends. Young as I was, at first I thought that adding bipeds wouldn't be much different. But it wasn't easy. I had to learn not to pee indoors, or chew the furniture, or bark at the mailman, or fight with the resident cat. My family gave me lots of love—and plenty to eat. (*Those* were the days.)

My very first home was at the Seeing Eye Breeding Center, outside of Morristown. I don't remember much, because I was only an eight-week-old pup when I left my mother, brothers, and sister. But I do remember that Mom had her paws full dealing with us energetic tots. Each puppy family had its own big kennel space with doggie doors leading outside. Through the inside walls, all of the families could see each other, and see the people who came in—because our spaces were arranged in a kind of circle (I learned later that this is called an "octagon") instead of along a straight hallway. We puppies liked knowing what was going on, and we felt safe in our big pack.

I think I was three or four weeks old when I first rode in the cart to the playroom. Puppies from all the families were there. We had fun things to play with (like balls and rubber bones) and on (like stairs, ramps, and slides). There was music too, and sometimes worse noise— to get us used to annoying sounds (as the cart accustomed us to the way automobiles move). There were no other four-footed creatures around . . . except outdoors I did spot some furry fellows with long tails, jumping around in the trees—squirrels. Looking way up at the top of the trees, I discovered birds. I loved to watch them fly—which I tried. (Ah, youth.)

All the mothers were proud of us when we left the Breeding Center for our second homes. My Mom said I was cut out for adventures and she knew I would be very happy. She was right. My new family lived in the country, outside Princeton, New Jersey, in a big, old house set in the middle of a huge meadow. I spied adventures all around me there. A stream ran through a little forest at the back of the property. A variety of creatures lived nearby—more squirrels and birds, but also some I'd never seen before, like rabbits, deer, and even foxes (which I thought at first were other dogs). Unfortunately, I was greeted by a four-footed animal *inside* the house: Ophelia—an aged orange, striped CAT. I'd heard some things about cats—not all good, und Ophelia was bigger than me, so I watched her pretty carefully. My new human family had a boy of twelve, a Mom, and a Dad. They seemed very eager to make me feel at home. I began to think of my own dear mom, and I missed my siblings, especially Henna, the only girl in our litter. We were special playmates . . . and Ophelia was *not* going to be a substitute for Henna. I could tell that right off.

Our Breeding Center home had been plenty big for all of us, but this house was huge. When I was allowed to roam the whole place, I went exploring and sniffing. It was a whole new world. I missed my family a great deal, but I knew that this was a warm and friendly home. (Ophelia excepted.)

With Young Master, I played tug with a rope, chased a Frisbee in the yard, and fetched the sticks he threw. This is where I discovered Music, because the Mom taught piano at home. Her students were human puppies, ranging from eight (which I quickly learned is *much* younger than canine eight!) to late teens. I thought that she herself played beautifully—which is more than I can say for some of her pupils. She was amazingly patient with even the least talented. I learned much about classical music and composers like Bach, Chopin, Beethoven, Mozart, and Brahms. Did you know Schubert wrote a growling dog into one of his songs? I loved it. The family also owned many classical "recordings" of orchestral and choral music. I especially liked something by Wagner, called the "Ride of the Valkyries." I learned they were a gang of liberated ladies who flew around on horses, fetching dead warriors and taking them to what I concluded later was a kind of immortal Hall of Fame. (The real horses I saw in Princeton ran so quickly that they almost *seemed* to fly.) The Valkyries' music sent me galloping around the living room, fetching toy bones. But I continually knocked over the lamps that got in the way, so the family stopped playing much Wagner.

My dad—"The Guv"—had grown up in England. In our house he kept what to my puppy eyes appeared to be a box. He called it the "telly." When he flicked a switch, several little people ran around in it, all talking like him. When I grew up, of course, I learned that those people had been actors in programs called *Masterpiece Theatre* and

Upstairs, Downstairs. As an adult I thought about the downstairs people—they were like Seeing Eye dogs; their job was to serve. And then I thought it would be fun someday, after my job was done, to be like the upstairs people—waited upon and harness-free.

The Guv taught literature, primarily English and American writers, at a private high school near Princeton. He often took me to class, where I settled down by his desk while he discussed all sorts of interesting authors. My very favorite is American: Mark Twain. Like Oliver Twist, Tom Sawyer is a hero of mine. He surely knows how to trick people into doing what he wants; he has a lively imagination and a repertoire of daring plans. So do I. *Some*times, when The Guv talked about a very dull book like *Pilgrim's Progress*, I couldn't help getting up, stretching back and forth, and yawning wide and long. This greatly amused the students, who paid more attention to me than to John Bunyan. At those times, The Guv leaned over to scold, "Now Hickory, don't be beastly—there's a good lad."

I met many of my family's biped friends, including a nice man who came regularly to visit them, and especially me. I heard him speaking with The Guv, Mrs. Guv, and Young Master about what they called my "progress." I deduced that he represented a famous school that trained dogs like me to be guides for people who can't see. My family told him how well I was behaving (!) and described my times out of the house too: at the beach, on the streets of Princeton, and in a nearby park where I played with other canines—some of them very different from me and my family at the Breeding Center.

After a few of these visits, I understood that they were checking my progress in "socialization." I began to realize that *I* was in the running to be one of those special guide dogs. Then I heard that Henna was, as well! Training at the school and being a guide dog sounded like a great adventure. Plus, if they chose me, I'd be able to see Henna again—and maybe my brothers. I crossed my paws for luck, kept my tail wagging, and did my very best to please my puppy-raiser family and Nice Man From The Seeing Eye.

I worked hard for a happy year and a half—and I succeeded! I was chosen to move to The Seeing Eye. Everyone was happy and

Lloyd Burlingame

excited. (Especially Ophelia, though she didn't show it; she's a cat. We two had agreed to share the house—when I began to outweigh her.) Yet my leaving these beloved friends was difficult for all of us. My family was pleased to have helped me pass my "puppy tests," but sorry to part. I owed them a great deal and was sad to depart from another happy home. As Nice Man and I drove off for The Seeing Eye, I saw Young Master—my best pal—wipe away a tear. Ophelia yawned, rubbed up against his leg, and grinned like that Cheshire cat.

* * *

My new home, the kennel at the school, was so different from my Princeton house and yard. I was excited and nervous, knowing I must be alert and open to new and strange experiences. I certainly didn't lack for canine chums. This was a doggie hotel with many small, low-walled rooms—each of us had his or her own. Our doorways looked out on the hallway, so we could greet each other and the trainers. Henna *was* there! I was thrilled to be reunited with my beautiful sister. (All the names in our litter begin with the letter "H." I had learned at the puppy kennel that this is true for *every* litter—but each litter uses a different letter. That seems to be the way our trainers kept track of us.)

This new home was clean and comfortable, and we had spacious grounds for our play time. But I soon learned that we were not there to fool around. We were dogs on a mission, learning basic commands and actions: come, sit, down, rest, forward, left, right, and many more. On the second day of training we began wearing the weird handle-like contraption called a harness. It took some getting used to, I assure you.

After a month or so, I noticed that some of the dogs in our entering class were missing. The buzz around the kennel was they had been judged not suited to guide duty. But no one told us exactly why. I had seen that one or two of the missing were much too easily distracted by squirrels, which made the Trainers unhappy. Others didn't seem interested in learning or could not grasp the basic actions and commands. The rest of us wondered—and worried—about where they had gone. One of the older Labs told us they would all have good homes with bipeds who can see. Sometimes people wait two years to adopt the dogs who haven't finished the program, because even they have been trained so well!

Halfway through the program, those of us left were entering the big time. Now my master was not a young boy, but an expert adult instructor named Will. He was a perfectionist, but always encouraging and filled with praise when I did good work. I enjoyed the work and strived to earn that praise. The harness came to feel natural. Training on the sidewalks of the little city of Morristown brought new challenges. I "got" the guiding part easily—for instance: stopping at curbs, pulling at a steady pace, and ignoring other dogs when in harness.

My problem—though *I* never called it a problem—was that I could not resist lunging for anything on the ground that just might be edible. This nearly was my downfall. Morristown's streets are boringly clean . . . but not *always*. I'm so tempted by tidbits—a half-eaten roll, an apple core, candy bar wrappers, spilled ice cream, twigs, discarded Kleenex . . . In this area Will and I had our work cut out for us—but I refused to become a dropout. I had watched dogs in the class ahead of ours working with people who couldn't see, walking quickly down the sidewalks and confidently crossing the street. I knew I could do that, too. I wanted to convince my instructor and the head of training: a prince of a man named Pete.

I can't say that we eliminated my fascination with food . . . oh, glorious food . . ., but with hard work, my Trainer and I improved my willpower. I passed all the other tests—even those that admitted me to the small, select group of dogs who could handle the demands of a big city. I had loved our two days' training in New York City. I liked its high-voltage life and challenges—missing in laid-back Morristown. My Trainer's high praise delighted me when I plowed through crowds, ignoring the noisy rough-and-tumble of Manhattan. I began to hope for a "big city" Partner.

By mid-October, our numbers had been a good deal reduced. All of us who had successfully completed the first four months' training were eager to be matched with biped partners. Henna had done very well. She was one of twenty class members who left our kennel one day for the school's main building. We had learned from a golden retriever in the group ahead of us (they enjoy gossip) that this was where the human trainees lived. I nuzzled Henna "good-bye." Though I was proud of her, my tail drooped as she was led away; I didn't know if I would see her again. The golden had said our training would end in a month.

Twenty of us were left behind. I was troubled . . . had I not been chosen for a partner? Was something wrong with me? I couldn't complain about our good life in the kennel, but I was ready—more than ready—to move on to the big time, not stooge about in some sort of holding pen. My Trainer had praised my sunny disposition to Pete . . . and I am *usually* cheerful. But I became more and more downhearted over the next two or three days, which left me still among the dogs-in-waiting. Once I glimpsed Henna in harness, working with her partner— a young lady who might have been a college student. My sister guided her expertly as their instructor, just behind them, gave corrections and praise. I was ever so happy for Henna . . . but I envied her, too. "Why," I sighed, "can't that be me?"

Four days after the selected dogs from our group began partner training, Franz returned to the kennel. He was a mighty German shepherd—a star of our gang—and now he felt that he had failed. He told us he had missed his trainer terribly. And though he had tried to bond with his new partner—a retired professor from Manhattan—his heart hadn't been in it. I felt sorry for Franz. But he *was* of solid German stock and soon shook off his disappointment. He knew he was very good at his job, and now he understood the goal of that job was to bond with a new and needy partner. He resolved to make his next match work, and I admired that.

Back then I didn't think about the professor—the other half of the failed partnership. I thought the big loser was Franz: he had almost made it to *Manhattan*, where I wanted to work. But a few days later I would change my mind.

The afternoon after Franz returned, I was surprised to be met at the kennel by Tom, one of the more experienced instructors. He directed me to "heel"; we walked over to the handsome red-brick school building . . . and I entered the big front door for the first time. Passing through the elegant lobby, we went down a carpeted hall to a kind of living room. It was bigger than my puppy raiser's, but just as comfortable. I could think of only one reason to be here, but I was afraid to get my hopes up. My heart beat so fast and my tail tried to keep up with it—but the suspense was so strong that it couldn't move at all. Might I be the replacement dog for Franz? Then I saw a tall, white-haired man coming down the hall, tapping his long white cane . . . *could* this be the professor from Manhattan?

I stood patiently by Tom's side as the man took a seat across from us. He seemed friendly, but nervous. Tom walked us slowly toward him and introduced me quietly: "His name is Hickory." The man—Tom called him "Lloyd"—held out his hands for me to sniff. I caught a whiff of cat on his jeans. (Bother.) "Hello, Hickory, I'm glad to meet you," said this Lloyd, his voice friendly and warm.

He didn't have a harness either, so he gave the "heel" command. As we walked, he held my leash with one hand and used his cane with the other. We climbed a flight of stairs to the second floor and walked down a wide, long hallway, past several closed doors, then stopped at one. The man opened it and we entered what he called his room. Next he took me off leash—so I could explore the space. It was much larger than my kennel cubicle, but far smaller than the Guv's house. I sniffed my way around the four walls to discover a desk, a large bed, and an easy chair by the open window where the sun streamed in. I saw a laptop computer on the desk, and later I learned that Mr. Lloyd used it to keep a daily journal about his progress at the school. Another open door led to a bathroom much like the Guv's in Princeton; it had a toilet, sink, and shower. Everything was almost odor-free—much too clean for informative sniffing. But I did catch a whiff of Franz. That made my heart sink—this Mr. Lloyd *was* Franz's professor. I wondered if I was only "on trial" and if I, too, would go from here right back to the kennel. Mr. Lloyd showed me my bed—my pad—on the floor; it was right next to his. This was all very different

Lloyd Burlingame

from both my Princeton home and the kennel. I didn't know what to expect. The professor still seemed nervous; he kept his distance and angled his head—he seemed somehow to be watching me. I wondered if he, too, was thinking, would *this* match work?

Later that afternoon, in harness, I guided Mr. Lloyd around the leisure path on the broad front lawn of the school. On our first turn around the big oval, we both moved carefully. But on our second and third turns, we picked up speed. I realized that he *could* see, just a little—only the outside edges of things. On each circuit he seemed to gain confidence in me. When at last we returned to our room, our cheery moods reflected the bright sunshine. I had been incredibly happy outdoors, charging ahead with my now-delighted companion. Later he told Tom, "I have not been able to move safely that fast for years. Hickory really knows his stuff. I've got my fingers crossed that partnering with a dog will be the answer to my prayers. Who's disabled now?!" I crossed my paws, hoping *I* was the dog to do the answering.

It was a couple of days later that I learned Franz wasn't the only one disappointed when his partnership with Mr. Lloyd fell apart. In fact, I found out, it was even worse for Mr. Lloyd. I was lying on my pad, considering a nap, when he telephoned his friend Charlie. My ears pricked up when he told Charlie he'd had a rough time at the school. Here's how he remembered the call in his journal:

> *Only when it was the last resort, I turned to partnering with a guide dog as the potential solution of my mobility problems. On first arriving at The Seeing Eye, I was pushing down my deep skepticism about working and living with a dog. Then my worst fears were realized when I was partnered with a German shepherd. Franz seemed fierce and anything but friendly and loveable. Day after day, training in Morristown, he led me into traffic; and night after night he kept me up, whining and barking for his trainer. It was truly a nightmare. I took my concerns to the director of training and he told me I either could keep trying to work with Franz or could request a new dog.*

I called my sister, Susie—wise, owner-of-many-dogs, and trusted adviser on the biggest life questions. I laid out the situation to her, and asked for her words of wisdom.

"NEW DOG!" she shouted, without hesitation.

My sleep-deprived, muddled brain welcomed a flash of clarity. Even though Franz kept me awake for much of the night, I snatched a few hours' peaceful sleep. I had made my decision. The next morning, I requested a new dog, was instructed to give Franz a goodbye hug, and caned my solitary way back to my room.

Sitting alone in what felt like a fog of failure and discouragement—and doubt about my ability to partner with a dog—I wondered if the new one would be any different from Franz . . . or, dear God, even worse? What then? I determined to put the best face on it possible and to once again give the benefit of the doubt. The alternative of returning to the cane was too distasteful. I crossed the fingers of both hands, and awaited the summons to meet my fate and the new dog.

Listening to Mr. Lloyd talking to his friend explained a lot. I was surprised to hear that Franz had behaved so badly. But now I understood why Mr. Lloyd had been so nervous when we met . . . *And* I understood the call he had made to his friend Charlie after our first leisure path walk. Mr. Lloyd wanted to cancel the car that Charlie had ordered to take him back to New York. Now, putting two and two together, I realized Mr. Lloyd had been so discouraged about ever working successfully with a Seeing Eye dog that he had given up. Luckily for both of us, he had taken just one more chance—which was me. What an unhappy situation I had walked into! I was glad and grateful that he believed things were looking up for him. That meant they were looking up for me, too.

Over the next four weeks, Mr. Lloyd and I got to know and trust each other, training as a team. Early on he asked about that: "Why are we here to train for such a long time? Hickory's had four months of schooling; there are not too many commands for me to learn. A week should prepare us to take on traveling in the real world." Coached by Tom and another top instructor, named Jeff, the professor soon found out how much there was to learn. So did I. We had a few difficult and discouraging days, but most were filled with the joy of discovery as we made rapid progress. The funny thing was, instead of feeling four weeks were too long, eventually my new partner felt they were probably too short. In the last week he made many requests of our instructors: he wanted to learn more about night travel, and to review our training with revolving doors and escalators. This professor was an eager student; the more he learned, the more he appreciated the school . . . and, I think, me.

We had a bizarre happening at the end of our first week's training: Instructor Tom's group of five biped students met for a lesson in combing and brushing us canines, in the small grooming room downstairs in The Seeing Eye's main building. It was Halloween, October 31, 1998. (Remember the date.) I don't know why, but the school does not give exact statistics about us guide dogs when we first meet our future partners. The instructors wait a week to state our weights, heights, and birth dates. These are announced with great seriousness. I was the last one reported on. "Weight: 61 pounds; height (to shoulders) 21 inches; birth date: October 10, 1998." Across the room, Henna looked puzzled. The professor—always full of questions—asked again for the date; it was still "October 10, 1998." He and I found this answer more Halloween trick than treat. I saw a twinkle in his eye when he replied, "Well, that makes Hickory three weeks old today, and he already weighs 61 pounds. If he continues to grow at this rate, the one-bedroom apartment I've just bought for us will be much too small. I'll have to find a garage or high-ceilinged loft." The instructor laughed; he said he'd check on the date.

A few days later, the news came back that I was really born almost two years before the recorded date—on October 27, 1996. We were all pleased to know that I wouldn't grow into a giant. Imagine harnessing a guide Lab as big as Paul Bunyan's blue ox, Babe!

If only our other unique problem had been so easily solved. This one was medical. It arose like a small dark cloud forming in our usually clear blue sky—and it grew much larger when we moved to the city. Mr. Lloyd paid the most careful attention to Tom and Jeff's every instruction. For a biped working with his first canine partner, there was a great deal to learn and process. The professor said it was like learning to drive a shift-stick car: There was steering, parking, shifting the gears, signaling, accelerating, braking, and on and on. (The humans understood this, but I didn't.)

It turned out my new partner was an art teacher (which didn't explain why he used such big words). He used to tell his students as they learned to paint and draw: "Just stick with it. One fine day it will all come together and you'll wonder what the problem had been." It was too bad he didn't entirely follow his own teaching. Instead he ignored one of the corrections that Tom often repeated—about proper body posture while walking with me. The "guidee" holds the harness in his left hand, and naturally there is pulling to move him forward. Sometimes the pull is too strong, and that can cause problems in the left shoulder. Standing tall and keeping shoulders down and back can avoid this. Mr. Lloyd said he had heard enough of that sort of posture-correction while in the Army. He didn't understand that Tom was not concerned about looks, but about physical well-being, so he paid no attention to his instructor's orders to walk tall. Little by little, my companion's shoulder began to ache, but he soldiered on, not complaining. He told me the discomfort would pass.

Not knowing that little cloud would keep growing, we graduated from The Seeing Eye. We were filled with optimism; my partner declared he eagerly looked forward to "playing our parts on the big-city stage."

Lloyd Burlingame

Hickory at home in his "yard" playing with a new toy

CHAPTER TWO

Two on an Island: Off and Running in Manhattan

November 1998 – May 1999

There were no clouds in the bright blue sky the morning Jeff drove the professor and me from Morristown to New York City, where we would begin our new life together. I sensed that My Partner was excited and nervous; we both were. I watched the New Jersey countryside—my native state—whip by the window. I missed it a bit already. Whizzing us up the Turnpike toward the entrance to the Lincoln Tunnel, Jeff called to us in the back seat, "Look, you can already see the Manhattan skyline! The Empire State Building and the Twin Towers stand out bright and clear!" There they were, gleaming in the morning light. Today I would call this great city home; my heart beat faster and my tail kept it company.

Coming out of the dim tunnel, we turned right, heading "downtown" to the little Village called Greenwich—a district in the big city. After a few weeks, I figured out the geography: Greenwich Village is halfway between the Empire State in "Midtown" and the World Trade Center way downtown. I had trained with Jeff and Mr. Lloyd in the Penn Station and Garment District area. Those are west of the Empire State—and New Jersey is farther west, all the way across the Hudson River. In Midtown, so many modern tall buildings crowd together that the streets are shadowy and you can hardly see the sky. In "The Village," which is older, the buildings are smaller and lower; they have what the humans call "quaint charm."

When Jeff pulled up in front of my new home, I saw that all the buildings on the block were apartment houses. An energetic man named Steve came to meet us at the curb. His job was to keep watch and open the door. He welcomed me like a long-lost friend and I took to him immediately. I learned later that he had worked with dogs while in the Army, so he understood us better than most people do. He helped the two of us move our gear to the elevator. This was new to me then— we hadn't tried one out at The Seeing Eye. A pair of doors slid open and I saw an empty closet. I was a little surprised when Jeff and the professor walked me in there. The door closed, something whirred . . . and it felt like the whole room moved. Then the door opened. What was that all about, I wondered. We walked down a narrow hallway that I hadn't noticed when we entered the closet, and we came to a door that the professor opened with a key. In we went—to a light-filled room *high above the street.* Oh! *That's* what elevators did—they moved you upstairs. This was exciting—what else would I discover here in New York?!

It didn't take me long to figure out that many other bipeds and families lived on this floor, and on other floors—separately, and all stacked up. When I discovered other canines there, too, I decided it was just a bigger, taller kennel than we had had at The Seeing Eye.

My host-partner gave me a tour of the apartment—which was

Lloyd Burlingame

much smaller than my Princeton home. I sniffed around the big main room, where we had entered; it was a bit like a small version of my Princeton living room. It included a "dining area," and I liked the sound of that. There were also a bathroom, a good-sized bedroom, and—most important—a *kitchen*. (I was getting hungry after our trip.) I had a new "false wicker" bed near the window wall, giving me a direct view into the cooking area, just a few feet away—that was thoughtful. Jeff inspected the whole apartment to make sure it was safe for me, then we all went back to the elevator. I learned that they go down as well as up, because the doors opened onto the lobby. I wagged my tail goodbye to Steve and the three of us headed for the street, to explore where I'd be guiding my partner.

One big deal was to find a sheltered place for me to "park." (That's Seeing Eye for "peeing and pooping." The professor calls it a "euphemism." *That's* a long word for something that means something else. He likes long words.) Our problem was that cars are not allowed to park on our side of the street. ("Parking" with cars, of course, is not the same thing.) So we had to locate another kind of shelter. About twenty feet to the left of our front door, we found a very large green metal box with no top, filled with old doors and other trash—and a *very* interesting mix of smells. Jeff said this "dumpster" was a perfect shield against the fast-moving traffic. He reminded us that I'd have to visit the street four times a day, more or less on the same schedule as at The Seeing Eye. We were pleased to have arranged that important part of my life.

Next we three went strolling on the sidewalks. I was in heaven, sniffing an amazing variety of scents. No fireplug in Morristown offered such a mishmash of messages as the one near my new home. But I had to postpone this bit of heaven. Jeff said we weren't there to play games, so I focused on minding my training manners. We went around Washington Square. My Partner called this a "park," too— which confused me at first (Sometimes bipeds use one word for too many different things.) A lot of old-fashioned brick houses stood on the "uptown" side. (That's north, by the way.) There was also an enormous arch with sculptures of the man the square was named after—showing him as "president" on one side and "general" on the other. Impressive . . . tempting . . . but clearly not to be peed on. Around the other three sides of the square—the professor said it was really a rectangle, but who's measuring?—were many buildings owned by his former employer, New York University. Hundreds of college kids rushed helter-skelter to and from their classes. Jeff seemed to think they might be a problem for me, but I liked weaving in and around them. Sometimes I couldn't help lurching toward a scampering squirrel or a pecking pigeon in the gutter—I had never seen so many pigeons!—but I got leash corrections for that extracurricular tugging. The professor looked unhappy. My lurching and tugging pulled painfully on his left shoulder. Jeff noticed his wincing and told him (again) to stand straight, with his shoulders back and down. He did this, but I had a bad feeling that we were in for trouble if his problem didn't clear up soon.

Jeff was very thorough. To end our lesson, he even walked us two extra blocks west, to that dangerous crisscross intersection at Saint Vincent's Hospital. Of course, at this point I didn't know about the professor's frightening experience there, almost a year ago, or that he hadn't been back since. But he was much more relaxed after Jeff showed us exactly how to manage the crossing.

I had a wonderful time that afternoon, discovering many new things—especially the fabulous sniffs of the big old city. There were many off-limits snacking opportunities, but with Jeff watching everything, I had to mind my p's and q's. Mr. Lloyd seemed wonderfully happy to have begun partnering with me in this Village neighborhood, where he'd lived for many years—both with and without his sight. He was thrilled to have his freedom of movement restored, he told Jeff, and thanked him especially for the useful and encouraging final lesson. Jeff seemed just as happy. He wished us all the luck in the world as he drove off, back to Morristown. As we watched him leave, I think the professor and I both realized with a gulp that now, for the first time, we were on our own.

But that night, as he filled the water and food bowls for my supper, the professor paused and murmured, "God's in his Heaven, and all's right with the world." I felt that way, too, as soon as I'd eaten.

36   Lloyd Burlingame

Even with Jeff gone—my last connection with The Seeing Eye and all my friends there—I felt . . . well, content, and safe. I belonged here, and I liked it. I realized I had dropped the formality: no more "Mr. Lloyd." I had moved in with "My Partner."

I was getting sleepy and thinking about kneading my new bed into shape for the night . . . when four big amber-colored eyes caught my line of vision. I had forgotten about the cats—though their scent was all over—a pair of small, coffee-colored felines. Just like Ophelia in Princeton, they skulked: in corners, behind the sofa, and on the pass-through from living room to kitchen. My Partner introduced them as Hugo and Clemmie. They weren't very happy to meet me. I wasn't surprised, since Mr. Ll . . . My Partner had told me they'd lived with him for a long time. They'd never had to share him before, and now they had a large yellow roommate. None of us knew how they felt about it. I hoped we could work out a peaceful arrangement. Ophelia and I had managed that. But this was two against one. I kept one drowsy eye on them until I fell asleep.

* * *

The first months in Manhattan were both a huge hit and a near-disastrous flop. Our team travel went well in many ways, and that was encouraging. We walked fast around Washington Square Park early every morning for forty minutes. This was my "core" exercise time (our daily minimum), so we walked rain or shine—but not snow and ice. I enjoyed observing dozens of canines of all breeds and sizes in our neighborhood, though socializing with them was strictly out of bounds for me. (One of the biggest drawbacks of being a working dog.) My Partner, however, began to dread these outings: He said the necessary tension on my harness was turning into torture for his left shoulder. A red-hot poker seemed to stab into it every time I tugged or lurched on the job. His mood darkened as his pain grew worse. I could tell he was becoming anxious about taking me out, and that made me nervous. My Partner called the school for advice, and I heard Pete, at the other end of the telephone, offer to bring me back for a few weeks until the medical problem was solved. The Old Prof seemed grateful for the offer, but I could tell that, as much as he was hurting, he did not want us to part. I certainly didn't want to leave my new home and happy working situation to go back into the kennel.

Another dark cloud suddenly appeared: As we left our apartment building early one day, My Partner greeted Doorman Steve with a cheery "Good morning." Steve didn't look cheery. "I'm not sure you're going to think it's so good, he replied. "They took away the dumpster last night, so there's nothing to protect you and Hickory from the traffic on this side." The Old Prof was dismayed. Jeff had told us that this was the side of the street for me to park. The Prof was intent on following those instructions exactly; he didn't want to make any mistakes. Now he thought there was nothing to do but hope the crazy traffic would swerve around us.

My Partner became terrified each time we stood in the street. He said this was like "lunatic Russian roulette" and that eventually a racing vehicle would hit one or both of us. Worse, it was nearly mid-winter, so three of our four daily outings took place in the dark. My Partner wore a florescent orange vest to alert drivers, but he didn't believe that it helped. He nervously urged me to hurry up my parking. But I couldn't do that; finding just the right place to pee takes time, even in risky situations.

The poor Old Prof told our friend Charlie that this parking arrangement was growing intolerable. As he had back in Morristown, when he and Franz hadn't been able to make their partnership work, now My Partner felt the "dark shadow of impending failure." He feared that his inexperience with dogs was an impossible handicap—that he could not reach "the bright promise of independence" offered by *any* guide dog. He had cherished such high hopes for our partnership. I was sad to see these fade as he became desperate to find solutions for my parking and his shoulder.

My Partner called another good friend—David—who had worked for a long time in the city with *his* guide dog. He suggested we had a double problem: First, the Prof was new to living with a dog, and that needed adjustments. Second, he was new to working with a *guide*

Lloyd Burlingame

dog—and that needed more, unique, adjustments. David said that patience and "sticking with it" would make our partnership work. That was encouraging . . . but after another month of shoulder torture and in-the-street high anxiety, the Prof very much doubted that we would make it.

After talking to David, My Partner had started "intensive physical therapy" for his shoulder problem, which is called "tendonitis." I learned that "intensive" also means "long," because this went on for many months before he felt cured. The moves he made at the physical therapy place were really weird—even weirder than the exercises he did at home. But I had begun to get used to "weird" from him.

At last one problem was solved; the Old Prof figured it out for himself. One day he simply realized *why* Jeff had insisted we use the dumpster for parking—it was the only protection on *our* side of the street. The other side of our street, where cars park all the time, offered plenty of protection. By now we had crossed a lot of streets together . . . why not this one? In the spaces between the cars over there, I could pee safely and take all the time I needed. After all our worrying, this solution was a no-brainer. I wondered why neither of us had thought of it before—especially him. (Though I'd already seen evidence that being a professor doesn't mean you're always smart.)

A few months later, our second problem faded. Stubborn as he is, My Partner stuck with his physical therapy: his shoulder healed and his posture improved. By early spring, with patience and practice, all the elements of teamwork had come together. The once-gigantic black cloud had nearly disappeared. We were smooth travelers and happy partners.

* * *

At home when I'm off duty and out of harness, I have play dates with my schnauzer friend, Homer. We get up some speed, zooming around the dining room table and roaring back into the living room. My open space has a cheerful green rug covered with leaves. My

Partner calls it my "yard." It's *much* smaller than my puppy-raiser family's back yard though—and they had *real* leaves. Since the apartment is so small, too, I let the Old Prof do his exercises in my space . . . for which I get little credit. In fact, he seems annoyed when I drop my big, heavy, plastic Nylabone on his head during what he calls "sit-ups." Patience is not always mutual around here. Ah, well, he's only human (and a wimp).

I have a small collection of Nylabones and red-rubber Kong toys at one end of this miniature yard. With just ten bones and five toys, I'm always glad for more. I don't mean to complain, but he only plays tug with me for a total of about thirty minutes a day. Any reasonable dog knows that two hours of daily tugging is the bare minimum.

My yard is multipurpose—it's taken over for professional activities, too. The Seeing Eye has us practice the commands of our discipline exercises every evening. I dutifully respond to "heel," "come," "sit," "down," and "fetch." I'm eager to do my best, because we repeat this routine just before my tasty—but very *small*—dinner. My yard is also the grooming area where I'm combed and brushed every evening; my fine, pale yellow hairs fall on the leaves of the carpet. My Partner's cleaning lady says she likes this light green rug, because it doesn't show my hairs like the dark green rug in the dining area.

Eva is fond of me and says nice things in Polish—well, I think they're nice, and I think it's Polish. She and the Prof are disgustingly sweet to the seven-pound Burmese twins, who think they own the place. I was very polite to Hugo and Clemmie when I first arrived, because they'd been with the Prof for four years—and, after all, I was moving into their home. But when I learned they'd only lived in *this* apartment for five weeks, I began to throw my weight around. After all, I have a real job to do around here. I'm the one who guides our Meal Planner to the store so he can buy their little cans of Fancy Feast while they lie around all day. They greeted that point with a yawn. Which is pretty much their response to anything logical. After *weeks* of getting nowhere, we finally agreed: The floor and anything on it is mine—all

Lloyd Burlingame

mine. The cats keep the upper spaces: sofa, table tops, book shelves, bed, heating unit . . . and the stereo amplifier next to the telly. They don't much care about the music, but they've figured out that the amplifier, like the heating unit, keeps them warm.

Since My Partner has "20/20 hearing," but near 0/0 vision, he is, foremost and first, a classical music lover. I agree with the cats on one subject: You can have much too much of a good thing—like Bach, Beethoven, Mozart, Mahler, Shostakovich, Verdi, Bellini, Strauss, Puccini, and on and on. I made it clear to the Old Prof that I appreciate all these music makers . . . but maybe twelve hours of masters daily is going too far? "Get over it!" he growled.

"My Place" is in a cozy corner of the bedroom where I have a second bed. This one, like my new bed in the yard, is made of real wicker. (I ate the old yard bed in ten days . . . as I've said, not much food around here.) Both of these current beds taste *awful*. My Partner sprays them with a nasty liquid called "Bitter Apple," so I won't snack on them. (I call that low. I had hoped to enjoy the Big Apple, not be starved by a bitter one.) I get no praise for taking initiative: Last month, I was having a fine time snacking on a dime and a nickel when The Prof spoiled it by playing what he calls "the extracting dentist." He says if I keep trying to swallow coins, he'll name me, "The First Hickory Savings and Loan." I don't get it.

On the other hand, the Prof has told several people how good I am, not pestering him too early in the morning. We rise every day at 6:55—much later than The Seeing Eye's training scheduling. I put my nose over his bed at exactly 6:54. I'm not allowed the least little bark, not even a low growl, by Seeing Eye law. Hugo bothers both of us by yowling at six or earlier, and gets away with it. So unfair. (I've noticed that bipeds expect far less from cats than they do from dogs; that's the disadvantage of our superior intelligence.)

Now that it's spring in the Park, our morning walks are great treats for My Partner and me. Sidewalk traffic moves in both directions, so we meet a large number of friendly joggers. We've only been crashed into twice in five months. Fast-walkers usually let me plow right on through teams of two or more. The Old Prof scolds that's rude, but I'm not here to fool around. He says the oddest thing about what he calls my lack of sidewalk manners: "Hickory takes no prisoners."

One basic distinction that any self-respecting Seeing Eye "cadet" must grasp and practice is which direction is left and which is right. I understood that immediately, though not everyone in the class did. As we walked around the Village a week ago, a young man came up to us with his Lab. "I'll bet my dog can do anything your dog can," he claimed. We knew this poor Labradorean was not a trained guide dog (no harness), and I wondered how My Partner would respond to the near-challenge.

"I'll take that bet," he said with a kindly smile. "For starters, let's begin with the basics. Can your dog tell left from right?"

"Well, errrr, no, he can't," replied the crestfallen challenger.

"You lose," said My Partner. Giving the regulation little hand movement, he pointed to the right and commanded, "left." Off we went around the corner to the right. I wondered what the young man and his dog thought of this. The Prof had given two different directional commands, so I had just tossed a coin in my head and gone in the direction he pointed. After he said, "Good boy, Hickory!" I knew I had guessed correctly. By now I had had plenty of practice; this problem began during training in Morristown.

My "Emeritus Professor" continues to confuse left and right, saying "left," when he means us to turn right and therefore should be commanding (hello?), "right." Usually I understand what he means even when he can't say it right. Then I save the day by guiding him in the correct direction. An emeritus professor is supposed to be smart; mine even has a medal saying so. (I've never seen him wear it!) To be fair, he apologizes every time he's wrong. And he seems to appreciate my extraordinary intuitive powers. In fact, he often says I'm a great help in guiding him around New York's ever-changing sidewalks and streets. He also thinks that because people like me so much they offer him more assistance than they did when he traveled with his white cane. (I should think so: nothing warm and furry about an aluminum stick.)

* * *

These days when that "stick" appears, it's usually bad news for me. I figured this out the first time My Partner left me behind at Creature Features—until then, one of my favorite pet stores. I had been of two minds about leaving the apartment, because he was carrying the cane: Why would he need it when he was walking with me? A few blocks later when I caught a whiff of pet store smell, I forgot about the stick, expecting a treat or a new bone. But I was being *tricked*, not treated: I was there to get my first bath—my least favorite thing in the whole world—since leaving The Seeing Eye. I don't care that we Labs are supposed to love water; I *hate* getting wet. At the pet store I balked when a strong-armed thug dragged me into the bathing room. What had I done to deserve this treatment? Now I knew why My Traitorous Partner needed the cane: Giving the excuse that he had nowhere to sit during my torture, he deserted me. Ordinarily I would have been sorry for him, leaving the store unhappily with his cane, feeling handicapped again. But none of this was *my* idea.

Professor Judas told me later that he got his comeuppance for his betrayal: It was lunchtime on a sunny April day (people were eating; *I* was getting bathed), as he tapped his way along the crowded sidewalk. He is always afraid that he'll whack someone's ankle . . . so, of course, he did just that. "Ladies, that man just hit me with his cane!" shrieked a woman who had been chatting with her friends. They all made sympathetic noises at her and unsympathetic noises at him. Of course, he apologized: "Oh, I'm terribly sorry. I honestly didn't mean to hit you. Please forgive me."

When his "victim" gave a deep-throated menacing growl, the Old Prof was sure that police would arrive at any minute. Seeing his distress—almost panic—the "wronged woman" let out a huge, jolly laugh: "Oh, yeah," she joked, "I know your type. You were just trying to pick me up." Her friends laughed hard, too. Relieved, My Partner hesitantly joined in. Then the lady (he called her "Rubensesque") *really* surprised him with an enormous hug. Even though his adventure turned out happily, the Old Prof still dreads "incurring the wrath" of pedestrians accidentally hit with his metal stick. He says he feels like "Mr. Magoo"—a squinting old man who blusters around with his cane, and runs into everything and everybody. (Someone should tell *him* about The Seeing Eye.) But my Professor Magoo says he can relax when I lead him in harness; he just follows my broken-field weaving in and out of the crowd.

* * *

My Partner takes me on walks to explore the older parts of the Village. This way I get to know the territory and he tests his own sense of direction and locale positioning. After a few months of partnering in the city, we tried a big test: We returned to the "intersection-from-hell" at St. Vincent's Hospital—this time without Jeff to help us.

After spending many weeks together, building each other's confidence, I was ready for this excursion. But I could tell that My Partner was nervous about our trying it alone. He hesitated for a while, and listened really hard. Then he took a deep breath, said, "Forward" and gave the accompanying hand gesture. I breezed right out and got us safely across. Professor Magoo was extra pleased with me, I could tell. His hand relaxed on my harness and he grinned broadly. The curse had been lifted from that crossing forever.

* * *

After a couple more run-ins inside and outside the Village Diner, My Partner sent the owner a strong letter of protest. He received a call in response: Nick, the owner, was very upset to learn of our treatment by his staff. He apologized over and over, invited us for a free meal, and said that his daughter was visually challenged. He had total sympathy for us and total respect for the law. Now we're always welcome there, and Nick is another fan of mine. That's the best—when lessons learned mean new friends made.

Taxis can be trouble, too. The law strictly forbids them to discriminate against guide dogs and our partners. It also requires us to file a report when this happens—by calling in the cab number. See a problem here? If Magoo were able to read the number . . . *why would he need me in the first place?*

* * *

Regular dogs get to go to dog runs and the beach. All I was doing was going to theatres, art galleries, clubs, and board meetings on Park Avenue. (By no definition is this a "park.") At The Seeing Eye, My Partner had thoughtfully asked about taking me to dog runs, but he was told not to—because they can be germy, and if there's a dog fight, My Partner can't see how to help me. (Phooey. Those puny dogs in Washington Square are no match for me.)

Every week we went to the downtown branch of Tower Records, where the Old Prof added even more Bach, Beethoven, and Mozart to his dementedly large collection of CDs. He says before I arrived, the salespeople paid little or no attention to him. Now Ron the Buyer is our new best friend. He has a bulldog named Patsy, who I still haven't met. I'd love to know if she's forced to listen to as much of Johann Sebastian, Ludwig, and Wolfgang Amadeus as I am. (I like their names better than their music. My Partner's brother, my Uncle Michael, lived with a dachshund named Johann. Uncle Michael says his "Bach was worse than his bite." And I think "Wolfgang" would be a dandy name for a German shepherd at The Seeing Eye . . . if they ever get down to "W.") Thanks to me, the Prof and I get similarly good service at the local supermarket. And shopping for food is a great deal more fun than looking for music.

* * *

That first spring of our partnership, the Old Prof taught me a lot about the different kinds of places where people go in packs. Mostly these events are rather boring, but sometimes good smells—or food— liven them up. Throughout April and May I fought both boredom and temptation admirably, pleasing My Partner as well as myself.

To prepare for my first visit to an opera house, the Old Prof forced me to listen to a two-CD-long opera, *Intermezzo*, by Richard Strauss. We were going to hear it *again* at a place called the New York City Opera, where a friend of his is a director. This so-called friend arranged for us to go to a "final orchestra dress rehearsal." Oh. Joy.

Magoo played the CDs several times—to "accustom" us to the opera. ZZZZZ. On a welcome break, we met our neighbor Gail in the street. She was out with her pup, Ashley—a cute little Jack Russell terrier. Gail asked what we were up to. My Partner told her about going to the opera and listening to *Intermezzo* to prepare. "You play operas to prepare your dog?!" she exclaimed. (At this point, I was really envying Ashley.)

"Sure, doesn't everyone?" replied the Prof.

Never at a loss for words, Gail was . . . well . . . at a loss for words.

This is my unedited account of our trip a few days later, uptown to Lincoln Center. I dictated this to Maestro Herr Professor Boring right after we had (thankfully) returned home:

> *We went to the State Theater, where the opera people live. Inside, a lot of other people were standing around in this big room called a lobby. They were very noisy, and their tempting mingled smells made it hard to focus on my job. Then we were led into another big room, where a man took us to a long row of seats and sat us down—near an exit, just in case I joined in singing. Having heard the thing before we went, I didn't much want to do that. But forget the music—this theatre place was worth the trip.*
>
> *I had never been in any room this large, or tall; it even had high porches they called "balconies." The weird thing was that all of the many, many chairs faced the same way, toward a blank wall. Very odd. The Old Prof and all the other bipeds acted as though this was perfectly normal. Even odder. I got comfortable in the aisle—then, suddenly, the power failed and all the lights went out. That put me on the alert—what was*

Lloyd Burlingame

going on here?! Then the blank wall of the room went up into the ceiling, and we saw another, smaller, room where there had been no power failure. It reminded me of a giant telly screen, much bigger than what we had in Princeton.

Pretty soon the music started and the singers entered that other room ... so it was time to sleep. But just as I had dosed off, the singers started slamming lids on suitcases and trunks. That wasn't in the CD; it was fascinating. I got back to a nice nap in what is called the third scene, but jangling sleigh bells woke me up—they were exciting. More noise from the singers—handclapping this time—came at the end of "The First Act." Too bad that wasn't in the CD, and too bad it didn't last longer. Things got boring again, but I was able to sleep till the end. My Partner said I had behaved admirably and my soft snoring blended in with the celli.

It took too many more operas to figure out what celli were.

* * *

Not only had I become a big-city dog in New York; after six months there, I was finding my way around Washington, D.C., too. This was my first train ride since The Seeing Eye, where the Old Prof and I had been taught how to manage these noisy giants, on a fifteen-minute trip between Morristown and Madison, New Jersey. This time our train was named Amtrak. The Washington trip took much longer, but I had plenty of room to spread out and found the not-so-clean floor entertaining.

There were more new smells, sights, people, and dogs when we arrived at our destination. We stayed with My Partner's sister—now my Aunt Susie—her husband, Ed, and their husky and little poodle, named Sophie and Meep. We all got along very well. The Prof introduced me as "My pal, Hickory." I liked that. There was amazement at my ability to find objects to chew on: a boot here, a sock there, a fork, and a napkin under the table. My aunt thought she'd puppy-proofed her house—well, she'd never met a growing Lab!

Washington offers many fine places to park; green grass is everywhere. We went to the Kennedy Center—another theatre—where the Old Prof was added to an old folks' honorary artistic society, as part of a festival of college theatre performances. The honoring took place in a great banquet hall, where we sat near a little stage. I checked the place out, found most of the people a little dull and a lot stuffy, and settled down for a nap. Suddenly loud music woke me up—*not another opera!* Luckily it wasn't. Instead two young dancers leapt onto the platform, and it became a booming drum. Their sliding, gliding, and stomping had my complete attention. I jumped to my feet to make the duet a trio, but My Pal's firm hand on my harness reminded me of my manners. It was difficult not to dance and not to bark. I could tell the Old Prof was proud of my self mastery, but that temptation seemed an unfair test for both of us.

* * *

Back in New York we went to another kind of meeting—no one danced. This was called "The Annual Meeting of the Board of Directors of *Choice Magazine Listening.*" My personal professor says he cares a lot about this organization, "because it gives blind and visually impaired people high-quality audio recordings of articles from important magazines." My Partner was new to the board and I guided him to 101 Park Avenue—as I said, hardly a park. Months before, he had been interviewed to earn the honor of sitting through these meetings. He startled the board members when he said that because he can no longer *see* to read, now he reads twice as much by *ear*. I can vouch for that: He reads while making meals, exercising, grooming me, and on and on. I bet he listens to four or five books a week (mostly histories and mysteries), recorded by the Library of Congress. I'm starting to recognize the voices of some of the top narrators and actors who bring the books to life for us. What a relief to leave Mozart, Beethoven, and Verdi for stories by Tolstoy, Agatha Christie, and Fitzgerald. All of us—the Old Prof, me, and the cats—gather for Jim

Dale reading *Harry Potter*.

So, our meeting was on the 45th floor of a glass-and-chrome office tower. I had never been up so high and was stunned by what I saw outside the huge windows. We were really close to the top of a beautiful building called The Chrysler. I envied the birds outside and remembered trying to fly like them when I was a pup. How wonderful to swoop around the "topless towers" of Manhattan! *Our* tower was a disappointment—the elegant deep-pile carpet was revoltingly clean; I knew I'd have to be patient until lunchtime. The meeting started with a lot of talk about money. I thought some of the people needed diversion during this boring gobbledygook. So I went to work on my big, heavy Nylabone: "crack, chomp, crunch, crick, gnaw, chomp, crack . . ." My dog-bone sonata had everyone smiling—except for the no-nonsense money man. Singing for my supper worked; the large bits that always fall off of hard rolls showered down on me throughout the meal.

The Old Prof introduced me to another kind of New York meeting—an "event." (An event is a meeting where something actually happens.) This was at New York University—NYU to those of us in the know. We were invited to "The Opening Night Reception of the Design Department of The Tisch School of the Arts." It was another "annual" thing—an exhibit of student work. My Partner had been in charge of that school for more than 25 years, so many people knew him and greeted him. More than a few knew me, too, since some had visited us at our apartment or at The Seeing Eye. This exhibit was really special—because I was allowed out of harness for the first time in public! I did my best to deserve this happy surprise, and later the Prof said my good behavior had "exceeded all expectations."

After the two-and-a-half hour event, we went to a place nearby, called The Cactus Café. Inside I lay quietly under the table, still as good as gold. But hunger pangs hit half an hour later . . . so in a weak moment I ate half My Pal's paper napkin. (Mexican restaurant napkins are spicy and delicious.) My reputation is growing as the prince of napkin thieves. Unfortunately, the Old Prof keeps teaching diners to be alert, lest they suddenly lose their napkins mid-meal. Outwitting him and them livens up my boring hours under the table—and adds a meager supplement to my pitiful rations at home. *Mi gusto mucho*!

*Hickory and the Old Prof endorsing 'talking' books at
The Andrew Heiskell Library for the Blind*

CHAPTER THREE

Taking Center Stage

May – December 1999

My Partner became a senior citizen on, as he put it, "the last day of the old millennium." We sent invitations to family and friends for a big birthday lunch. For the cover, I gave him permission to use a close-up photo of me gnawing on a huge plastic bone. That may well have amused the biped invitees, but it was a cruel jest for this quadruped who went hungry under the table. No wonder my heart goes out to poor Oliver Twist.

* * *

We had been living happily for eight months in our new East Ninth Street co-op apartment when My Partner was invited to be on something called the Jefferson Tenants Board of Directors. After thinking about it for a while, he did join. I figured that for me this would just mean lying under another big table, being another kind of "bored." The annual meeting of the Board and the apartment owners was my first in front of an audience. I lay before the Old Prof, who sat to the far right of the other five Board members, all of us facing the forty owners.

We were in the parish house of Ascension Church, which seems to believe that cleanliness and godliness are closely related. The rug was disgustingly, boringly clean, offering little sniffing activity. I was wide awake, so my only alternative was practicing my stretches: I can make myself quite long and flat and extend over a great distance, like pancake batter, when the mood strikes. After pancaking, I rolled over to get more comfortable and stretched my legs up in the air. I was hoping for some action—the Prof had said there might be some yelling about an "assessment." I'm not allowed to growl, bark, bite, or do much of anything that I like, but I do enjoy watching a good fight . . . but the meeting wore on and everyone was disgustingly cordial, to the point, and constructive. Boring. The only things of interest were the elegant, gleaming shoes of the president, so eventually I pancaked over to him in the center. I got a really first-class sniff and, just as the meeting closed, added to their shine with a couple of big licks.

Many owners called this the best-spirited session in years; they said much was done in a short time, with great good will. When My Partner eventually figured out what I had been doing at the far end of my leash, he said he thought my "entertaining floor show" had a lot to do with the meeting's success. He's begun to suspect that it's really me they wanted on the Board. (He is sometimes pitifully slow to catch on.) I'm soon going to organize a Canine Co-Op Board—with Homer, Rudolph, Granite, Peety, Cosmo, Valentine, Mercury, Blue, and Mia— to protect our rights, and insist on equal bones for all and a dog biscuit

52   Lloyd Burlingame

from the doormen each time we successfully return from the outside world.

* * *

After the meeting, we went to an Italian restaurant, on University Place, for a working dinner of the Board. Heather (Homer's mom), My Partner, and the other four men sat around a table. The thing I liked best was that our table was on a balcony, so my place on the floor was not so boring as usual. I could look right through or under the railing at the diners just below us, whose shoulders were at the height of my nose. I could sniff their foods and choose what interested me. For over a quarter of an hour I had been closely watching a woman shovel unruly strands of spaghetti into her open maw. I had a surefire plan for an aerial attack. Like a stealthy leopard on a tree branch, I waited for the exact second to pounce. The unsuspecting lady raised her fork and leaned forward . . . *just* as my open mouth approached her juicy meatball. She let out a hideous shriek. She was startled to find my cold, moist nose and gleaming, white teeth a millimeter from her own nose, mouth, and meatball. A cruel jerk on my leash robbed me of this golden opportunity to experience the joy of Italian cuisine.

I just don't get it: I'm never given enough to eat, and I try to be philosophic about this. I assume that the Old Prof is too poor to feed me properly, and my heart goes out to him. After all, retired school teachers are not exactly captains of industry or investment bankers. But when I take some initiative to relieve the situation, to take pressure off the poor old man, what does he do? He thwarts me at—almost—every turn.

* * *

You guide dogs reading this know how to occupy yourselves while stuck at rest beneath a table, foodless as the people overeat, dropping only the occasional crumb. There's the traditional snatch-of-the-napkin: One of the humans may have wiped off marinara sauce with it—delicious. Naturally you'll have checked and continued to hunt for any bits of food left by previous diners. And there's always the narcotic of a good snooze. I have discovered another under-table activity that I wish to share with you. Now, this works only with single-pedestal tables, which are vulnerable to a special diversion: simply (1) stand up, (2) arch your mighty back, (3) tilt the table top to rock it back and forth, (4) repeat, and (5) continue repeating.

To the humans above deck, this will feel like dining on a ship during a very rough storm at sea. At first, they won't know what's causing the water and soup to slosh out of glasses and bowls. They won't even think of you, abandoned and starving in the hold. They'll start to batten down the burgers. Eventually they'll discover that *you're* the storm and will enjoy the joke. At this point you may expect at least a roll to drop from the table. Footnote: The tables at The Village Diner are wonderfully unstable and make for very stormy dining. *Andrea Doria*, thinking of you.

* * *

Hurricane Floyd's torrential rain didn't stop the Old Prof from dragging me into the street early on the morning of 16 September. *How* wet did I get? Here's how wet: I dried off about seven hours later. He had scheduled another bath for me at Creature Features that afternoon—this was only about six months after my first! We should have begun building an ark, not going to another torture session at my least-favorite place in the whole world. I was relieved to see him waver, then postpone that ill-advised appointment for two days.

They went far too fast. On Saturday, we walked past fallen trees laid low by Floyd's high winds. What the Old Prof calls his "scrap of far peripheral vision" helped a bit in trying to avoid the fallen branches. Finally we arrived at the torture chamber—I mean the Great Bathtub—on Great Jones Street. In return for my careful guidance, once again I was deserted: Magoo unfolded his long white cane and tapped off toward Tower Records, a block north.

Here's what he told me about this solo visit to Tower:

He arrived at the glass doors leading into the classical music department. By now we had been entering these together for a year. Expecting our customary warm welcome, he was surprised when a voice demanded, "Where's your dog?" My Partner recoiled, then soothingly explained that I was fine—just getting a bath nearby. (Personally, I don't think "fine" and "bath" belong in the same sentence.) "Humph" came the reply, as though the hearer was not entirely sure that I was safe. After an awkward pause, the Old Prof continued his walk. Another voice stopped him: "There's nothing wrong with your dog, is there? He's not sick?" The Prof reassured this one, too, and kept walking. (He was beginning to notice that no one asked after *his* health.) At last he reached the back desk—where Steve cried, "Where's your dog; nothing's wrong, is there?" Again My Partner gently explained that I'd be back within the hour. But he had begun to feel himself on trial—as if accused of somehow distressing everyone's best friend: me. Tolerated only because he promised a quick return of . . . me.

The Old Prof felt compelled to prove his innocence, so next day we walked *together* to Tower. The rain had stopped, the sun shone forth, and I felt particularly fit—ready for a smart series of tail wags, my head held high. As we entered the glass doors, a friendly voice called, "Hickory!" I flashed my most brilliant smile and lunged forward to return the compliment. Magoo seemed less than pleased by my surge. ("Tough," I thought, "*he* wasn't half drowned yesterday by a brute—nor assaulted by the loud, high whine of a hair dryer.")

Another voice called gleefully, "Hickory!" Clearly, I was returning not only dry, but triumphant. At the back desk Ray, John, and Alex cried (you guessed it), "Hickory!" As Ron, Patsy's dad, hurried down the side aisle, also calling my name, My Partner grumbled something about "Carol Channing," a spotlight, and the " 'Hello, Hickory!' number." I was over the moon with their welcome . . . though I saw no edible token of appreciation—not one measly dog biscuit.

There's much talk at The Seeing Eye about who is Alpha Dog on the team. Presumably it's the human, but these back-to-back visits to Tower showed the Old Prof who really plays second fiddle in our duo. At home he said meekly that he felt ("in a microcosmic way") like someone named President Kennedy, who on a visit to Paris, called himself the "humble escort" of his wife, Jacqueline. He said he was there to open doors and hold her chair while she was being seated. Perhaps our family President has learned there's a downside to drenching me against my will? I live in hope.

* * *

Our venture into film acting didn't do much to restore My Partner's self-esteem. This began with a call from his friend Agnes Beck, a librarian at Manhattan's Andrew Heiskell Braille and Talking Book Library. She asked him to appear in a training film for library employees (doubtless knowing I would be accompanying him). Of course he said, "Yes." (I think he likes to show off.)

At the library, the film crew seemed cordial enough to Magoo—but they fell all over themselves when greeting me. I, of course, responded in kind. I greeted them with my dolphin-out-of-the-waves spiral leap, as well as my more-sedate circular moves with fast-wagging tail that so many admire. My Partner told me to restrain myself, sternly reminding me that I was still in harness. I wondered if there was some jealousy here? He was overweight and couldn't jump in spirals anymore (if ever). I didn't say too much—he's thin-skinned, if not thin. Besides, the poor man would soon realize again that he was merely playing a supporting role to me.

First the gentleman with the camera put us into the right position for filming. He asked the Old Prof if I must always stay on his left. Magoo explained this was true when walking in harness, but not in less-formal situations. The crew liked that and put me on his right when we sat at the table with the Kurzweil personal reading machine. We both knew all about this thing because we have one at home. It looks over the words in a book (the humans call this "scanning"), then a voice in the machine reads them out loud. It doesn't just read *books*, though. When My Partner types on his computer, our voice—we call him "Perfect Paul"—reads the writing out loud. Paul says each word as My Partner types it in, and reads stuff back to him too, for proofreading.

For the film, someone grabbed a book off the shelf and opened it. When the voice started reading, it sounded *just* like Perfect Paul at home. While I was trying to figure out how Paul's voice got to the library, he said the "F Word"—whatever that is—and all the people started gasping and giggling.

When the bipeds had settled down again, the crew began filming us with me stretched out on a too-clean carpet, facing the table. Now, my tail is good, but it's certainly not my strongest point, so wisely the cameraman asked me to turn around, with my head pointing toward him. Luckily no one told My Partner that the camera was on him for maybe three . . . well . . . two . . . seconds, and on me the whole rest of the time. I flashed my brilliant smile, gazed most soulfully, and displayed my long-nosed classic profile. There was general praise of my performance. I honestly felt sorry for the Professor. Who stars in this partnership is becoming more and more clear to him. I don't want his bit-player status to crush his spirit, so I try to buck him up whenever I can.

* * *

With practice, the Old Prof began to see the benefits of my taking center stage. For instance, he became less nervous about public speaking. He knew that however dull he might be, with me beside him, his speechifying would not be a total loss for the audience.

I was a big help when our friend Susan Niederman invited him to talk to a group in New Jersey. They wanted to learn about his having had a prominent theatre design career and then adapting to losing his sight. We both stood onstage in front of the audience of about fifty middle-aged ladies who were involved in Jewish "philanthropy." (That has something to do with money.) There was a microphone on a tall stand in the middle of the platform, but my pal didn't need it—so one of the ladies moved it just to the side of us.

First, the lady who had greeted the Old Prof talked about their previous guest and the one to come. She said everyone agreed that last month's speaker was one of the best they had ever heard, and next month's would discuss "Noah and the Rainy Season." My Partner started off by saying how much he admired last month's speaker and how he feared himself "not quite able to achieve her high level of presentation." Yawn. He was absolutely *sure* that his subject matter "did not have the archetypically cosmic depth of 'Noah and the Rainy Season.' " Yaaaaaaaaaaaaaaawn.

I decided to liven up the proceedings by whacking my mighty tail against the base of the mike stand. By now I had learned something about music (whether I wanted to or not), so I whacked rhythmically, each blow of my tail making a glorious racket. It boomed out through the speakers, sounding to my delight as if a man with a big bass drum had led a parade into the room. I think the ladies liked this a good deal. But the Old Prof was more than a little peeved that someone was stealing his thunder. He began to peer from side to side, trying to figure out who the competition was and why no one had made them stop. Boom! Boom! Boom! I was really into it now. Suddenly a lady zoomed up and moved the microphone away from my tail. Party pooper. My tail continued its commanding thumps, but they could hardly be heard beyond the stage, so I lost interest and decided to think about a nap. All the same, everyone laughed heartily at my diversionary concert— except You Know Who. When the mike-snatching lady told him who the drummer was, he gave me a watery little "I'll get you for this" smile. Well, it's not my fault he doesn't know how to start a lecture with a bang.

After the talk, as we stood near the exit door, several ladies came up to speak to us. One of them, maybe about seventy, told My Partner, "There are four reasons why you should do more speaking."

"Really? Four?" he replied pleasantly.

"Yes, four: First, your subject matter is interesting. Second, you are a good speaker. Third, you have a sense of humor, and fourth

Lloyd Burlingame

[she paused], you're not so bad looking."

The Old Prof laughed. "Well, I don't know about that last one. [Now *he* paused.] Come to think of it, a dear old friend told me last week that I was getting to look more and more like my dog. I thought that a great compliment, since I think Hickory is very handsome indeed!"

Now *I* thought this was very good of him—elegantly put. I began to forgive him for that "I'll get you" look. But the lady seemed mystified by this response.

"You think you look like your dog?" she asked, totally bewildered. She began to work through this mystery. She stared hard at my face, then studied the Old Prof's. Back and forth, comparing one face to the other—as if making the judgment of Solomon, or Paris . . . well, *one* of those Greeks. Again she paused. Finally, deliberately, she pronounced, "No, Mr. Burlingame, you are better-looking than your dog."

Well, that seemed wantonly rude to me. She was probably just trying to cheer up the poor old fellow. To be honest, I don't think he believed her—and that, at least, is some crumb of comfort for me. I've asked to be excused from doing more events like that in suburban New Jersey. Let's just see how well he does without my presence and quick-witted moves to perk up his presentations.

* * *

Nearly every morning when I take the Old Prof to nearby Gristedes supermarket, we're greeted with joyous cries of, "Hickory!" "Hickory's here!" "How are you doing, Hickory?" It gives me quite a lift to be welcomed with such enthusiasm. I'd guess that only two out of a dozen helpful clerks know My Partner's name—and they seldom use it. To his credit, he has grown to take his near-anonymity with a fairly good grace; he seems even a bit bemused by it.

When we are shopping very early in the morning, an elderly woman barges into the store. She always demands that the staff stop serving other customers and wait on her immediately. As the Old Prof orders his potato salad or rice pudding, she interrupts, loudly demanding to know if the bagels are fresh or why the chickens weren't barbecued before her arrival.

On one shopping trip, she surprised us with a polite approach: "Hello, Hickory."

"He's resting right now," My Partner managed to reply, "but I know if awake, he'd wish you a good day." The woman looked puzzled and corrected him: "I don't mean your dog. I'm talking to you—isn't your name 'Hickory?' Everyone calls you 'Hickory.' "

The Old Prof laughed his little President Reagan, "heh, heh," and explained, "Hickory is my dog's name, but people usually greet us as a team with Hickory as the lead partner." He smiled as though to show that he was accustomed to playing the role of junior partner.

She seemed most dubious and challenged, "Okay. If your name really isn't 'Hickory,' then what *is* it?

My name is "Lloyd."

She narrowed her eyes suspiciously, reluctant to accept this lesson from the Prof. "*What* is it?" she shot back.

"Lloyd," my pal repeated.

"*Lloyd?*" She shook her head. "That's a funny sort of name." She spat it out as though she'd just tasted something nasty. "I never heard of any such name."

. . . She now unfailingly calls him, "Floyd."

* * *

I had pretended to ignore that whole stupid interchange at Gristedes, but, frankly, I can understand the woman's disbelief. "Lloyd" is a good enough name, I guess, but "Hickory" is, by common consent, one of true distinction. I am generally quite pleased with it— although it, too, occasionally causes confusion. For example, the other day in the elevator, a kindly little old lady sweetly asked My Partner, "Now what's your dog's name again? Is it 'Whiskey?' " She pronounced that with a charming quaver, so I thought adopting it for a while might be fun. But Old Spoilsport said that "Hickory" suited me admirably—and that was that.

If You Can Break It There, You Can Break It Anywhere

One day in November I overheard Charlie and My Partner begin to plan a party for my third birthday—for friends who had asked to play with me out of harness. The two came up with a list of thirty of my fans. But then My Partner reconsidered—fearing that being *socially* involved with so many people in the neighborhood might distract me from my duty. Now that *is* a party pooper.

At least he didn't completely ignore my big day. In lieu of the gala, there were small events. We had a new friend, Barbara Backer, who walked with us around Washington Square every morning. Early on this special morning, the three of us went for a six-mile fast walk along the Hudson, as far south as Robert F. Wagner Park. We paused for a rest and Barbara gave me a sturdy tomato-red rubber Kong toy. The day was cool and crisp. The sun was warm and many fine orange leaves had fallen from the trees, to sniff and try to eat. On our way home Barbara warned My Partner that just ahead of us a flood of people was streaming across our path, from the Weehawken ferry boat toward their Wall Street jobs. That bothered me not in the least. I simply put my mind to Moses parting the Red Sea and we sailed right through. My parting of the sea of brokers impressed Barbara. I can't think why; I'm a no-nonsense pro.

I was given an okay bright cobalt-blue rubber bone by the Old Prof; and an orange plastic ball, complete with bell, by the cat cousins, Hugo and Clementine. I was surprised by their thoughtfulness. (Not exactly common in a cat.) They have good taste, but their gift was just a little too large for me to swallow—making it a good toy, but not a great one. There were long-distance calls wishing me well, and even an animated E-mail card of singing Labs. That came from Barbara Cokorinos, My Partner's "administrative director" at NYU, who had visited us at The Seeing Eye.

In the evening, Jane from Dr. Zimmerman's office came to

visit. (He's My Partner's "internist" . . . whatever that means.) She gave me a tug toy . . . she also brought toys for the *cats*, which was inappropriate on my birthday. But those toys are small, so maybe I can eat them when no one's looking. Jane is the dearest, smartest, kindest sweetheart in the whole world and has a dog named Shayna whom she loves even more than her fiancé. She writes all of the good doctor's appointments in a date book and gives this to him to plan his next day. Sometimes she enters an appointment of her own. Today Dr. Zimmerman came to her desk to ask, "Who is Hickory, and why am I going to his birthday party?" Jane said she replied coolly, "Hickory is Hickory Burlingame, and you are not invited to the party, I am." The people all found that pretty funny. But next time I invited Dr. Zimmerman.

Bill Marbit, the owner of Reader's Stationery Store on Tenth Street, came as the other of our two invited guests. He brought me a big rubber bone that had been "pit bull tested" for strength. Well, if I'd had sleeves to roll up, I'd have done so. That kind of boast gets my juices flowing and my jaws primed to show who can do what to which. Besides, it was a slur against Labs. The two men chatted away for a few minutes, then suddenly Bill said, "Look, Hickory's tearing the bone apart and about to eat a large piece of rubber." My Partner – jailer snatched away the bone *and* the tender morsel I was about to devour. Bill said he was taking the bone back to complain and replace it with something stronger. Pit bull – tested indeed. Since then the Old Prof has called me "Napoleon Bone-apart." (The previous Christmas, I had proudly destroyed in record time 85 percent of the toys given me. Clearly the bipeds were wising up, making it harder for me to live by my motto: "If it ain't broke, break it!")

All in all, my third was a pretty good birthday. At least Magoo didn't overreact as he had on the one-year anniversary of my living and working in Manhattan . . .

Maybe I did go a bit too far on that 19 November: My Uncle Michael had come to visit, and before biped breakfast—but two long hours after my skimpy repast—I was innocently playing tug with him. The thick rope toy takes some mighty strong pulling to really have a

Lloyd Burlingame

good time. Like any good Lab and good host, I threw my strength and my determination into the game. With reckless abandon I leapt in the air. True, I had not paid much attention to the clear glass top of the coffee table—who could even *see* it? I landed directly on top of it and the stupid thing shattered. That was even more of a mess than my Christmas rampage. This *really* bothered the two brothers. My so-called Partner scooped me up and tossed me in the bedroom with some overly dramatic exclamations: "Thank God you're not cut!" was the calmest. I decided to take a little snooze to get back my strength. Meanwhile, evidently they cleaned up the jagged shards and little bits of glass that had flown all over the place—so I never did get a good look at the full effect of my strength. The cats were such ninnies they'd dashed away at the first crack of glass.

Soon after, two strangers moved in a new wooden coffee table. One of its legs looked mighty tempting, but the Prof managed to spray the whole thing with Bitter Apple before I could sink my teeth into it. That stuff is *vile*. Still, all chewing aside, I thought the new table looked sturdy enough for one of my famous four-paw landings . . . but I decided to save that stunt for New Year's.

* * *

After my morning walk—always too short; it's only two miles—we return home to be greeted by our building's doorman, Steverino. We usually take the elevator to seven (push the fourth button from the top on the right), and My Partner has a little system for finding our apartment: Make a right and trot down the hall to the next-to-last-door on the left. In front of it lies an ugly doormat, which Professor Magoo bumps with his toe to know he's arrived at the right place.

One day we left the elevator and headed to the apartment door, he with his key at the ready. I knew instantly by new and wonderful odors in the carpet that something was different. It's a source of ever-growing wonder to me how very limited his sense of smell is. You don't have to be a brilliantly gifted sniffer like Dr. Doolittle's dog,

Gyp, to sense something radically different in the air. Nose-wise, the meanest all-American knows more than the Old Prof, or any other human I've met. This can be profoundly discouraging—as it was on this occasion. I raced around in my mind how best to signal to him that he was putting his key in the right door—on the *wrong floor*. I didn't want to annoy—or alarm—whoever did live here. He fumbled with his key, stubbornly trying it this way and that. Inspiration hit: I sniffed the stupid door mat like mad, going left, tugging on the leash, going right—trying to get him to stop and get out of there. His peevish response was only, "Well, you certainly have discovered a whole new world of scents in our old door mat." (Honestly.)

I renewed my effort. If only I could get him to feel, or even dimly see, that it was not our cream-and-black, diamond-patterned mat. *Finally*, after checking his keys and scratching his head . . . he got it. Then with horror he remembered the hostile, mean, lawsuit-loving tenant who lived behind that door—and we got the hell out of there. If it had not been for my quick-wittedness, who knows what could have happened. I never like to take too much credit, but I must admit my solution showed a touch of genius. On returning home, two floors higher, I pointedly ignored our boring, ugly doormat—thinking an appropriate award for my good work would be a far more interesting replacement.

THE MIDDLE YEARS: 2000 – 2003

Hickory meets Fala at the
Franklin Delano Roosevelt Memorial in Washington D.C.

CHAPTER FOUR

Why Don't You Listen to Your Dog?

By my third Christmas in the Big Apple, I was becoming an experienced dog about town. Just before New Year's, the Old Prof and I rode Uptown, to Saint Barts at 51st and Park, for a concert of Bach Cantatas. We met our dear friends, Carrie and Nathan (both bipeds), and got seated—separately because Carrie has "allergies" . . . to *me*! (Perplexing; I'm not allergic to her.) A kindly lady in the pew in front of ours befriended us, keeping people from entering our row to cross over. I had a lot of space between pews in which to spread out, and my behavior was exemplary. But the soprano's singing was not—it was vinegary and shrill. Whenever she soloed, I began to whimper. My Partner called that honest music criticism.

After the concert, we zoomed farther Uptown, to the Carlyle Hotel, for dinner with our friends and their friends: Martha and her dinner companion. Everyone seemed to love me. Several smartly dressed young women dashed up to admire me. The staff was most courteous and accommodating. The Old Prof knew Carrie had made sure that they were dog-friendly, but we'd had no idea they'd care so much about my well-being. Later during the meal, I overheard that the brother of one of our party owned the hotel.

* * *

I guided My Partner to a luncheon to honor Recording for the Blind & Dyslexic, an organization located in my old hometown, Princeton. The Prof said my great popularity might have had something to do with my being not just the handsomest but the only canine present. (A rather petty comment.) Whatever the reason, I was widely photographed—I consider myself a stellar representative of The Seeing Eye.

That same week I represented my alma mater again, in an "academic procession." It was held at historic Cooper Union, just a few blocks from where we live in the Village. Fifty colleges and universities sent deputies to honor George Campbell, who was being installed as the Union's new president. My Partner proudly marched with me, representing his other alma mater: Carnegie-Mellon University. He got to dress up in an academic gown with a brightly colored Scotch plaid hood. Even though I wore only my usual plain harness, I was photographed more than him—*and* more than the new president, Senator Schumer, Maya Lin, Virginia Fields, and Milton Glazer. Professor Magoo was proud of my most skillfully negotiating the many ins and outs of stairs and street crossings.

Lloyd Burlingame

During the two-hour feast of speeches, I spread out in the wide aisle next to My Partner's seat. He said he was sure my handsome, pale-yellow figure cut a distinctive silhouette against the dark red carpet. After the ceremony we lunched at a nearby restaurant and encountered one of the speakers, Maya Lin. My Partner expressed appreciation for her work, especially the design of the Vietnam Veterans Memorial on the Mall in Washington. "And I admire your handsome dog," she replied. "Trying to concentrate on delivering my speech, I could hardly keep my eyes off him!" (Ahem.)

* * *

One very hot afternoon, the Old Prof and I walked to the Andrew Heiskell Library, to pick up a new cassette player. I have to admit, I was off form heading north on Fifth Avenue. I'm afraid I dragged him left and right to a half-eaten bagel here and a baby in a stroller there. With my concentration way off, My Partner's corrections grew sterner and sterner as we neared the library on 20th Street. Pulling myself together, I remembered to turn left going toward Sixth Avenue. But I became distracted again, so he leaned hard on me to walk quickly, straight ahead. Near the end of the block, I tugged and tugged, but My Partner paid no attention. Finally we arrived at Sixth Avenue—having passed the building he had visited dozens of times. A fellow pedestrian helped us turn back to the front entrance, where we were greeted by the lady in charge of the door. "I saw you go by," she told Magoo. "Your dog pulled you to come in and you wouldn't pay attention to him." She folded her arms, shook her head in mock exasperation and demanded, "Why don't you listen to your dog?" (He should have asked himself— rhetorically—"Now, who's off form and messing up?")

Inside, a charming, capable, and eager young librarian offered to help find some books on tape. The Old Prof didn't know her so he introduced himself: "My name is Lloyd . . . and his name is Hickory." She drew a blank hearing his name, but lit up like fireworks on the Fourth of July hearing mine. "Hickory!" she exclaimed. "I've loved reading your journal reports. You're so witty and charming. She returned to the Old Professor: "I'm sorry, what was your name again?" We headed home with the new cassette player, both of us back in form—perfect representatives of The Seeing Eye's rigorous training.

* * *

I made my well-prepared Carnegie Hall debut on Valentine's Day in the first year of the new millennium. "Maestro" (as I call My Partner when he's in musical mode) had been invited by his pal Sal to attend a gala performance of an opera by Donizetti. This was one I hadn't heard (hard to believe around our apartment), called *Lucrezia Borgia*. But I knew well the voice of the soprano who would sing the title role: Renée Fleming. We listen to many of her CDs.

Now, the Maestro had been a bit cautious about exposing me to what he calls "the last bastions of high musical culture in our fair city": Avery Fisher Hall, The Metropolitan Opera, and Carnegie Hall. My Partner told Sal the invitation was hard to resist, but that he was nervous: I might react badly to the cheering and wild applause that would doubtless greet Ms. Fleming. So the Old Prof decided I should be even more thoroughly versed than usual in the opera itself. He played a CD version for me over and over. I felt like Liza in *My Fair Lady*, fed up with all the drills forced on her by Professor Higgins. Even Hugo and Clemmie retired into a box, covering their oddly pointed ears to escape the onslaught.

The Maestro had what he thought was an "inspired" idea. (I didn't.) He found a recording of a performance from 25 years ago: Montserrat Caballé's debut in *Lucrezia Borgia*, also at Carnegie Hall. This has the loudest, wildest, most unbridled applause and cheering you could imagine. Not since my training at The Seeing Eye to keep me steady in Manhattan traffic had I been forced to listen to so much ear-insulting noise. The Professor wouldn't quit, and I had no way to avoid Madame Caballé and her delirious fans—he has speakers in every room of the apartment! If I didn't go mad first, I was ready to stay totally calm—by now I would not be surprised by even the loudest bombardment of Macy's Fourth of July fireworks.

But the opera's plot really disturbed me: La Borgia didn't mind offering her guests a little "arsenico" in the Chianti or the osso buco. Magoo does all he can to keep me away from possibly toxic treats on the streets of New York. Yet he continued to expose me day after day to this story of a professional poisoner who finally murders her own son. I was only four years old! Shouldn't some productions be rated to warn the parents of young dogs? I still think this one deserves an "XXX."

The big evening arrived. I jumped into the car that would take us north to 57th Street— slightly shell shocked, but eager to experience the smells (though maybe not the sounds) of the famous Carnegie Hall. We waited in the lobby for half an hour before being seated. Several new best friends approached to greet me and offer assistance. My companion asked them not to pet me while I was in harness, but since he can't see too well, they snuck in several pats on my head. I responded with a few good tongue-lick kisses. Old friends whom the Prof not seen for years greeted him and met me. The Maestro reunited with one old friend when his date happened to call out, "Look at that handsome dog." I was having a high time with all this commotion and attention.

The fun pretty much ended when the house manager seated us at the rear of the orchestra floor—a good position because when all the people finally sat down, I was able to spread out comfortably in the aisle. The loud overture started and the lady directly in front of us kept darting anxious glances at me over her shoulder. She seemed to fear I might misbehave. True, I lurched every now and again, finding an odor I had missed on first meeting the deep maroon carpet. (What maroon-blooded canine wouldn't?) Still, after the first scene—which seemed about two days long—I signaled to my pal that returning to the lobby and meeting more jolly people would be better. I had already had enough of the smooth, long-breathed "legato line"—heaven knows, I had heard it often enough at home—but my suggestion was ignored.

Miss Fleming was singing softly in the stratosphere. I thought she needed some reinforcement, and since I knew her part by heart, I tilted my head heavenward to join her in canine. I sure got some dirty looks and sharp tugs on my leash, but it was my turn to do the ignoring—he'd had his chance to leave. That woman in front of us glared at my companion. He was cringing, about to gather up all our supplies: extra paper towels for an emergency, little dog-bone treats, plastic bone, water bottle, and folding water bowl.

Then the music grew louder, and helping out so forcefully had made me tired. As Professor Maestro told it later, I concluded my much-admired "fil di voce" (that means "vocal thread"—whatever *that* means) and ended duetting with my "stunning diminuendo" (whatever *that* means). Except for the Nervous Nellie, the people around me seemed pleased with my magnificent concluding note. I went to sleep—to heck with it. At the end of Miss Fleming's aria, the audience yelled, stamped, bravoed, and carried on like crazy. I rose to check that out—Nellie was screaming with the rest of them. (I guess she saw audience participation as a one-way street.) Clearly, no more help was needed from me . . . I did my old "what's the use?" plop onto the floor and stretched out quite comfortably for the rest of Act One.

Intermission was more fun: visits with friends old and new. The second act was as dull as the first, so I got in some deep sleep.

The second intermission was another story. I was taken outside onto 57th Street, to see about parking. I could go either left to Seventh Avenue or right toward Sixth. I chose Sixth because I spotted a magnificent upright support for a canopy that extended out to the curb from some restaurant. I went right up to one of its poles and expressed myself with operatic extravagance. Sal and the Old Prof laughed. They said the just-refurbished restaurant had been "re-christened " 'The Russian Pee Room'!" The joke escapes me.

For Act Three I was as silent as a Borgia guest after his first (and last) swallow—and was rewarded with four small Milk-Bones. Considering what I had learned of human (mis)behavior while we were boning up on the performance, I gave each and every treat a good sniff before gulping it down. After the last hurrahs, even Nellie in front of us gave me a big smile and wished me a kind goodnight. You have to be

Lloyd Burlingame

careful not to rush to judge bipeds too harshly on first meeting.

* * *

If only that had been my last musical outing . . . no such luck. The Old Prof was invited to Brooklyn for a private harpsichord recital, given by the talented daughter of an old friend. He said I'd like Brooklyn because it has many trees. He said nothing about how I'd like hearing the harpsichord. I was on guard instantly, because out of the *hundreds* of CDs around our apartment, only one features a solo harpsichord—and that's never played.

The parents of the harpsichordist picked us up. They were dog lovers, so I was allowed to sit on the back seat and observe a new part of the world. The view crossing the Williamsburg Bridge really held my attention. We arrived on a pleasantly tree-lined street near a nice-sounding place called Prospect Park. I immediately parked to announce my arrival to fellow canines, then went upstairs in the old brownstone to the "floor-through" apartment where the concert was to take place. A harpsichord is a bit like a small piano. The strings inside that make the music are plucked with some kind of quills. (But I never heard a bird make such a racket.) The sound is high—pingy, jangly, chingy—and *hard* on dogs' ears. Humans' ears must be as bad as their noses, because they all sat there smiling as Purcell, Byrd, and Bach high-pitched their way forward, for *days*. I'd heard music by these fellows before, but it hadn't sounded like this. I hunkered down as low as I could, clamped my paws over my ears . . . no use. Not meaning to—because the playing itself was accomplished—I let out long, high whines of pain. Every once in a while I lifted up my head beseechingly toward My Partner and tried to ask if this torture would ever end. He patted my head and stroked me reassuringly—which offered no comfort at all.

At last, just as I thought it was safe to uncover my ears, the little audience demanded an encore! An *encore*? I couldn't believe it! My ears buzzed, rang, and only began to return to normal half an hour after the agony ended. Back home, I was solemnly promised that

I'd never, ever again be subjected to another harpsichord concert. The remorseful Maestro had not only put me through this ordeal, but had forgotten to give me my dinner. All in all, a day I hope to forget.

We were put through noise-distraction training at The Seeing Eye. Only the top dogs in the class could work in big cities with their jack hammers, pile drivers, air brakes, car and truck horns, trucks backfiring, occasional gunfire, and police, ambulance, and fire engine sirens. But no one had ever prepared us for the horrible harpsichord. I'm writing to the A.S.P.C.A. These things should be labeled: "Caution: The Surgeon General warns that harpsichord listening can be dangerous to a dog's health."

***

Barbara Backer has become such a close pal, I call her Aunt Barbara. She brings me treats and we travel all over the city together—not only around Washington Square Park and down to Wagner Park, but uptown to Times Square and the enormous Central Park. Magoo tags along, thinking she's his new best friend. (Wrong: she's mine!) My Partner has told other friends that the "Hickory Connection" brought her happily into his life, and I'm given great credit . . . though I'd prefer extra boney treats.

The Old Prof and Aunt Barbara sometimes talk to each other in German (also called "Deutsch," which is harder to spell). It sounds like mutts barking—or as if they were constantly clearing their throats to spit out raspy-sounding words. This amuses them and somehow they seem to know what each other says. I just take a nap.

Barbara's family comes from Germany, which is in a faraway place called "Europe." She and My Partner plan to introduce me to the Old World there, which sounds very interesting. My Partner says he'd like to return to a city that he loves, called Vienna, in a country called Austria, which is part of the Old World. So they're making plans for us to cross "The Pond" to get there, in October. (I wonder how big that pond is and whether my feet will get wet.)

Austria and Vienna will be new to Aunt Barbara, and that

seems to interest her. I overheard My Partner write her a little note to explain why revisiting Vienna excites him. I can't remember all of it, so we inserted it here:

Meine Liebe Barbara,

Gruess Gott! Just a little note to let you know how happy I am that you are up for a trip to Vienna with Hickory and me. I had not told you why that city means so much to me and thought you'd like to know.

I had very much planned on retiring to Vienna when I left the University, loving music as I do. But I got cold feet when my eyesight became so limited I needed to partner with a Seeing Eye dog. Vienna has felt like home to me from the first time I accidentally arrived there as a 24-year-old soldier on leave. I thought I had bought a train ticket to Venice . . . and was mighty surprised to find only one canal and everyone speaking German! Venice is grand, but Vienna, for me, is near heaven—hearing Mozart, Haydn, Beethoven, Schubert, Mahler in spaces where they first played their own music can be close to a religious experience. (In the Central Cemetery outside the old city are, in a circular pattern, the graves of Beethoven, Schubert, Brahms, and Johann Strauss, Jr. Nearby lie Gluck and Schoenberg. My brother, another music nut, and I call this "the sacred grove.")

I spent four slugging years learning Deutsch, preparatory to living in der Kaiserstadt: at NYU in the fall, winter, and spring, plus two summers at the language institute of Middlebury College in Vermont . . . not to mention my tutorials in New York and living in Vienna on a Fulbright research grant seven years ago. The "slugging" was with ears only, because my sight had already failed badly. My text books (both grammar and literature) were prerecorded by volunteers at the Recording for the Blind & Dyslexic, but I was handicapped by a primitive "talking German dictionary." I look all of my tests (the Germans love tests) aurally, with a special tutor. Middlebury is famous for its rigor, which lives up to an old German expression: "Deutsche Sprache, schwere Sprache" ("German language, hard language") . . . oh, that Teutonic wit.

To tell the truth, even though I've lost most of what little sight I had then, I still wonder if it's not possible for Hickory and me to live in Vienna at least half of the year; I'd like to check this out. Also, it would be great fun to introduce you to my favorite museums, cafés, churches, and good friends. I think that Hickory would have a great time, since several of those friends have dogs. Most of all, he'd like it that dogs are allowed in restaurants. Of course, here he goes to any restaurant he wants to, but he's usually the only dog in the room. In Vienna he would have plenty of company.

Alles gute!
Dein,
Lloyd

Vienna restaurants sound promising! Here in New York I miss being able to socialize under the table with other canine friends, as I was used to doing at The Seeing Eye. If there are no harpsichords in the "City of Music," as My Partner calls Vienna, this sounds like a great adventure.

* * *

Except for the two red rubber Kongs, an orange rubber ball with bell, a blue rubber bone, several red rubber tug-toys, some brown and white tug-ropes, and an assortment of white plastic bones, the apartment (where I'm forced to spend a good deal of time) is unimaginatively, boringly decorated. It's all sooooooo regular and planned out. My yard has the moss-green Indian rug with a pleasing leaf pattern, but the rest of the place is all khaki, olive drab, and brown wood—it gives "neutral" a whole new meaning. You'd think a professional designer could do better than this. In my spare time, I've tried to figure out how I could bring a little zip to the place.

On entering the apartment from the hall, you come directly into the dining area where a round table sits on the dark-green rug. On the right are a little hallway and the sliding pocket-door to the bathroom. On the left there's the piano against the wall and beyond that a deep alcove where the Prof keeps his files in oak cabinets. We needed a strong and simple design statement that would take the eye from the navy-blue-and-white-tiled bathroom all the way across the apartment to the wall cabinets . . . something like the center line on a highway. How was I to effect this?

First, I must tell you about the unfair obstacle. It was created to allow the cats to slither into the bathroom—where their perpetually filled little bowls offer a feline smorgasbord—but to keep me out. A chain on the sliding door allows only about a three-inch vertical opening—just wide enough for me to insert my nose and smell all that food. Imagine the temptation! I always keep a weather eye out, waiting for the Old Prof, guests, or the cleaning lady to forget about the chain. At last, one fine day Magoo himself—Mr. Ever-Vigilant—was so engrossed in something he was writing that he dashed from the bathroom to his work station—*hah!*—and left the sliding door wide open.

Unfortunately, this time the cats had emptied their dishes, but I snatched my opportunity to create: I walked quickly, but not so as to attract undue attention, into the tiled room, took the end of the new(!) roll of snow-white paper in my mouth . . . and in one grand, unbroken gesture, dashed across the dining area into the office alcove. Like an expert skywriter, I left a perfect trail of pure white, running 35 feet from west to east. (I also snacked on a morsel of the end of the tissue: a little reward for a big job expertly done.)

What gave me up was that roller thing holding the paper: it squeaked. That caught the ear of the local gestapo. He hurled himself in my direction and peered at the something new. Since his vision is hardly X-ray, he had to get down on hands and knees to inspect my post-modern, low-tech decor. He didn't even give it a chance. He let out a howl of mingled mirth and derision, then tried to re-roll my centerline. He did not accomplish this in a professional manner. I most certainly did not help.

* * *

On September 11, 2001, I went out at noon with My Partner to park. On our half-block walk to Broadway, he was unusually quiet. At the southeast corner of our block we paused and were astonished to see hundreds of totally silent people streaming north on Broadway—Manhattan's main street, usually full of cars but now traffic free. Young, old, men, and women—a total cross-section of humanity—fled Uptown. They seemed stunned. Even if I hadn't heard the awful news on the radio just after our morning walk, I'd have known from the mixture of bad smells all around us that something big was wrong. But I hadn't imagined this gloomy parade from lower Manhattan. It had been three hours and they still kept coming. We stood, also stunned. The deep silence of that September noon will always be with us.

All over the city, people wanted to *do* something: How could they help? . . . How could we? Next morning, Maggie Raywood called. This good-hearted head of the NYU Design Department costume shop *was* doing something—for the rescue dogs at Ground Zero. She planned to make booties to protect their feet, and she needed to measure mine for the patterns. Thinking of my fellow canines working so gallantly just a mile and a half south, I did this gladly. I stood on a sheet of brown paper and was still as still could be while Maggie drew around my paws. It wasn't *much* of a contribution to the cause, but it was the best I could manage from here.

That afternoon My Partner and Aunt Barbara sat again at the dining table to talk about Vienna, but this time they were very gloomy. Because of what happened yesterday, now we lived in something called a "frozen zone." Flying long distances could be dangerous, so my friends sadly canceled our plane reservations. We were all disappointed, but this loss was nothing compared to the suffering of our

Lloyd Burlingame

country—of the world. I hoped my booties truly were helping fellow service dogs at Ground Zero.

* * *

Instead of flying to Austria in October, we took a train to My Partner's hometown—Washington, D.C.—on 17 September. At Penn Station, the Amtrak conductor found just the right place for me to spread out in comfort, but I sat up for most of the journey and looked out the window. Above ground, after crossing the Hudson, it hurt to look back at New York—to see empty sky where the towers used to be. But the Empire State Building still stood—and the Statue of Liberty in the harbor. We sped south, very fast, on a new train called the Acela Express.

At Washington's Union Station we met up with the Prof's brother, Michael. His large car has a spacious back seat and I was allowed to sit on it. (I can't do that in taxis in the Big Apple.) Uncle Michael lives on Capitol Hill, famous for its many trees and much grass in dog-friendly patches, medians, and lawns. Some buildings are also especially interesting. But since the area was crawling with police and military, the Old Prof strongly discouraged me from leaving messages for canine companions of senators, representatives, judges, and the like.

We were invited to Aunt Susie's again, in Chevy Chase. (I get the "Chase" part, but what or who is a "Chevy"?) She, Ed, and two canines greeted us at the door. Meep had a new companion: a cute border collie named Hedy. The family has several fine trees and an ample front lawn—which we don't see much of, living stacked up in Manhattan. Aunt Susie has problems with seeing, too, so I can usually look forward to Magoo and her dropping at least a napkin or a roll. But that night, though we had a jolly time, very little of interest fell from the dinner table.

The next morning, dark and early, Uncle Michael, My Partner, and I went out for an exercise walk. Here we didn't have to trot around and around a small park as in New York. We went by a white marble building called the Folger Shakespeare Library and past the Library of Congress where my uncle was working on his biography of Abraham Lincoln. We passed the Senate and House office buildings, but no one was working that early except the many guards. The Capitol dome was all lit up and I thought it was wonderfully handsome. There were many big flower pots and little walls and such all over the sidewalks. They made walking great fun; Uncle Michael said it was "like slaloming," but he explained they're meant to stop bad men who mean mischief . . . which was sad to hear.

We went down a hill and saw a wonderful sight: a huge—I mean enormous—lawn called the Mall. Wow! In the middle of this, a pinnacle called the Washington Monument glowed brilliantly against a dark sky. Most impressive. We continued in a circle, going back up the hill to the other side of the Capitol. Uncle Michael read the *Washington Post* headline in a newspaper dispenser right there: "Anthrax Attacks Capitol!" Oh, did those brothers get quiet fast. I fought off the notion that My Partner may have been a bit irresponsible, taking us from our frozen zone street in recently attacked Manhattan to bad goings-on in D.C. Later that afternoon, we passed government workers lined up on the sidewalk, waiting to be protected from possible anthrax poisoning. We were all pretty quiet again.

I was taken to monuments honoring three presidents (by now I knew what a "president" was): Jefferson, Lincoln, and Roosevelt. At the Lincoln Memorial I was impressed by all the white marble steps that led up to the statue of "Honest Abe." A kindly guard asked the Old Prof if he would like to take the elevator to the main level. My pal was astonished to learn that there *was* such a thing. He had visited the memorial often since he was first brought there (in 1940!). Sure enough, we went in a side door, found the lift, and up we went. Going up stairs is not so hard for Magoo, but coming down is pretty tricky for both of us. We were glad to be spared that. President Lincoln thought of everything, and for that and much else we all thank him.

The new Franklin Delano Roosevelt (*you* try to spell all that) Memorial was very interesting to walk through. I liked the sculptures of the President and his wife, Eleanor. Imagine my delight when I came

Lloyd Burlingame

upon a statue of the President's Scotty, Fala. Wow! It was about time that canine accomplishment was recognized. Historian Uncle Michael asked, "Where would we be if FDR couldn't have cited Fala's resentment of unfairly negative criticism leveled at him during the 1944 presidential election campaign?" (I still don't quite know what that meant.) "Fala helped his master achieve the Voltairean desideratum of making his enemies look ridiculous." (I completely gave up on that sentence—but I did understand the next, and I wasn't surprised.) "In essence, Fala got FDR re-elected."

My picture was taken at all sorts of grand buildings and monuments . . . but the photo I like best is that of me with my friend Fala.

Not far from the Lincoln Memorial is the Kennedy Center, which we had visited on my first trip to Washington, before I knew who President Kennedy was. My Partner and Uncle Michael hoped to get tickets for a concert there that featured Verdi's *Quattro Pezzi Sacri*. (There's no escaping this stuff.) A few hours before the performance, we arrived at the box office and joined the line of ticket seekers. The tired, cranky ticket seller told biped after biped that this evening's performance was completely sold out: "No standing room, no chance of returns, read my lips, sold out." We got to the window and it was our turn to ask. She wearily began to repeat herself: "We're completely sold out . . ." Then she paused, leaned forward, and took a good look at me; I gave her my most winning smile. She exclaimed, "Oh, what a handsome dog!" She turned to one side, typed on her computer, turned front again, and purred sweetly, "I have two excellent seats in a box, with plenty of room for your beautiful dog to stretch out in." (Don't kill the messenger—I'm just quoting what she said.)

As the ticket lady had promised, the box well suited the brothers Burlingame and me. At intermission we went outside to sniff the air and see about parking. There were about six million white marble columns that I was not allowed to investigate. Finally we found a single tree, which was judged perfectly fine. (Go figure.) While we were out, the head usher had thoughtfully brought me a bowl of water—*and* had moved us to even better seats, on a broad cross-aisle near the front of the orchestra. Smiling, My Partner told Uncle Michael, "That's the magic of the Hickory Connection at work yet again." (Frankly, my idea of real magic would have been not getting the tickets in the first place.)

I enjoyed being in the world of lawns, trees, bushes, houses, and other dog friends. It was more like my childhood days with my puppy raisers in New Jersey. There's much to be said for living in Manhattan, but Washington will always have a place in my heart.

Our Acela trip home was uneventful—except for a carful of idiots holding little boxes up to their ears and yelling they were on the train. The Prof seemed anxious about being met at Penn Station in New York, and getting home from there. As we neared Penn, my nervous companion gathered up our belongings, put me back in harness, and stood, thinking a conductor would come to help us onto the platform. Suddenly Uncle Charlie appeared out of nowhere, laughing, welcoming us home, and taking some luggage. He was a wonderful surprise! I tried to give him my usual frantically happy greeting . . . but the narrow aisle and all those bustling passengers prevented my running even in tight circles. My Partner was delighted and wondered how Charlie could have known which car we were in. He's clever, alright. He gave us the best ending to an excellent trip.

* * *

Walking north on the east side of Sixth Avenue, at 15th Street, My Partner and I were greeted by a lively woman in her thirties.

"I love yellow Labs! Can I pet your dog?"

"It's better not to when he's in harness," explained the Old Prof for about the four hundredth time, "because he can be distracted from his job as a guide dog."

"Oh, okay. I just love your dog. I want to be a puppy raiser for guide dogs."

"That's a generous thing to do," the Old Prof replied, adding, "Hickory's from The Seeing Eye in Morristown, New Jersey."

The woman answered brightly, "Oh yes, I'm leaving all my

money to The Seeing Eye— I hate all my relatives."

Her reasoning was hard to applaud. My Partner managed to gulp, "Errr, well, good for you." But I figure The Seeing Eye deserves support, whatever the reason. I thanked her with both my flashiest smile and fastest series of tail wags.

Don't Ignore the Sign

When I'm taken out to park, My Partner needs his hands free for leash holding and clean-up. So he dutifully removes my harness and slings it around his neck, creating kind of a horse-collar effect. The harness boasts a bright chrome-yellow sign with strong black lettering: "Ignore Working Dog." One day the Old Prof's fashion-conscious niece, twenty-something Jessica, accompanied us on a park outing. "Gee, Uncle Lloyd," she exclaimed in admiration, "you sure know how to accessorize!"

Jessica hasn't been the only one to comment on the Old Prof's odd neckwear. One night at my final park time, a well-dressed gentleman about his age politely asked, "May I point something out to you?" I could see the "Oh, Lord, not another nut" expression on my companion's face. He had become used to loony questions and suggestions. He managed to muster a nod and a weak smile while urging me to focus on the business at hand.

"That sign you wear around your neck," began the helpful stranger, "do you know it's upside down?"

This would-be Good Samaritan thought my pal was wearing an old-fashioned "sandwich-board." (The Prof later explained to me that these were just advertising signs hung around people's necks—not tables full of goodies.)

"Thank you," My Partner gently explained. "Actually, it's not *my* sign, but belongs to my dog. When I put the harness back on him the sign will be right side up."

"Oh," replied the man, doubtfully eying my seemingly feeble-minded pal. "I understand." Neither of us was entirely sure that he did.

* * *

Uncle Charlie's partner, Sal (different from Sal of Carnegie Hall), kindly took the Old Prof to the early-morning start of his five-hour stress test at the NYU Medical Center. Of course, I came too, but since the tests were in small back rooms crowded with machines, there was no space for me. Sal and I waited in a hallway-cum-waiting room. He had brought a long, hard-cover novel to read. I lay quietly at his feet, wearing the harness and the "Ignore working dog" sign. People quickly came and went along the busy passageway. A doctor and nurse rushed by, glanced at Sal and me, and halted abruptly. Bug-eyed with amazement, the doctor gasped, "Look at that guy with the Seeing Eye dog: he's reading a book!"

Sal kept a straight face. Later he told My Partner that he had been tempted to respond, "Yes, I arrived here early for a procedure; now, only two hours later, thanks to a miracle of modern medicine, my vision is once more 20/20 and my dog can get out of harness." Sal also wondered if the doctor and nurse had thought him a total fake—right out of Dickens, using me to get sympathy from strangers. We should have brought a tin cup.

The Old Prof had been having less fun down the hall. The stress tests showed that his heart needed more study, so a few days later we were back at the NYU Medical Center—this time with Aunt Barbara as our companion. My Partner was there for an "angiogram." Somehow this thing watches what's going on in the heart and can see if it needs to be fixed. Aunt Barbara is a retired professor of nursing, and before the angio-thing started, she grilled the young surgeon just outside the operating room. I could tell my pal was cringing, and his expression made me nervous, as she demanded to know how many "procedures" like this the doctor had done. "Hundreds," he replied, reassuringly. When Aunt Barbara nodded her approval, My Partner managed a feeble smile of relief—he'd been sure the surgeon would hold her questions against him. I felt better too.

They wheeled off My Partner without me. I got nervous again, but Aunt Barbara stayed with me and said nice things to cheer me up—

so I guessed things would be okay. She and I went into the waiting area. Almost everyone there was very anxious, silently waiting for their own friends and relatives in surgery. As usual, my presence brought a smile or two, and a few people asked my name. When Barbara saw my cheering effect on this nervous dozen, she decided to remove my harness and sign. This meant that the people were allowed to pet me— which some did with great affection, and even delight. I could tell what my role was here and did my best to befriend one and all. I flashed my own brilliant smile and vigorously fanned the air with my mighty tail. Before we knew it, the dark mood had brightened (for me, too). Everyone was smiling, chatting together . . . and saying *very* complimentary things about me and The Seeing Eye. Aunt Barbara shook her head and murmured, "The Hickory Connection strikes again."

But I was not happy to be shut out of the operating room. My Partner and I lived together literally 24/7, and this separation had gone on for more than two hours. On the other side of the operating room doors they were fixing my pal's heart. When they wheeled him out on this rolling-bed thing, I was so glad to see him that I dashed up, dragging Aunt Barbara behind me. I gave him many happy, juicy licks on the face. Everyone laughed, including my Magoo . . . though Aunt Barbara wondered if this was quite sanitary.

* * *

I always look forward to a little extra sniffing time at our midday walk. The elegant apartment houses next door have particularly fascinating scents. One afternoon I was energetically inhaling these when a young man approached My Partner. "What kind of work does your dog do?" he demanded.

We both figured the questioner had read our "Ignore Working Dog" sign. (What did he think my harness was for?)

The Old Prof replied with his own question, "Errr, are you making a little joke?"

"No. Is he sniffing for gas leaks?" guessed the young man.

Since I was exploring perfectly maintained buildings, I

imagined My Partner thinking, "Yes, amid the rubble and smoking ruins of East Ninth Street." But in his Mr. Rogers-nice-guy-voice he explained aloud, "No, he's a Seeing Eye dog."

"Oh, yeah?" the young man challenged. "How come you need a guide dog? You seem to be walking with no trouble."

The Old Prof replied (*very* slowly and nicely—with infinite patience, as if speaking to a small child): "That's . . . because . . . I . . . have . . . a . . . Seeing . . . Eye . . . dog."

Hickory wistfully contemplating the remains
of a forbidden banana

CHAPTER FIVE

A Canine *Rashomon*: Three Versions of an
Incident on a Greenwich Village Sidewalk

Since my Partner's vision is almost nil, sometimes he must rely on his friends to explain the events around him. On some subjects—like food—he'll even take their word over mine. This happened a few summers ago in the Village, when one very promising afternoon was ruined by "our" friends.

"Ruined" was *my* opinion; Uncle Charlie had a different one, and the stranger we met that day had a third. Uncle Charlie is a movie buff. He said our disagreement reminded him of an old Japanese film called *Rashomon*, in which four different people tell four different stories of the same bad event. He suggested we write our own *Rashomon* script. Charlie and I would each tell his own version. Then, since the stranger was long gone, we agreed the three of us would try to describe the event from his point of view. I wasn't too sure about this, since it was two men against one Lab . . . besides which, the Old Professor declared he would start the script off with a prologue—more like an "apologia," if you ask me. (I learned that from the Guv.) So the whole project was against me from the start.

Just read this Prologue from the Prof:

Like many Labrador retrievers, Hickory was born with the besetting imperative urge to eat anything, anywhere, and at any time. Suffice to say, he's ingested or attempted to devour anything from discarded chocolate bars to old tennis balls. Chocolate can act as poison on dogs; and tennis balls, once ingested, cannot be digested. Swallowing one left our next-door neighbor's Rhodesian ridgeback with 62 stitches from abdominal surgery. Hickory is not only my miraculous means of traveling, but has become a beloved companion. He must be protected from himself concerning his gourmandizing propensities. Random snacking is strictly forbidden!

Like most Labs, Hickory can put on weight by straying the least bit from his Seeing Eye – prescribed diet. Gaining unwanted pounds can lead to hip dysplasia, which forces guide dogs to stop their valuable work early. At the time of this story, I recently had learned from our vet that Hickory had gained nine pounds in less than a year. This was a slippery slope down which I didn't want him to slide any farther. We had changed his diet to low-fat, low-calorie Kibbles and the dangerous extra pounds were slowly coming off. This explanation is to make clear the grave necessity for Hickory's being hounded by Charlie and me to obey the strict dietary laws.

I'm leaving all of that nonsense in my journal only because it shows the bias I've been up against. Now, try to forget it and keep reading:

Lloyd Burlingame

Charlie's Story

First off, you need to know how much I love Hickory. He's sunshine on a dark day and always lifts my spirits when they're down. I call him "Vitamin H." Every Saturday I work with his partner in the apartment and Hickory sits or lies near me. He usually has his own work, gnawing an enormous plastic bone—supposedly dog-chew-proof, but only sort of so. Hickory can make inroads into just about anything he chooses to chew. I'm the ever-watchful sighted one in the apartment, snatching up rubber bands, dropped quarters, and plant leaves that his partner can't see. I know Hickory often considers me The Grinch Who Stole Christmas, but his safety comes first, last, and always.

I'm aware that as much as Hickory resents my sharp censoring eyesight, his master appreciates my vigilance on our forays around Greenwich Village to stores, the bank, and the vet. This Lab has the mouth of a billy goat, but the delicate stomach of a pampered aristocrat. I give nothing potentially harmful to Hickory—including the benefit of the doubt. Nothing.

Here's what happened: One gloriously sunny July afternoon, Lloyd and I were chatting with two friends encountered on the sidewalk. Shoppers and tourists strolled by in both directions, but Hickory Sunshine seemed content to sit, waiting until we moved on. It was lunchtime, so many passersby were either munching candy bars, chomping on bagels, or licking ice cream cones. All seemed in expectedly good order. However, out of the corner of my eye, I caught sight of a shabbily dressed man veering unsteadily toward us. Granted, people's dress in the West Village is often strikingly unusual, but this guy wore one red sock, one tan sock—and no shoes. Maybe this was a new fashion trend coming west toward Fifth Avenue from the funky Lower East Side. I certainly did not recognize this man and I wondered why we were being approached.

Peeling a banana, the stranger smiled with pleasure, anticipating his first bite. Suddenly he rushed forward, knelt down, and offered the dog a taste. Hickory lurched forth, almost connecting with the forbidden fruit. Our friends and I yelled, "No!" and Lloyd immediately yanked back on the leash. The newcomer may have meant his offering kindly, but he evidently didn't see the sign that urges "Ignore Working Dog."

I had to add, "He can't eat that!" The man, who seemed as baffled as the dog, accidentally knocked most of the banana onto the sidewalk, where it lay. Hickory began to drool as he fixed his gaze on this gift he had been offered, then denied. "Kick it in the street," I yelled, fearing Hickory would try for it again. One friend obliged and the banana landed in the gutter. The stranger rose, turned, and began a slow retreat. "Man," he mumbled, "Man, it's only a banana."

The Banana Man's Story

I dunno know what happened to my shoes; I musta lost 'em somewhere along the line. Anyway, the day was nice and sunny and my feet weren't cold. Besides, I like walking in my socks.

So, I was walkin' along with all the other folks, groovin' on the day. Seemed like just about everyone was eatin' something while they walked: little kids chewin' big bagels and teenagers lickin' dripping ice cream cones. I got real hungry and spent a dime of what little change I had on me to buy this cheap banana. I strolled along, peelin' back the skin. Just as I took a bite, I spotted this cool pooch. He was with some old guy who was holdin' some kind of big-handled thing attached to the dog's back. It had a sign saying, "Ignore Working Dog."

Well, that dog looked kinda skinny to me. Maybe he was workin' too much and people weren't feedin' him. His great big sad, dark eyes made me feel kinda bad for him. I thought, "What the hell, he could use a little somethin' to eat.

Lloyd Burlingame

I'll give him a bite of my lunch." He looked like such a friendly dude, sorta smilin' at me and starin' at my banana. I bent down and held it out to him. He jumped forward with his mouth open and almost got a bite. But then these three guys all hollered at me like I was hurtin' the dog. They scared the livin' daylights out of me. The guy with the handle yanked the dog back. This other jerk yelled, "He can't eat that!"

Jeeeze! What was with them? Well, I thought, at least I had my banana back. Wrong: most of the damn thing got knocked off and fell on the sidewalk. I stood there with just a little bit of one end of it, the stupid old skin danglin' down. The rest of the banana just sat there on the concrete. The poor dog dove toward it and the old geezer tugged him back again like it was poison. What the hell did they think I was givin' him? I still felt sorry for the dog—but I wanted to get away from those nuts. "Man, it's only a banana," I told 'em as I left. That dog looked downright miserable. The turkey who yelled at me got the sorry remains of our lunch kicked into the gutter.

That's the last time I try to give a dog a treat. Maybe those dumb bozos didn't know what a banana was. Me and the dog—we may have been shoeless, but at least we weren't clueless.

Hickory's Story

My mostly loving partner and I are locked in this tug-of-war about my inadequate diet and his need to monitor what I can and can't eat. I hear all kinds of nonsense that supposedly support his stinginess, but I don't buy any of that it's-for-your-own-good drivel.

Not only am I stopped when I try to help myself, but when kind people take pity on me, they are forbidden to give me anything at all to eat. God knows I've tried (and failed) to understand where Magoo is coming from about the food. Recently at the supermarket I decided to make a compromise that suited my diet restrictions and my need to chew. I chose cinnamon-flavored Trident Sugarless gum from a low shelf by the checkout. I had just about chewed through the foil wrapping when . . . guess whose hand was in my mouth. Sometimes I think he sees too well.

So, on a hot July day Uncle Charlie and I trotted along University Place with My Partner to see his Dr. Zimmerman. On the way we ran into two cool guys from our apartment house and those four started telling stories that seemed to amuse them greatly. Mercifully—since one of us wore a fur coat—we were standing in the shade. Those guys were about the only people on the street who weren't eating something. I watched a parade of tempting goodies pass by. It was torture. Even the pigeons were pigging out. It had been over six hours since my tiny breakfast and I was feeling mighty peckish.

Sitting at My Partner's side, I subtly looked around to see what could be done about the food situation. It was like a fairy tale: This angel—shoeless, just like me—came out of nowhere to my rescue. I took to him immediately. Real skinny; maybe he was on a diet like mine. He walked toward me holding a banana. (When you peel the skin away, the fruit inside is just the color of my fur.) We locked eyes as he came toward me, offering to share his treat. How neighborly! Naturally I didn't want to appear rude, so I lunged toward this heaven-sent snack. Then all hell broke loose.

"No!! No!!" Charlie and our two neighbors barked.

I got yanked back, like being rescued from the jaws of death.

Charlie yelled out, "He can't eat that!" (And this from a man I love.)

My angel was in shock—baffled, and hurt—and why not? Then things began to look up for me: Suddenly most of the banana fell to the sidewalk. I figured I could finally get at it and my drooling increased to full-faucet strength. Then, just like the restaurant meatball, my prize was snatched away—this time cruelly kicked into the gutter. I felt bad for me and terrible for my new chum.

He turned to go and said sadly, "Man, it's only a banana."

My four so-called friends seemed smugly pleased with themselves, having cheated the poor stranger and me out of our lunch and scared the poor guy nearly out of his wits.

I guessed some pigeons would come along soon. I was right. They swooped down to start pecking away at my forbidden fruit. I got mad at those stupid birds, but then figured it was only right that the rejected banana be of some use—even if only to them. Sometimes I think I'd have been better off as a pigeon. All they do is fly around, deliver a few messages, and eat as much as they can find—no food police on their cases . . . maybe they aren't so stupid after all.

* * *

So, that's our *Rashomon*—only we improved on the movie. In the film, the viewer had to decide whose version was true. But that afternoon, we had a judge—and a very good one, I think. When Dr. Zimmerman heard all three views of our incident, he smiled: "I'd have let Hickory eat the banana."

Hah!

Lloyd Burlingame

THE LATE YEARS: 2004 – 2006

Hickory longingly wondering if he can get away
with surreptitiously swiping a piece of cake

CHAPTER SIX

A Birthday Cake in Peril:
Theme and Variations

This photo on my Christmas card was taken at Uncle Michael's birthday party in September. The Prof compares it to some painting called "*Aristotle Contemplating the Bust of Homer.*" But that day I felt like one of those other Greek guys—Tantalus—because the cake I longed for was cruelly whisked away just before I could taste it. The Guv used to talk about some queen who *wanted* her subjects to eat cake. You'd think Magoo, who I work for like a slave, would feel the same about me.

Still, the odds at Christmastime are usually good for me—because three events can yield a slipped fork or a lonely mince pie: Christmas Eve supper, Christmas Day dinner, and the New Year's Eve celebration of My Partner's birthday.

My own birthdays, though, are like Tantalus and Sisyphus (an*other* Greek) combined. It's the same sad story, over and over again. At the party for my eighth, I, as usual, endured, while all the bipeds gulped down red velvet cake. Nary a *crumb* for the honoree! What made that particular birthday even worse: they wore little conical hats with a picture of a big red hound dog. Please—a cardboard *red HOUND*? While they ignored this starving yellow Lab?

Back at my seventh birthday party, Aunt Jennifer (a longtime close friend of my pal) had left the room . . . *and* her slice of key lime pie. I leapt to this opportunity of a lifetime. Tantalus, you are avenged! Was Jennifer ever surprised when she returned! I stared at the cats, throwing suspicion their way. That ruse failed. But I got the pie.

* * *

A tantalizing event occurred in June 2004 when Aunt Barbara, uncles Charlie and Sal, and I took the Old Prof to a gala 75th-anniversary reunion of working dogs and their partners at The Seeing Eye campus. Over 150 canines and companions, plus another two hundred guests, had a sit-down supper under a tent on the front lawn. The 149 other dogs slept quietly under the tables. Only I sat vigilant, ready to catch any crumb that might fall off our table or from a waiter's tray.

That fall Aunt Barbara, the Old Prof, and I enjoyed a jolly trip to Mystic, Connecticut, to visit Aunt Lois, Uncle Michael, and Cousin Jessie. We all went to a very long stretch of sand at a place called Watch Hill Beach, in Rhode Island (which is next to Connecticut). This was my first visit to the ocean. I was introduced to the Atlantic and it came forward to meet me. I'd have been happier if it had kept its distance. I prefer *dry* feet, so I "nimbly skirted" the incoming waves. I also managed to snatch some sort of vegetable marine life at the water's edge. Kelp is a bit salty for me . . . and no substitute for red velvet cake.

Music and Medicine

One opera should be enough for any Lab, but *Lucretia Borgia* was only the beginning. I learned too soon that my home away from home would be the Metropolitan Opera at Lincoln Center, 56 too-short blocks north of our Greenwich Village apartment. Now, the Maestro is not only an opera fanatic, but a Mozart devotee. Put those together and you get *The Magic Flute*. We were invited—I thought unfortunately at the time—to a final orchestra dress rehearsal at the Met. Julie Taymor was the director, and George Tsypin had designed the sets. He's a former student of the Prof's—a talented prince of a guy and one of my fans—so I agreed to go.

Because my harmonizing at *Borgia* had gone unappreciated, these days I simply slept through most performances. (My screen saver mode is widely admired.) But I actually enjoyed *The Magic Flute*! The usher took us to a box. We like those because they give me plenty of room to spread out—all the way to the end of my tail, which is in mortal danger on an aisle.

The lively overture was a good sign. Then the curtain went up . . . and on slithered a huge dragon! It was about time the Met put an animal on stage He was chasing the hero, who promptly fainted. (Some hero.) Papageno, a bird catcher and kind of a feathered critter himself, livened things up even more. Big on eating and drinking, he was my kind of guy—unlike that silly, swooning prince. Papageno even called himself a *Naturmensch*: German for "good old boy." Later the prince proved good for something when he played his magic flute, calling up bigger-than-life—I mean *huge*—white bears who lumbered around in a friendly dance. *Then* on came these twenty-foot-tall dancing flamingos! I thought I would fall out of the box in excitement. If I'd been bigger—like that big red dog at my birthday—I'd have liked to join the fun on the stage.

After intermission—which for once didn't feel too short—My Partner suddenly looked worried. He seemed to know something I didn't. Pretty soon I knew it too—there was a blinding series of lightning flashes, then ear-splitting thunderclaps. I just about leapt out of my skin. I really hate thunder storms and never dreamed it would rain in a theatre. I leapt to the door of the box, giving my pleading look to the Old Prof. "We're out of here, right?" I signaled desperately. He soothed me with pats on the head and doggie-bone treats for my tummy. I lay down, reluctantly, fearing what was to come. I was sure a heavy rain must follow, so I went to the front of the box and scanned the gold-leaf ceiling high above. No threatening, dark clouds. I was much relieved. When I finally figured out the lightning and thunder were just part of the show, I relaxed inside. But I pretended to cower with each flash and boom. This fake fear got me about a dozen Milk-Bones—not bad for one afternoon at the opera. I was sure the wily Papageno would be proud of me for pulling that one off. I later found out that Magoo had been so carried away by Act One, he'd forgotten to tell me of the *Donner und Blitz* to come. Now that I know how he handles this, maybe I can persuade him to take us to *Rigoletto*, *Die Walkuere*, and *The Barber of Seville*—all lightning operas. Yum.

* * *

In mid-June, during our seventh year together, My Partner and Aunt Barbara took me (for who knew what reason and without a by-my-leave) to a building I hadn't seen before. They might have warned me that this was the Upper East Side Animal Medical Center! This time, I was the one alone in the operating room. I was there to lose five "fatty cysts" that had been worrying my pals. The doctors were the best, but the operation was no fun. My so-called best friends came to bring me back home the next day—about time! I couldn't wait to see them, but I was *so* embarrassed! I had this huge plastic lampshade around my neck. I looked like some kind of demented flower and I was moving like a drunk with a lampshade over his head. I could hardly squeeze into the car.

When I hobbled into our apartment, the cats were terrified and disgusted at the sight and smell of me. Their cheery welcome certainly made my day—feeling groggy and betrayed had been bad enough. I did my best to soldier on, but I felt like such a klutz: crashing into

Lloyd Burlingame

doorways, furniture . . . even frightened cats. After a few miserable days, I'd had enough of being so hang-dog handicapped. Time for revenge. I had found that I could crash from the bedroom into the dining area, accidentally-on-purpose knocking over one, maybe three, of the tall-backed dining-table chairs. People were so understanding and sympathetic, "Poor old Hickory," they murmured—more fools they. As Attila the Lab, I managed a lot of getting-even mayhem, turning that stupid collar into my own private cowcatcher. I urge fellow canines to consider this kind of payback, though I wouldn't wish the indignity on a cat.

Oh: Magoo had to have all four dining chairs re-glued in the early fall. *Ha!* Having recovered fully in a month, I am now cyst-free and handsomer than ever.

* * *

My Partner says he has a "glass back" (don't ask me), so I guide him regularly to the University Pain Center near us. It's in an old building whose elevator is the slowest in town. One August morning my arrival at the lobby was greeted, as usual, with pleasure and praise. As I sniffed for food and worked the crowd—five men and a woman— waiting for the elevator, the woman suddenly shrilled, "Get that dog away from me!" I was shocked, and clearly the other bipeds thought she was, well, odd. So was her explanation: A year ago, at a wedding, she'd been "all dressed up in a designer gown." Another guest had arrived with a new dog who (she said, but I can't imagine) "fell in love" with her and "kept jumping up" on her. "He simply *ruined* my gorgeous gown," she whined. The Prof (and everyone else) had listened patiently. At last he asked, sweetly, "Are you in a designer gown now?" "Oh, no," she simpered, "this is just an old rag from a thrift shop." Long pause. My Partner stuttered, "Y-e-e-s, I understand perfectly." . . . None of us did.

At last our elevator arrived at the eighth floor, and all of the folks who needed physical therapy hobbled, rolled, and stumbled off. Each and every one, except for that woman, wished me well: "Take care, Hickory!" "Have a great day, Hickory; you're the best!" Well, five friends out of six ain't bad. But I think very highly of that jumpy dog at the wedding.

We were early for the Old Prof's physical therapy appointment and waited quietly in the large reception room. On our left, about fifteen feet away, two women held a lively conversation; one of these simply fascinated me. Back in the physical therapy area, my many friends—both patients and therapists—greeted me warmly. Sherry, My Partner's PT, put him on the high bed-table to attack the problems in his lower back. As usual I was tied to the sturdy leg of another table, watching all the weird contortions bipeds oddly choose to make. Toward the end of the Prof's exercise session, that interesting lady from the waiting room approached him. She noted in her charmingly soft voice, "Your dog kept staring at me in the reception area."

"Yes," he replied, with no subtlety at all, "Hickory loves the ladies."

"I'm not joking," she countered. "He didn't take his eyes off me."

"I'm entirely serious; he's a shameless masher. I apologize for his cheekiness."

Seeming to doubt this explanation (I don't know why), she politely switched to another topic: "Do you ever listen to books on tape from the Library of Congress?"

"All the time," he said excitedly, "I hear four to five books a week."

"Oh, I'm glad to learn that," she declared, then paused. "I record books for the Library of Congress regularly."

"You do?" my pal asked brightly. "Please tell me your name."

"Yoland Bevan," she replied, in her slightly accented English.

The Prof sat bolt upright, exclaiming, "You're fabulous! I've heard dozens of books you've recorded—and so has Hickory."

They both had an "Ah ha!" moment, *finally* figuring out that I had recognized her distinctive voice back in the waiting room. They both laughed and looked at me. I sprang to my feet and gave Ms. Bevan my special one-eyebrow-raised-with-brilliant-smile greeting. She truly is a wonderful actress, superb reader, and intelligent woman. As for the masher business . . . she's also not at all bad looking.

* * *

The Old Prof often lightly refers to the Hickory Connection as a benefit of our seven-year partnership. I think he should be more thankful. In March I guided him and our friend Lenore to the Metropolitan Opera House—*again*. This was for the final orchestra dress rehearsal of Tchaikovsky's opera *Mazeppa*. The Prof says it's almost never heard outside Russia, but that didn't stop him from finding a recording (bother)—which, of course, we listened to about forty times in advance. All I wanted to know was if there would be a lot of thunder and lightning as in *The Magic Flute*. If so, I sure wasn't going. The CD sounded noise free (except for all the singing), and since George Tsypin was the designer again, I decided to risk torment.

Our seats on the aisle in the Grand Tier gave me plenty of room to stretch out and snooze, but the first act kept me riveted; there were all kinds of high jumping and sword slashing. At the first intermission, head usher Gabriella—another admirer—asked My Partner if I'd be more comfortable in a box. Well, yes—and so would he—so the Maestro accepted with delight. Gabriella led us to the best seats in the theatre. These are called "the parterre boxes of the Diamond Horseshoe," and we were seated right in the middle! The Prof said that in Europe this would be "the King's loge," and he got a kick out of hanging my leather harness where royalty would have hung their expensive wraps. I settled in, pleased to hear him declare, "It's important to know dogs in high places."

The second act was almost a total bore—mostly politics and love stuff—so I had a grand snooze in our grand accommodations. But late in the act, that rat Mazeppa had his girlfriend's father's head cut off. I sat bolt upright just in time to see it roll down the slanted stage to the footlights. More operas should end like that.

* * *

Two Seeing Eye Dogs Take Manhattan! ...a love story

A close friend of Aunt Barbara's, named Bill, had generously arranged for a big car to drive me to and from the Animal Medical Center for that stupid operation and the follow-up check-ups. Very thoughtful, since wearing that lampshade I couldn't fit in a taxi. A year later, I was worried to learn that now Bill was in the hospital—and it was serious. Aunt Barbara, My Partner, and I arrived at the front desk of St. Vincent's, where each got a pass. We were pleased to find Bill out of bed, sitting in a chair. But he seemed gloomy, staring through the window. He immediately brightened when we entered: "Hickory! You've come to visit me," he cried out in delight. My companion removed my harness. I trotted right over to Bill and gave him many loving licks. Aunt Barbara feared again that these might not be quite sanitary, or approved by the attending physician. Bill said, "It's the best medicine I could ever think of." We all had a good laugh—I laughed with my tail wags. The longer I stayed, the better Bill seemed to feel, making me one happy Lab.

After half an hour a nurse came to give Bill shots, put him back in bed, and shoo us out. Bill was beaming when he tenderly hugged me good-bye. Aunt Barbara said I'd done him a world of good. That made my heart sing; I was glad to return his kindness to me.

Ten days later we learned of Bill's passing. Aunt Barbara, the Old Prof, and I went to his memorial service at Grace Church. We sat in our side-pew box, as we do for the Christmas concerts. The dark-suited usher, a pal of Bill's, hesitantly asked, "Are you Hickory, Bill's friend?" I smiled and wagged my tail "yes." "Bill spoke so excitedly about your visiting him in the hospital," the usher explained. It was mighty nice to hear something bright on this dark day.

After the formal service I was surprised to be visited by at least six older men in dark suits—all knowing my name and everything about my visit to Bill. He had told every one of his visitors about my coming to cheer him up. Aunt Barbara cried and laughed; My Partner choked up, smiled, and lovingly stroked my head. I think after this, we both took the Hickory Connection more seriously.

* * *

Lloyd Burlingame

Not long after, we were at a celebration of the work of our friend George Stoney. He is a much-honored documentary filmmaker (the Old Prof finds his work "poetic"), and this event featured excerpts from his films of more than fifty years. The large audience included many film and theatre colleagues of both George and Magoo. My Partner had been asked to speak, and I did nothing to upstage him (no microphone this time), but I must confess I felt the audience's attention focused on my every move.

After the presentation, friends came up to visit us. My Partner was delighted to recognize the husky, shining voice of Rosemary Harris, an actress he calls "magnificent." As a costume designer, he'd worked with her several times. The Old Prof seemed particularly happy to introduce the star and me to each other. She was warm and charming; when she bent down to pet me, I gave her many kisses, adding my brightest smile and fastest tail wags to show my pleasure. (After all, she was not only my new best friend, but Spiderman's Aunt May.)

A few months later, I heard Uncle Michael tell My Partner that he'd accidentally met Miss Harris. Uncle Michael and Aunt Lois, his fiancée, had seen a matinee of the Noel Coward play she was doing, and then had gone backstage to greet a friend in the show. Afterwards, they got lost in a maze of corridors and couldn't find the stage door. Several times they passed the open door of a dressing room. Miss Harris saw them reflected in her makeup mirror and asked if she could help. Lois and Uncle Michael were happy for the help, but even happier to meet and congratulate this wonderful actress. Uncle Michael mentioned that My Partner was his brother, adding how highly the Old Prof thought of her. She listened with pleasure. "Yes, there's a family resemblance," she declared. "Lloyd's a nice person and a good designer." She paused. Her face lit up . . . she flashed a brilliant smile . . . *"He has the most wonderful dog!!"*

Lloyd Burlingame

*Hickory the Flying Labrador leading an active life
in his new yard on Sunny Meadow Lane*

HICKORY'S EPILOGUE

Retirement Approaches:
A Successful Visit to Vienna

23 August 2006

Back in the summer of 2003, My Partner and I had accidentally encountered a retired couple from Virginia. We thought they were lively and charming . . . and neither of us knew they would change our lives. Jay and Lolly Burke had come to New York to visit an old friend living in our apartment house. It turned out the couple was deeply committed to The Seeing Eye. When they saw the TSE logo on my harness, they knew I was an alum. Visiting in front of our building, we five found we shared a good friend in Rosemary Carroll, the Director of Development at TSE. We parted, wishing each other well, and I gave the Burkes my best supersonically fast tail wags in farewell.

Three years later it was time to give the Old Prof my notice.

Eight years is a long time to work as a guide dog in a stress-filled big city. I knew I was losing my edge, literally cutting corners—and I had the feeling My Partner thought so too . . . though he wouldn't admit it. He said that eight years ago he could not imagine living with a dog; now he could not imagine our parting. He wanted to keep us together and agonized over how to do it. The Prof knew I would have to play second fiddle to a younger guide dog and could not get to many of the places I'd grown used to visiting. He worried too that a new dog would feel overshadowed—and that wouldn't be fair. But our only alternative was putting me up for adoption.

My Partner went around and around with this dilemma. Then one day the answer became clear: "What is right for Hickory is right for me." Though I tried not to hurt his feelings, he knew I was ready to say goodbye to the Met and hello to a country meadow. Once he accepted this solution, he threw himself into making it work. Friends feared he would be miserable at letting me go. "Not at all!" he answered. And I knew his enthusiasm showed how much he loved me. The Prof had been assured of The Seeing Eye's excellent method for placing retired dogs with loving families. But for him that wasn't enough; he seemed driven to find me the perfect retirement home.

We both worked very hard to find it, but our three-month search went nowhere. All our possibilities had fallen through, so My Partner asked Rosemary Carroll for help. He said my new home ideally would be with an active, retired, and dog-loving couple in the country— someone like Lolly and Jay Burke, for instance. With them as our example, we kept on looking . . . and getting more discouraged.

Three weeks after My Partner talked with Rosemary, she sent us a stunning E-mail: She had contacted the Burkes for us—and they were eager for me to live with them! But first they wanted me to meet their two rescue poodles. The Old Prof and I were invited to visit the whole family at their home in Fairfax County—the middle of horse country. It would be a kind of audition for me. I hoped the poodle pair would be more welcoming than the cat cousins, and I vowed to be on my best behavior. I was delighted to think of living in the country and having close canine friends. I could hardly wait to see the Burkes again.

Lloyd Burlingame

My Partner and Aunt Barbara happily and hopefully planned our trip south. The Prof said that my finding a home in Vienna, Virginia, would be a wonderful coincidence . . . since the three of us had been unable to visit Vienna, Austria, those years ago.

In late August Aunt Barbara, My Partner, and I took the train to D.C., where Aunt Susie and Uncle Eddie met us and drove us to Vienna. The Burkes had a big, friendly home. I loved its acre-and-a half fenced-in lawn, where we all met. I thought I'd write a song, "Do Fence Me In." The poodles, Cheri and Rusty, scampered out to greet me . . . we hit it off right away! Inside, they eagerly showed me the whole house, "upstairs, downstairs and in my Mistress's kitchen."

We all relaxed and happily visited at lunch (even though, foraging under the dining table, I snagged only one napkin). The Burkes knew all about dogs and made me feel right at home. I passed the audition! I was thrilled—so was my pal. If you really want to know how we felt, play Beethoven's "Ode to Joy" and turn up the volume very loud! (I *like* that one.)

My partner had grown up in Arlington, Virginia—the next county over—and he loved that I would be a resident of that state. It was a precious gift to grow up in suburban New Jersey and then to work on New York Island, with all its fire hydrants, lamp posts, and ever-changing smells. But the Prof says there's an old song called "Carry Me Back to Old 'Virginny,' " and I'm glad that's where I'll be—exploring acres of grass and varieties of trees. (All that worries me is a place nearby called Wolf Trap Farm, where there's opera in the summer—the wolves don't scare me, but the opera does.)

Jay, my new-dad-to-be, asked me if I liked to ride in cars. I shot him my brightest smile and enthusiastically thumped my tail; I'd seen several vehicles in his garage. He bowed, laughed, and said he would be honored to be my chauffeur. He added he could well imagine me as "Squire of Sunnymeadow." That reminded me of my puppy days in Princeton, seeing *Upstairs, Downstairs* on the telly. In New York, the Old Prof had joked about my "aristocratic streak" . . . but now I was joining the First Families of Virginia! "Squire" sounded very *Upstairs* to me.

Jay talked a little like the telly and the Guv. I liked it and found myself doing the same. I saw myself chauffeured in the convertible—a blue Porsche with its top down—wearing my Snoopy goggles, my long silk scarf flying: The Yellow Baron, Sir Squire of Sunnymeadow!

* * *

So much love has been showered on me in my eight human years (56 canine years). My heart overflows with love sent right back to all of my friends and fans. With the gift of this journal, I wish all of you every joy and thank you for many kindnesses. (I especially thank those who have given me *food*.)

My Partner kindly thinks of me as the most wonderful dog. I say he's not such a bad dad himself.

PART TWO

Squire of Sunnymeadow;

Students at The Seeing Eye

Lloyd Burlingame

Not yet two years old, Seeing Eye dog in training, Kemp, already instructing Transportation Security Administration Big Wigs in Washington, D.C.

CHAPTER SEVEN

A Fateful Meeting

October 2006

19 October 2006: E-mail to the Old Prof, from Hickory at his new home in Virginia

Dear Old Prof,

I arrived here in Vienna in good form. My chauffeur and his wife were excellent company, and the limo was very comfortable (though I'd have preferred the convertible!).

But I want to share with you a scene that you missed; it still catches in my throat: Lolly, Jay, and I had just left you and Aunt Barbara. We were waiting on Ninth Street for the light to turn green at Fifth Avenue when my dear old friend Lenore saw me and blew me a kiss. Lolly—I think I'll call her "Mistress" from now on—put down her window and asked if the lady knew me. Lenore replied that she was only one of my many friends so sad to see me leave. She had seen us saying goodbye, but not wanting to interrupt, she had quietly walked on. Then spying me in the limo, she had to signal her fond farewell. Mistress was overcome with emotion. So was I—so much that I could only nod my warm thank-you before the light changed. I turned to the back of the limo, and through the rear window I saw you and Aunt Barbara waving goodbye. You grew smaller and smaller as we drove west. I realized that I was leaving my Home. Goodbye, dear Old Prof-and-Dad. Goodbye, beloved Barbara, Charlie, Sal, and all my treasured Village friends. My throat ached and I felt a tear move down my muzzle.

I miss the Village and my people very much. But this is exactly the country retirement I wanted. And I was given a proper reception the minute I arrived: Cheri (she's a sweetheart) could not have been more welcoming, and Rusty showed me the better sniffing spots around my new grounds. Already a neighbor and her little girl, Katja, have arrived to pay their respects and check me out, thank-you-very-much. We three went to the garden, where I gave a praiseworthy "fetch-and-drop" demo, with a new toy glove. I lost sight of it on the early throws, because they threw it higher than we did in the Village. (Outdoors, they don't *have* to toss low—things are different in the country!)

It's coming up food time and so far so good: Himself (don't you think that suits Jay?) and Mistress have seen that I get my accustomed treats, and I certainly expect the same at dinner. That's not to say that the long journey from New York—about five hours' worth—and all the romping I had to do to impress the locals doesn't warrant a little something extra in the old bowl . . . if you know what I mean. Let's see if Himself figures that out.

Now, dear Old Prof, I have some grand news! Remember, before I left New York, that we talked about asking Himself to be my new scribe? I was really nervous, because I wanted so much for him to say "yes." I took a deep breath, told him about our happy collaboration as scribe and dictator-dog, then asked if he and I could do the same. He lit up like a Christmas tree. He said he knew that you and Aunt Barbara would love to get my news—that he was delighted and eager to be my new a-man-u-en-sis. (That *does* mean "scribe," right? After all that

Lloyd Burlingame

English I learned from the Guv, now I must bone up on Greek and Latin!) I am ever so excited, and I look forward to telling you all the news of my new life here in Dixie. These Southerners are a different breed. I'll give a rebel yell of joy—as soon as I learn how!

I feel a bit of a nap coming on; it's been a big day. I will close for now with you warmly and kindly on my mind and in my heart. I'm sure you'll be in my happy dreams.

Love,

Hickory

21 October 2006: E-mail to Hickory from the Old Prof

Dear Hickory,

Wonderful to hear from you! I was so glad to receive your first E-mail from Virginia, and even happier to be reassured about your carefree retirement in the country. I love knowing you are adjusting easily to your new lifestyle, your harness-wearing days behind you. And I am delighted that you and Himself (yes, that name fits well), have already worked out an arrangement like ours. What a relief to know that we will be correspondents; I have so much to tell you.

You've been gone three days and I'm in a kind of limbo for another week until I return to The Seeing Eye to train with your successor. I can now fully understand why our school insists that a guide dog is not a "pet," but so much more. We have been together eight years, night and day, seven days a week, twelve months of the year, at work, play, and rest. You have known my every wish and mood, as I have yours. Suddenly I feel handicapped, diminished . . . and old. I felt none of these while partnering with you, much-beloved friend.

In the awful vacuum caused by your absence, I have been brought up short, forced to use the long white cane as a poor substitute for my trusty guide and best friend. You would easily have found the grocery store, bank, and barber shop. Without you, I fumbled and flailed around with the cane, overshooting the entrance to the gym, the main door to the library for the blind, and so many of our favorite haunts. Once again, I feared whacking sighted pedestrians' feet with my cane sweeping; I dreaded enraging touchy New Yorkers. Without you, I have been bereft—half of me has suddenly disappeared.

Lenore's farewell as you rolled south toward your new home was only the first message from your legion of friends up here. They stop me on the street to wish you well, as I tap my companionless way around the Village. Clemmie and Hugo do what they can to cheer me, but their cool feline vibes can't compensate for your warm canine energy. Uncle Michael comes today to stay with me until I return to Morristown. That will go a long way to helping me feel less mournful. His visit and my knowing that you are happy with your new home encourage me to look on the bright side. At long last, you have plenty of outdoor romping and sniffing room—and two canine companions to share it.

Please keep the E-mails coming; they bring me shots of Vitamin H. My very best to your new Dad/Boswell, Mistress, Cheri, and Rusty.

Much love, tummy rubs, and hugs,

Your Old Prof

23 October 2006: E-mail from Hickory to the Old Prof

Dear Old Prof,

Oh, dear, it isn't fair that I am in heaven while you are in limbo—not at all fair. But be of good cheer—soon you will be guided by a well-educated Seeing Eye dog who just now is finishing up his (or her) four months' intensive training. That pup will be as eager as I was to start work; I feel it in my bones. For now, I hope that you and your cane will stay away from that intersection from hell by Saint Vincent's.

To tell you the truth, going solo felt quite strange to me, too—not hearing you give the old "forward," " left," and "right," commands. Even stranger is that I am harness-less and free of many "shalt nots," which makes me think of Tom Sawyer playing hooky. I have Cheri as my Becky, though Rusty is definitely no Huck Finn.

(He's shy on zip.) My paws are crossed that you get a winner of a new dog, maybe a chum who *enjoys* going to the Met. (I most certainly do not miss Verdi and Wagner—a little blue grass plucked out on a banjo suits this newly countrified boy just fine.)

I'm having to introduce myself to the Burke family in small increments, as too much of a good thing—me—can be overpowering. The People Staff do need some help in adjusting their schedule and expectations, but they are reasonable and we have reached suitable compromises. That cannot be said for the Canine Staff: Cheri is smitten. She goes gaga in my presence, when what is wanted is a more controlled subservience. Rusty, deluded poor soul, continues to act the "prince-in-waiting," not having grasped that the waiting is over: I Am Here.

For example, last night all of the Staff seemed shocked when I took my position upon the sofa in the family room. I cannot understand why: I did not crudely leap, bound, throw, or pile myself up onto the furniture; I smoothly slinked and slithered myself into a superior position. In every way I showed perfect grace and manners. Admittedly, I did give a few well-placed—but necessary—nose bumps to Staff unaware of my space needs. As a result, tonight my access to the sofas was unquestioned. Rusty, who clearly lacks proper training, was impatient with my routine. He seems to think that just having AKC papers makes him well bred, and he referred to my good manners as "the practice of common dogs." I explained that truly well-bred canines circle at least three times before settling and generously coached him on the proper way to sit. Tonight he is practicing three circles with enthusiasm.

This afternoon, my new human friend Katja came over and we had a most wonderful session of tummy rub and rope tug. Somewhere in my memory must be buried a recollection of children and wonderful times, because I so dearly love to play with this one. We roll on the carpet and run about; "sit," "fetch," and "roll over" are so much fun that I even make happy throat noises. Her parents won't let her stay though; when she began to leave tonight, even my most plaintive whines and begs could not keep her. But she returns tomorrow and the fun will continue. Katja is training nicely.

This afternoon, I took Himself out for our first area stroll. You would have thought that innocent sniffing was the same as eating something vile, what with his constant, "Leave its!" But Himself is a quick learner. I needed but a quarter of a mile to shape him up. Besides—there is nothing here to eat! No pizza pieces, chicken bones, burger bites, bagel buns . . . no nothing. It's all autumn leaves, grass, squirrel and raccoon scent, deer dew, and fox hairs. Still, by the end of the hour, I was on the long lead and Himself was quite happy with my sniffing.

The attention, affection, and ambiance here almost—I say almost—offset the need for a bit more food. I expected some latitude in that area when I retired. It's shocking that there is not more of what is needed.

However, I'm working on the problem.

Hickory

25 October 2006: E-mail from Hickory to the Old Prof

Dear Old Prof,

First off, the morning mail brought me two—two—birthday cards. I wasn't wearing my spectacles, so couldn't make out the words myself, but Himself and Mistress read them to me, and Himself held them so that I could give them a super confirming sniff. Indeed, my heart gave an extra beat with the wonderful memories from that sniffing. Thank you, Aunt Barbara and dear old Dad. (I hope that at my birthday party we will be served up extra portions of something. After all, reaching the magic "ten" is no small achievement and suitable recognition should be in order.)

I look forward to going out for a leash-free romp in the woods and grass with Cheri. We are getting to be quite an item. I am joyfully adjusting to being able to just take off and lark about. To be doing so with such a sweet little charmer is icing on the cake.

I interviewed my new vet, Dr. Chafetz, at three p.m. Wonderful man. He was raised in the Village and knew our vet, as well as others nearby. His dad owned a bookstore where all the East Village bookstores used to be clustered. Dr. Chafetz said it was very close to my home with you. We talked for about an hour and a half and had a most marvelous time; he gave me a number of treats. I already like him and if this is a typical visit, I cannot wait for my next appointment-with-treats! I am in good health—and I weigh only 70.8 pounds! Maybe you should suggest that Himself be more liberal with the treats; I do a lot of exercising around here.

You'll remember that Mistress and Himself are big supporters of The Seeing Eye, bless them. Mistress acted as a docent at the school when they lived near Morristown. Now she co-chairs the "Capitol Area Friends of the Seeing Eye" and is on an advisory board to the president of TSE. Mistress and Himself had dinner out tonight with new Seeing Eye President Jim Kutsch (his guide dog is named Anthony) and Walt Sutton, the senior trainer. The visitors had spent the day a few miles away, at the Reagan National Airport—teaching bipeds in the "Transportation and Safety Administration."

Walt brought a dog-in-training named Kemp, who took part in the teaching session. He'll be in the next class at Seeing Eye, which will start to work with biped partners in just a few days. I thought he must be a pretty sharp pup to be chosen to represent the school; he's not even two years old. Anthony went to the restaurant with the people, but Kemp and I were left behind with Cheri and Rusty. Kemp isn't allowed in restaurants because he hasn't graduated yet; and, of course, I can't go to them anymore. (This is the one tiny drawback to being out of harness: no more lying under restaurant tables, ever vigilant for fallen food bits.) This visit was a happy surprise for me, and I think for Kemp too. I took him on a tour of the house, which kept him busy sniffing his head off—upstairs, first floor, and large downstairs. We made quite a quartet with Cheri and Rusty tagging along.

After the grand tour, Kemp and I made ourselves comfortable on the deep pile carpet in the family room—time to get the latest news of my alma mater. Kemp filled me in on his four-month training period at the school. It was very much like mine eight-plus years ago. He had passed all the hurdles and was even quite likely qualified to work as a big-city dog. I got nostalgic, hearing him talk about the three training walks in Morristown: The easy one on Maple Street, the harder one on South Street, and the most challenging—the walk on Elm Street. I confessed that I had struggled against being distracted while working around food on the street and sidewalks. Kemp admitted that *his* Achilles paw was being distracted by other dogs. He's very outgoing and has an adventurous and athletic streak. Kemp seems undaunted by absolutely anything, and up for every challenge—now *he* could be Huck Finn to my Tom Sawyer.

We took a break for some serious romping, involving some "bone, bone, who's got my bone," then returned to stretching out on the comfy rug. Kemp asked me about next week; he wondered what he might be in for when he starts training with his partner. I said he would probably find himself considerably sharper than his new companion about the commands. I told him about that problem you have: commanding "left" when you mean "right." Kemp asked, "What do you do then?" and I said, "Guess what he means, and do that." Kemp said this might be more easily said than done. (Sorry, Prof—but I agreed!)

I told Kemp that he'd only be training for three weeks if he got a "retrain" partner—you know: someone who's partnered with a dog before—but that training with a person new to partnering takes almost a month. As we did, he and his partner will go into Morristown in the morning and the afternoon to train together on the three routes. In the evening, he'd have to possess his soul in patience, when all twenty-or-so biped trainees listen to lectures in the big upstairs common room. Kemp gave a mighty yawn and said that sounded boring. I agreed that it's a big snore for us, but it teaches you humans about our proper care, dealing with traffic, and many other things that make life good for the team. Kemp said he already knew that the staff is very cool, smart, and caring, and he thumped his very handsome tail to applaud them. He's devoted to his main trainer, Jan, who is fair, and encourages him . . . but doesn't let him slack off.

I explained to Kemp that during the training period he'd live in

Lloyd Burlingame

a big room shared with his partner, where he'd have his own mat and place to sleep. He'd get breakfast there early each morning, and supper in the late afternoon, after the second session in Morristown. I told him one of my favorite places at Seeing Eye is what they call the "leisure path." (I really loved galloping around that big old loop on the front lawn.) Kemp's big brown eyes brightened—he seemed to look forward to that a great deal. He wanted to know more, but I said the best thing would be to see if his partner would take dictation; then we dogs could stay in touch by E-mail. Kemp said he was really getting "revved up" for the last phase of his training. He promised to send me his new partner's E-mail address if he could.

I asked for details about his session that afternoon. I said it must have been quite an honor to train those Transportation people. Kemp modestly replied that it was "nothing"—he was just showing them how Seeing Eye dogs and their partners go through security checks at airports. Then the kid settled in to tell the story:

"The TSA guy wanted to feel like he was blind, so he had a cloth over his eyes. There was this metal doorway, without a door, standing alone in a big room. First the officer walked through it by himself, leaving me on the long lead—y'know, I was sitting quietly. We pretended he was my partner, so when he gave the 'come' command, I trotted through and went to him. We did this lotsa times with different TSA people."

Of course, I recognized that routine right away, Partner. It's just what you and I did in our final week of training at the courthouse in Morristown; that was easy.

The youngster really throws himself into his job. He said he was glad to go through the routine at the Reagan airport; it wasn't a "big deal" . . . because he had done the same thing that morning! He and Walt had *flown* to Washington, from Newark Liberty Airport, in New Jersey. That *really* interested me, Partner. After all those trains, busses, subways, cars, and trucks we've taken together, I've still never been in a plane.

When Kemp asked about my new life with the Burkes, I told him it was great to be out of harness. But I tried to describe the excitement and all the things we saw and did in New York City. And the gift of having hundreds of best friends (even though most of them were bipeds).

Kemp and I had been talking for a long time when we heard the car pull in the gravel driveway. We all raced right to the front door— Cheri and Rusty barking their little poodle heads off, Kemp and I maintaining the silence expected of properly trained Seeing Eye dogs. When Mistress, Himself, Jim, Walt, and Anthony walked in, I could tell from the smells that they had been to the Burkes' favorite Chinese restaurant—and I thought I saw a "doggie bag." (They use that silly term down here too.) It had been a grand treat to see Walt again and to meet Jim and Anthony. And it was a great pleasure to meet and visit with Kemp. Mark Twain would like him.

I must tell you how I do miss you all. Your E-mails are wonderful. And, dear Old Prof, please take care when in Morristown. And don't worry: I am sure that a companion is even now preparing to partner with you at my alma mater. That will be one lucky pup. For me the heavens opened when I became yours, and your many friends, mine. Take the new boy and hug him to your heart just as you once did me. He will return that love and loyalty as I did, one hundredfold. I am the luckiest dog in the world: You gave me a rich and loving life and topped it off with a retirement made in heaven. I am blessed. Gracious me, I am blessed.

Yours ever,

Hickory

26 October 2006: E-mail to Hickory from the Old Prof

Dear Hickory,

This is the day before your tenth birthday and I am very glad to have heard from you. I must correct or amend one thing you write at the end of your most moving and welcome letter: It is *I* who am the lucky one—maybe I should say, the luckier one. I hope you will have a wonderful day romping with Mistress and Katja, not to mention la belle

Lloyd Burlingame

Cheri. Be kind to Rusty as befits a prince to a duke. Noblesse oblige.

I'm so happy to learn of your weight. When I took you to Dr. Kutcher two weeks ago, she said you weighed 75 pounds, and that worried me, since 70 is what we have been aiming at for all your Manhattan days. Have you really lost over four pounds romping in one week in beautiful Vienna? Or, is it that maybe Dr. K.'s scale is a bit off? At any rate, good going. How great you had such a good visit with Dr. C. and you could catch him up on what's going on in the East Village. What is really going on is people coming up to me from near and far, friends and strangers, asking after you. They are so glad to know of your heavenly retirement; and all—I mean, all—send you best wishes, love, and happy birthdays.

Susan Niederman took me to lunch at the Knickerbocker Bar and Grille yesterday; we sat at your table 56, in the "Hickory Corner." It felt so weird not to have you lying beside me. We met in your honor and toasted you, dear absent friend. You remember she is my cherished friend who taught me braille at the Jewish Guild for the Blind long before I was blessed with your love and guidance. That lunch was the tenth Manhattan event occasioned by your graduation to the country. Heavens.

How amazing that Walt Sutton and Jim Kutsch were able to visit with you. Did you know that Walt is to be the chief trainer of this class I will be attending? I spoke with him last week and humbly requested a yellow Lab to succeed you. I know that for me there is really no other choice, but I wanted to make sure we were all on the same page—and we are. I think a lot of Walt. I have not yet met Jim, but certainly know his lovely wife, Ginger, and am anxious to "see" them both in a few days.

Uncle Michael is here and seems at loose ends without someone to play long and hard at tug-the-rope. I suggest he could work on finishing his four-volume life of Honest Abe, but he just looks a bit wistful, missing you.

I think your new dad is doing wonderfully well taking dictation; in fact, I find that your descriptive power has been improved by the country air and the freedom of having lost that old harness.

A great thing is: Now that a week has passed and so many of your dearest friends know how very well you are doing in your new life in paradise, they have stopped crying on the phone when they call to check in. That helps me keep smiling and counting my many, many blessings.

The car will pick me up in just two days, at 11 a.m., with a ton of stuff, including my new laptop computer . . . and off I go to our favorite alma mater. It is just about the same mid-autumn time frame that you and I had eight wonderful years ago.

Keep your paws crossed that I'll be gifted with one of your relatives—would that not be wonderful?

My great love to you on your natal day; fond best wishes to your dear new mom and dad, to Cheri, that charmer, and to Duke Rusty,
Your Old Dad, and the whole East Village gang.

29 October 2006: E-mail from Hickory to the Old Prof

Dear Old Prof,

Today you are back at the Seeing Eye Campus; only two days until you get your new partner. This morning, while I was free-sniffing in the woods, it came to me that being free is what we're all about: my brothers, sisters, cousins, aunts, uncles, and I. It is the gift we've chosen to give to you. I know your new friend will always be there for you, as I was. As soon as I learn the pup's name I'll make the proper, but discrete, family inquiries. As you know, we Labs are a social clan and I've my contacts.

You've no need to be concerned about my well-being; life is good. I've now taught Mistress to put sheets on one chair and two sofas. The master bedroom was rearranged last Thursday and my bed now occupies a most cozy spot. I do miss, however, the dirty clothes hamper that somehow has disappeared. It was a source of great things to drag out and about. On the other paw, the food situation is working my way, however slowly. Himself has broadened my diet with the

Lloyd Burlingame

nicest little fruit treats at "treaty" time. I'm particularly fond of blueberries, raspberries, and carrots. These beauties are not at the expense of my regular diet, but in addition to!

Mistress just finished brushing and combing me, Himself dropped five berries into my mouth, Cheri just wiggled by me, Rusty is paying his respects, and dinner will appear shortly. Less than two weeks on the job and all is going my way. These Virginia folk train well.

Hugs and wuuffing to all, and a special hug for the new kid on the block—I'm eager to hear all about him.

Hickory

Lloyd Burlingame

Kemp lavishes affection on the Old Prof

CHAPTER EIGHT

"His Name Is Kemp"

November 2006

2 November 2006: E-mail from Kemp to Hickory

Dear Hickory,

You'll never guess what's happened! *I* am partnering with the Old Prof! Who would have thunk it? I think he's real happy about this. He said you wrote good things to him about me—thank you! He's going to keep on being scribe at the computer. That made my heart leap up. Now we can really stay in touch and you can help me out! Gosh, I'm so happy and excited that my tail has complained about serious over-wagging. (I told the tail to get over it and move on.)

We've been working with Instructor Dave for three action-packed days. But first I should flash back and tell you about the Prof's third day at school—our first day training together, Monday. (I guess Monday is always the day when new dogs are paired with their people.) There were forty of us living in the kennel-hotel, waiting to be partnered. My sister Kalina was with me, so we caught each other up on recent doings. In the morning we had last-minute visits to the vet and then were given baths. (Do you like baths? I do—getting toweled off after is fun.)

After people lunch, Trainer Dave took me to the main building on campus. We went to a nice sort of living room where we waited. A tall guy with white hair came down the hall, using his long white cane. Dave called him "Professor." I thought, how funny if I got a teacher for partner, like you did. . . . *Then* I thought, how funny if he actually *was* your pal! After the guy sat down, Dave brought me over to him, paused, and quietly said, "His name is Kemp." The Professor seemed kind of startled, then his face lit up in a huge smile. My tail started up again—this *had* to be your Old Prof! I figured he knew who I was because you had E-mailed him about us meeting in Virginia. We were both too surprised to speak. Then he put out his hand for me to sniff and said, "Hello, Kemp, I'm very happy to meet you." He took my leash, gave me the "heel" command, and we went down the long hall to "our" room.

To tell the truth, I was kinda nervous—following in your paw prints, and heading for my fourth home in less than two years. (Y'know—first the breeding center, then with my awesome puppy-raiser family, then four months in the TSE kennel with Trainer Jan, and now this new room with your Professor.) It was simple and pretty big. I checked out everything with expert sniffing: the big bed, the desk and its "computer" thing, the bathroom; I liked that there were windows. I could tell that the Prof wanted me to feel at home. He sat on the floor, and I let him know I was a friendly sort of pooch—I licked his hands and gave him many kissy licks on the face. His happy laugh and loving pats made me feel better.

Lloyd Burlingame

After a little while, the Professor put my harness on me (you trained him good), and we went out to that big "leisure path" you told me about. That *is* fun! It was a beautiful day for our first time partnering. And it was really cool to put all my training into practice. I zoomed around the path and the Professor flew after me—he said he was delighted! In late afternoon, all of us classmates went to the big "concrete plaza" behind the school, and we dogs parked, circling around our partners. I wasn't really into it, so the two of us couldn't go back in the school for a long, long time. I didn't think it was a big deal, but I guess I have to work on it. One of the goldens heard we'll all have to park four times a day—very early morning, before noon, late afternoon, and before early bedtime, he said.

Anyway, next, me and the Prof went to our first meal together in the dining room. All the people with dogs (we have 22 people-dog teams) were helped to their seats. Of course, we pups lay under the table at our partners' left sides. I didn't get a high mark for being calm, because I was *sooo* excited to see my old friends from the kennel. Sister Kalina had made the cut—awesome! I leapt up and strained at my leash. I was glad the Professor seemed to understand, even though it's his job to correct me to calm down. I cooled it after a while.

Hickory, see what I mean about other dogs being my "problem"? (What did you call it? My "Sillies paw"?) After final park time (when I delivered big time), the Professor and I hit the hay. It was a real exciting day for me—for him, too, he said. We *both* slept real good, I think.

I'll E-mail on the weekend about how the rest of this first week goes. Till then, dear Coach,

A cheery wuff, fast sniffs, and hearty licks to you, Mistress, Himself, Cheri, and Rusty,

Kemp

P.S. Hi, Hickory—a little note from me, Kemp's scribe. I'm a very happy camper. Oh, Kemp's nodding that he's happy too.

Much love,

Your former scribe, aka Prof Magoo

2 November 2006: E-mail from Hickory to the Old Prof

Dearest Partner of Yore,

Himself has been in touch with Trainer Walt at The Seeing Eye and has shared news of you and Kemp with me. I'm one happy dog to know all is going swimmingly! Kemp seems delighted that he's been partnered with you. He says my Old Prof is the best; well, that's not news to me. I'm told the Morristown lessons are going very well and you're a quick learner—already adapting to Kemp's style and habits. That's good and I'm proud of you. A slow learner is one thing, but an obstinate one . . . well, understandably something else. I'm sure Kemp wants to please you . . . but like any of us Labs, he'd be pleased himself by one of your splendid tummy rubs, when he goes belly up!

As for me, well—knock on wood—it's pretty good. The news from The Seeing Eye made my heart sing; you seem so happy. The kid, Kemp, has his collar on right. Of course, I had no doubts. (Still, one never knows with the younger generation, what with all that rap and slang.)

I'm still exploring the territory and trying to catalogue all the scents down here. Big project. Virginia is not Washington Square by a long, long shot! Do you know that I go for walks (Himself calls them "walkies") without a lead? Now, mind you, it's only out back—but "back" includes woods, greens, and a brook. At first I was a bit perplexed without your guiding hand and the expected command, but I've accommodated over the past two weeks. Running free is fun. Playing chase-and-be-chased with my pals Cheri and Rusty is better yet. And Mistress and Himself? Well, they seem to believe I'm the fulfillment of their dreams. (Rightfully so, I might add.)

 Good hugs and a wuuff to all,

Hickory

3 November 2010: E-mail from Kemp to Hickory

Dear Coach Hickory,

Hey, we're off and running—well sort of running. Last Tuesday morning, Dave drove the Prof and me, along with another student (Sally) and her guide dog (Gretel), into Morristown to begin training on Maple Street. Sally seems kind of unsure—this is her first dog—so Gretel is too, not knowing what to expect. Dave has us go together and he corrects us as we walk the sidewalks, stop at intersections, decide when it's safe to cross, get to the other side of an intersection, and then push on. I guess you must have gotten used to the Prof's way of doing things, 'cause he's kinda rusty on partnering techniques, so I'm tryin' to be real patient.

For starters, he calls me by your name almost every time he gives a command. Y'know, he's supposed to say "Kemp, forward," give the little hand signal pointing forward, and then I go. Instead I hear, "Hickory, for . . . errr, I mean, Kemp, forward." Then he apologizes and I give an understanding tail wag to signal no harm done. Sally and Gretel are given so many corrections that it's very start-and-stop for all four of us; after a while, that gets pretttttty old.

Oh, who knew the Prof would be so messed up on his left and right commands? Yeah, you warned me, but this is really silly. I follow your advice and I just turn the way I know we ought to go. Would you believe it—I get it right most of the time! I get the feeling he appreciates me saving the day, time after time, but I want to do my own job and let him do his. (Hint, hint.)

The Maple Street walk is pretty simple. I've done it a few times in training, no special problems and surprises—well, except for one: The Old Prof and I were trotting along, all going smoothly, when suddenly this car roared out from a hidden driveway, just a foot ahead of us. We both stopped dead in our tracks. That was scary, but Dave and the Prof said my quick reaction impressed them. Score one for me! Turned out Walt, our class supervisor, was driving the car—the whole thing was a setup to *test* me. (Did they do that to you, too? It's kinda sneaky.)

Every night, after a long and busy day, everyone goes to the big common room to hear someone talk. You warned me it would be a yawn for us dogs . . . were you ever *right*. The people were really listening, but I was bored and wanted to play. I scooted over to my left and invited a German shepherd to romp with me. He just looked stern and growled, "Nein." So I scooted all the way to the Old Prof's right to make friends with a very pretty golden retriever. Miss Goody Four Paws sniffed that I should behave myself. So I scooted to the *center* again, in front of the Old Prof, and rolled over on my back and squirmed around for a while with my paws in the air. I got so cozy I fell asleep and had a cool dream: I was in your big backyard in Virginia, flying off the deck and bounding for that way-off grove of pines . . . Well, I guess I was not completely quiet and I kinda made a spectacle of myself. I got a jerk on my leash—y'know, a "correction"—then I got all proper. But I had more fun than the super-serious shepherd or the stuck-up golden girl. The Prof pretended he was annoyed with me, but I think that sorta smile on his face showed he really wasn't.

After a coupla days, we finished with the Maple Street route and the Old Prof worked on his commands. He sure stands *straight*, doesn't he? He told Dave that this is so he won't get into the same mess with me that he got into with you—that thing called "tendonitis." He sure doesn't look like anybody else, with his back so stiff and all that white hair.

We've started the next part of training: the South Street walk. Remember? It's a longer rectangle than Maple Street and has more-interesting places where streets cross—some have traffic lights and some have stop signs.

People keep asking me how I learned to read the signs. I bet you heard this a lot, too, and the Prof has had lots of practice explaining. He always tells them it's *his* job to hear what the traffic is doing, and *he* decides when we can walk and when we can't. Once I get the "forward" command, then it's *my* job to get us to the next point on our walk. One lady kept telling him he was wrong, so he gave up and said, "Kemp learned to read at Princeton, where he was first in his class." That satisfied her—*I'm not making this up!*

At the end of the week, in the evening, everybody went to the big room they call the Eustis lounge. It's real fancy—all the chairs look nice and pillow-y and make you wish you were out of harness. We were there for a "grieving session," and it was pretty quiet. The

Lloyd Burlingame

students who'd been to The Seeing Eye before sat with their new dogs and thought about their former partners. Kalina said this was like the "Quaker meetings" she went to with her puppy family. Some students were there with their second dogs, like the Prof and me—others with their third or fourth, and one lady with her sixth. When they spoke about their other partners they looked sad and happy at the same time. The room even *felt* quiet.

When the Prof began to talk, I tried real hard to remember exactly what he said, so I could tell you. He spoke about the pain he felt when he knew you had to leave. He said parting from you was "about the most difficult thing" he'd ever had to do, and that once he got so upset he thought it would "just about kill" him. He used one of those big words—"profound"—when he talked about his "undying" love for you. The people cried a lot and I thought about how all of them had partners they loved too. Gosh, Hickory, how can us new partners be that good?

Then the Prof said he was "ecstatic" to finally find you a perfect retirement home. He said that helped "ease the misery" of losing you. He smiled big and things got happier in the room. He said he'll never forget this meeting, and he thinks The Seeing Eye is the "Eighth Wonder of the World." (How many are there—do you know?)

Oh, and Hickory! We get visitors this weekend—I'll meet the Prof's family—and my family-to-be, I hope. Were you as excited as I am? Do you think they'll like me? I have so much to live up to.

Thanx a million for telling me about "left" and "right" and all that. I hope you're all well and happy on Sunny Meadow Lane.
Great wuffs in loving greeting,
Kemp

12 November 2006: E-mail from Kemp to Hickory

Dear Coach,

I've been keeping a diary, too, just like the Prof. I thought you might like to kinda hang out with us, so you're in it, too. Here's what happened the week before today:

The Eighth Day: Saturday, 4 November 2006

Today we did the South Street walk. We were paired again with Sally and Gretel. (Did I tell you that our 22 teams are divided into five Groups for our walks and stuff? Our Group has five teams in it, and those teams get paired up in different combinations. So who we're hangin' out with is always a surprise.)

I like this crisp, sunny weather—even the wind. Dave was monitoring all five teams, but not so close this time. The Prof led off the Prof-Kemp and Sally-Gretel teams. He was listening hard for traffic and making the big decisions—when the light had changed, when traffic was okay at stop signs, and when we could safely cross when streets met like a "T," with no light or stop sign. I thought we did pretty well, but Dave said my partner rushed the crossing twice. Y'know—he pushed the harness handle to make me go faster crossing the street.

Dave explained this real good. He said the harness handle belongs to the dog, not the man. When I get the "forward" command to step off the curb, I do that and guide us to the curb across the street. Now I'm in charge and it's my job to decide how to be safe—like guiding us around an open manhole or something else in our way. The man is supposed to just hold the harness handle and be guided by the dog. If instead he uses the handle to push the dog forward, it's too confusing—the dog can think the man's in charge, which can lead to big trouble. That's why it's so important for the Prof not to push the handle. (Dave called this using the "high handle.") The Prof gets it now—but he says it's hard because being pushy is natural for a New Yorker.

Dave said the Prof does own the leash. He holds it in his left hand, like most everybody does at TSE (well, you know that) and corrects me by tugging on it. He uses it, too, when I'm "heeling"—when he's totally in charge and I'm walking at his side.

I was thinking so hard about the South Street Walk that I forgot this was the big day—I was going to meet the Prof's brother, Michael; and his good friends Barbara, Charlie, and Sal. In the early afternoon, I took the Prof to the lobby, to wait for them. It has a big, thick carpet that always smells new, from all the different people and dogs who visit there. Today it was extra strange, so I got real excited—and then I made a great puddle. Gosh, that surprised us all. Dave rushed to mop up and the Prof hurried me outside to park—some welcome party we made.

But Dave got everything cleaned up in time, and it was great to meet the Prof's people—even though they went by the rules and didn't look me in the eyes or pet me. Barbara told the Prof she was "deeply touched" to see us "confidently" walking down the long hall toward them. She said she remembered how sad it was to say good-bye to you, Hickory . . . just three weeks ago! We all went out on the leisure path and walked briskly down to this thing called a "Victorian-style gazebo," in the middle of the oval. Michael brought me your tug rope from Prof Magoo's home—awesome. This will be a lot of fun and good exercise. Thanx.

Michael and Barbara took a lot of photos. Then a chilling wind came up, so we moved into the warm Eustis lounge. Our visitors seemed impressed by my looks, but when I tried to eat the arm of what they call an "overstuffed wing-chair," the Old Prof was not at all impressed. (Well, it is "overstuffed." I was just fixing it.) Lots more photos were taken, including when I kissed the Prof on the chin. He said maybe this can be a Christmas card? (Oh, I like Christmas.) Our guests drove off at four, after a very happy visit. They seemed to take to me, and I really like them. I hope they will be my new aunt and uncles.

That night our group of five teams met Dave in the grooming room to hear "statistics" for us dogs. I am 22 inches to my shoulders, weigh 65 pounds, and was born on 16 November 2004. Right now I'm nearly two years old. Gosh, my birthday will be on the day we move to Manhattan!

The Ninth Day: Sunday, 5 November 2006

Late in the morning, Dave came to our room with a progress report. He liked how well the Old Prof and I are starting to work as a team. The Prof asked that I be helped with what he called my "in-house misbehavior." (He meant that day I parked inside. I know we're not supposed to, but I was so excited then 'cause we were having company, and there was that great sniff on the carpet, so I just lost it. It seemed kinda natural to me, but the people thought it wasn't cool. I'm gonna do better from now on—if I can.)

The Prof was worried 'cause we'll go to "performances" in New York—at places like theatres, concert halls, and opera houses. I guess they don't like puddles at the Met. I hope I like the Met better than Hickory did. (Hickory, I'm still not sure what you meant by "forewarned is forearmed" when you told me about going to operas—but it didn't sound good. You were awful gloomy when you talked about sitting still forever while people played with noisy toys and screamed. Thanx for warning me not to drink too much water before going there. But what did you mean about being "cooped up in a box"? Is it less noisy in there? It better be a big box.) The other thing the Prof told Dave is that he wanted to be corrected so he wouldn't push me across the street anymore. It wasn't a bad report!

At lunch my partner sat where he's supposed to, getting me settled on his left side—y'know, the school rule when we're eating at (or under) a table. Then a student named Betty showed up with her dog, Jill. Betty sat at the Prof's left, and clumsily got poor Jill to lie under the table, nose to nose with me. I sorta liked that. Jill seemed kinda wacky, but friendly— she sure didn't want a fight. Seemed to me, if anyone did, it was Betty, who didn't position Jill the right way under the table like the rest of us. The Prof asked if Betty wasn't going to put Jill on her left, but she refused. So he moved us to the empty seat across the table. Then he wrote Dave a note about all this, and mentioned a recent spat between two other dogs who got too close. At dinner the Prof was glad we were "officially" moved to a seat across the table from Betty and Jill. (Isn't it cool that the school thinks when there's trouble with us dogs, it's usually 'cause of their partners?)

Later the Old Prof had a long talk about this with Dave. He said there was an "ugly scene" when you were in training, Hickory—when another dog in the wrong place under the table growled and then snapped at you. The Prof didn't want that to happen again. Then he said even though he sees the edges of things a little, he can't see well enough to protect his dog from attack by another dog—like what happened to you in New York, Hickory. Gosh, he said a crazy rottweiler almost attacked you in a big pet store.

That night's lecture was about dog care and diet. All of us pooches perked up our ears for this one, Hickory! Afterwards, the Old Prof asked a Seeing Eye person to give us "application papers" for an Animal Care Foundation "identity chip," in case I get lost and need to be traced. I don't know how that would happen—it's my job to stick by him and I would never leave. He really seems to care about me, Hickory. That feels good. More and more I hope soon I can call him "My Partner" for real.

In the morning the Old Prof and I went with Sally, Gretel, and Dave in the van to Morristown to tackle the third walk: the Elm Street route. It was another bright sunshine-y day, with light breezes and nice temperatures. Do you remember the route, Hickory? It's about a mile, and it's more interesting than the other two, 'cause it goes up a steep hill and comes down on the other side of a kinda long triangle. We had another sneak attack by a car hidden in a driveway—ha! I stopped on a dime. The Prof was alert too, and screeched to a halt right along with me. We two kept right on going, with Sally and Gretel way behind and getting lots of corrections. (At the end of the walk Sally joked that she would give the Prof a camp stool to sit on, so he could wait for them to catch up with us.) We did pretty well for our first trip. The Prof was better about not pushing me across the street.

During the traffic lecture before lunch, I went to the vet to be tested to see if any medical reason made me "lose it" on the carpet. Results come back tomorrow. The people seem to think this is a big deal, so I sure hope everything's OK.

After lunch, Sally, Gretel, the Prof and I were driven back to town to repeat the Elm Street walk—this time with less talk from Dave. The Prof knew the route and led our team good. I outdid myself in racing up Park Street hill— "Charge!!" We four finished the route quickly and only needed a few corrections for Sally and Gretel. At the end of the walk, my partner told Dave that his old hang-up on these routes is totally gone. The Prof told me he used to learn the street names instead of counting blocks, and that got you two into trouble. He said in New York with you, he had put together a guiding "system" of counting blocks plus knowing avenues, streets, and some landmarks. (But sometimes he got you both lost and had to ask another walker for the street name or number.)

Hickory, y'know that E-mail you sent to Barbara? Well,

she sent it on to the Prof, and his computer read it to both of us this evening. He was real happy when he heard it—and this part is way cool:

> *"Himself was riding to hounds Saturday. Came back covered in the best smells: leather, horse, hound, brandy. I think he plans to take me to the stable soon. I heard him speaking with Mistress about it. Lately I've been riding in the truck (up front, of course) with my nose out the window, surveying my estate."*

The Prof laughed when you said that you decided not to give us advice, "Because I've got it good down here and I would not wish Mistress or Himself to think I was looking for work." But I'll take your advice any time! You're my favorite Coach.

The Eleventh Day: Tuesday, 7 November 2006

My test results said nothing was wrong with me medically—the problem must be "behavioral." Gosh, it only happened once, just 'cause that carpet was a turn-on. I hope "behavioral" means the Prof knows that and won't hold it against me.

We partnered with Sally and Gretel again. Our walk went good. The Prof seemed to try to be extra on-the-ball—no "high handle." I did forget to stop at one very low curb, but that's hardly anything.

. . . Oh, Hickory—the BIG news! It's bedtime, but I can't sleep. The Prof and I really are "Partners" now! Missing that curb and the test about the rug didn't matter. Tonight he started telling me about his home in New York, and how we'll be going there together in just nine days, and how happy he is that we're a team. He said he's so grateful to have two best friends on four feet!!!

Coach, I couldn't have done it without you. You deserve all those horse smells and trucks and sunnymeadows.

The Twelfth Day: Wednesday, 8 November 2006

My Partner! My Partner! My Partner! MY PARTNER!! and me went out of the building dark and early for the first park time of the day—to get pounded by a waterfall of cold rain and big gusts of wind. My Partner (!) wore one of those people raincoats and a hat, but my furry coat was drenched. I got right to doing what needed doing and we scurried back inside in minutes. My Partner said my "dog-on-a-mission" attitude "delighted" him and he was blown away because I was not at all aquaphobic. (I think that means I'm not scared of getting a little wet—but who knows with him?) Getting towel-dried is lots of fun—well, at least for me it is.

At 9:30 My Partner and me went with Sally and Gretel for the "grand finale" of the Elm Street walk. Remember? This is what they call the "solo walk," even though we go in pairs. Our team had to wait at every corner for Sally to catch up—all those breaks made it hard to concentrate. The heavy rain made huge puddles at the crosswalks. I plunged into them right away. My Partner laughed and said he was delighted at my intrepidity. (I guess it's OK for professors to use words that nobody except them knows what they mean?) We did just fine as a pair, in spite of the stop-and-start part of the walk.

These training walks get harder and harder. They'd be fun it they weren't tests we both have to pass. The instructors keep saying they're not tests, but we all know they are. The walks show them what work still has to be done with each pair. The Seeing Eye is always extra careful about the safe training of its students, people and dogs. (I guess you know all this,

Hickory, but I wanted to write it so I remember it.) I was real glad to pass all three tests, because I know the school won't say we're ready to leave if we're not. I sensed My Partner felt the very same way. Now the instructors start working on the special problems of each team.

In the afternoon we took a field trip to a "mall." There were five teams in our group and Dave drove us in the van. The mall was one story high with extra-wide aisles. That helped us work with our partners. Each team took turns visiting the different stores—especially the Walmart. They had a machine that made dog tags. My Partner chose a plain silver one and Dave helped him write his name and phone number on the metal. This is in case I get lost—like that chip he talked about. Humans think about that a lot. But it doesn't worry me. Something else bothered My Partner too. He was sorry this building had no stairs—or something called an "escalator." This thing has metal teeth at the bottom and the top. The Prof told Dave that I could maybe get my paws caught in this thing, so I should know how to handle it. OK, now I'm worried. (Hickory, have you climbed on escalators?)

After the last park session we went to our room. Now that the Prof and I are partners for real, it's good manners to introduce myself to his friends and family. So we wrote this E-mail together:

> *Dear Family- and Friends-to-be,*
>
> *I am the Prof's new partner. My name is Kemp, and in Old English that means either "champion" or "warrior." I like them both and I want to be like them. My friend Hickory has given me some good advice, so that helps. Hickory's nose is very handsome. It's longer than mine—but we're both expert sniffers. His ears are longer, too—but all of our ears are what My Partner calls "butterscotch" color. My Partner talks about Hickory with a lot of big words. He says Hickory*

*has "an aristocratic bent and is a gourmet with a
raffish sense of humor, like Cary Grant's"—whoever
that is. The Prof says I'm more like "Mickey Rooney"
[Hickory, who are all these people?], eager for
adventures and good times—he got that right!*

*But school rules say I have to be kinda low-key
when I come to my new home in New York—just 'til
December 1. Then I'll be off the leash in our apartment
and free to be me. My Partner says that by Christmas
I'll be "a dog-about-town"—and the official gift-
unwrapper!*
*I send everyone big, cheery wuuffs and many licks on
your chins, ears, and necks.*
Kemp

*P.S. Here's something from My Partner: He sends
much love and many thanks for all the good messages
about Hickory's retirement and my taking on the job!*

Well, Coach, I guess it's OK to tell you about our latest
training problem: I'm more up on the rules than the Prof! He
really is a "Magoo," isn't he? It's just like you warned me—I
have a lot of correcting to do. Now that we're doing the harder
routes through Morristown, I'm real tired at the end of the day.
It starts at 5:30 in the morning and ends at 9:00 at night . . .
zzzzzzzzzzzzzzzzzzzzzzzzzzzzz.

The Thirteenth Day: Thursday, 9 November 2006

We spent this morning training on streets without
sidewalks. Nuthin' to it—except for one short scare. We were
almost at a corner when Dave said, "We're going to pass a yard
with a couple of rottweilers, who are usually chained up." I
thought, "usually?" There were loud, angry, throaty barks and I

Lloyd Burlingame

thought we were in for it. (I remembered the Prof's story about you and the New York Rottweiler, Hickory.) But these two really were chained up. Gosh, with two against one, I'd have been their lunch.

Our photos were taken late in the morning: one of just me, one of our whole group of five teams, and one of My Partner standing by me. (I was sitting on a table to be at his eye level. I bet they never let me do that again.) This will be our "identification" card from The Seeing Eye. The light was super bright at noon—golden November sun. According to the Prof, the temperature hit 70 in the afternoon. He said he figured this was just about the last of such "glad-to-be-alive days" before the late-fall chilly, grey weather comes. Then it's winter time.

After lunch we went out for our second lesson of the day—this time with Dave, plus Martin and his pooch, Gus, from the next room down the hall. We went into Morristown and walked a long, complicated route around the city. We crossed the town square to see this statue of Morris Frank, who was co-founder of The Seeing Eye. In the statue, he's walking forward with the very first Seeing Eye dog at his side—Buddy. Awesome. I wished I could thank him for real, but I just licked the statue's ear instead. . . . brrrr . . . was it cold!

We went into a big store with lots of different stuff and smells, to see about getting Martin's braille watch fixed. While we waited for him and Gus, My Partner enjoyed a talk with a friendly saleslady. She had a lot of questions about guide dogs and the training at the school. I sat patiently at his side 'til it was time to lead him outside. The saleslady bent down to stroke my head. She was very nice and it felt good—but it made me nervous because I knew it was against the rules. The Prof politely asked the lady to stop. (Hickory, I bet you've heard all this before!) He said that a working dog can lose his "concentration" as a guide if he gets a signal that it's Play Time. This can be real dangerous if the dog thinks he's off-duty at a busy street crossing. The lady kept apologizing, but the Old Prof excused her 'cause she didn't know the rule. When stuff like this happens, he decides he's a teacher again and trots out his "It's a Lovely Day in the Neighborhood" voice, to explain gently, but firmly. He told me that in New York, even the big sign you wore didn't help, Hickory. Sometimes when he pointed to the sign, the strangers said, "I wouldn't dream of petting your dog" . . . and they kept right on! They didn't notice they were doing it. Like the Prof says, since we Labs like people so much, they just like to pet us.

Dave, Martin, Gus, Magoo, and me finished the Morristown walk, going up the narrow sidewalk of Dumont Street, which was filled with vertical poles, parking meters, and hydrants. It was all what they call "close-passage work." I aced it. It was fun, weaving around all that stuff. At 4:00, the normal park time at the school, I did stop progress to pee—on the sidewalk, which I shouldn't have done. No demerit from Dave. Whew.

The Fourteenth Day: Friday, 10 November 2006

Dave drove Martin, Gus, My Partner, and me to Morristown, parked the van, and led us many blocks to a bus stop. We climbed on and got off the bus without much trouble. The high steps needed a little extra attention, but no big deal. Dave said that I am "well behaved on vehicles." (Well, not counting the three times I wiggled free of my harness in the van. I thought I was pretty crafty, and the Prof called me another one of those names he keeps throwing around—this time it was "Houdini." But he and Dave were not happy.)

Our bus went from Morristown to Madison town in about twenty minutes. Then we stepped down, and started a whole new adventure. We zigged and zagged our way through Madison to an "elevated train station." To reach the high

140   Lloyd Burlingame

platform we climbed up more high steps—these were even crumbling a little. At the top were two deep "tracks"—long lines of metal and wood. I didn't know what they were for, but we stood way back from them. The Prof said that one led to New York—yay!—and the other one went back to Morristown. Pretty soon there was a noise that got louder and louder, and then this huge, long bus (it's called a "locomotive train") came roaring up to us. At first I didn't want any part of that monster, but all the people seemed happy to see it, so I figured it was safe. It turned out we were there to get on it and ride it back to Morristown. It was kinda like gettin' on a bus, so no problem. The men sat down, and Gus and I settled in at their feet. We reached Morristown in fifteen minutes.

We got off the train easy, but we didn't go right back to the school. Dave had us stay on the high platform—then he gave us a test. He told My Partner to face the tracks and give me the "forward" command. If I obeyed, we'd land on the tracks in front of a train. The Prof was real nervous—my harness handle shook! He was putting his life in my paws. But I remembered what Jan taught me about "intelligent disobedience"—a guide dog must not obey a command that will lead the team into danger. Both times My Partner ordered me "forward," I wouldn't go. I sat stock-still—just like Jan trained me to do. The Prof was so happy! "Good boy!" he cheered, and gave me many loving pats. Hickory, you should of heard the relief in his voice when he told Dave about the first time you two took this test. The Prof said when you intelligently disobeyed his "forward" command, you "redeemed" his "damaged sense of trust in living creatures."

We were back at Seeing Eye by 9:30. My Partner told Dave this trip was real reassuring for him—and he thought maybe for me too. (Fer sure.)

At lunch we saw Jan, and the Old Prof asked when he could give her a great big hug to thank her for training me so well. She laughed, "How about now?" They did, and he said he was delighted with my intelligent disobedience. Jan smiled big and said, "Kemp really wants to do it." I so wagged my tail—because I do. My Partner said now he knew that a dog who's not "enthusiastically up for meeting the challenges of partnering" couldn't make it in the big city. (Hickory, did you know only about ten percent of us who make it through guide-dog training are up for working in a "stress-filled urban environment"? Wow.) The Prof told Jan that a friend of his had to return his Seeing Eye dog to the school after partnering a year in Manhattan—the dog got more and more nervous and fearful there. My Partner looked kinda worried after telling about that poor guy's washout.

Back in our room, I heard the Prof write in his talking computer:

> *A quiet inner voice cautions, "The streets and sidewalks of Manhattan are ten times more challenging than those of Morristown." Kemp's doing just fine here, but how will he perform in the big city at lunchtime on crowded sidewalks, in traffic with cabs, cars, trucks, buses, fire engines, garbage trucks, street sweepers, ambulances, messenger bikes—and in the subway at rush hour? Let's not breathe too easy until next Tuesday, when Kemp will be put to the acid test on the "mean streets" of New York City. We're not yet home free, not until Tuesday. My money is on Kemp—but you never know.*

But I know, Hickory. And I'm rarin' to go. Stand back, Manhattan—here comes Kemp!

* * *

That afternoon, all five of us teams in Dave's group piled into the van. This time he drove us to Madison to the campus of Drew University. My Partner told Dave he knew the place because he'd been there years and years ago when his sister was a student. Dave came along to show us how to do our lesson—it was learning how to "pattern" a route that would be used a lot. I'm real good at doin' this, but it's hard to explain, so the Prof wrote it out for me. (Big-word alert, Hickory!) Here goes:

> *In this instance, our goal was the University Library, about one hundred yards distant from our starting place by the theatre. The path to our goal forked about halfway to the Library; the left "arm" of the "Y" led to the library, while the right went to another part of the campus. By tapping several times with my foot at the start of the left path, I signaled to Kemp that he was to follow that section of the walkway. Arriving at the library, again I tapped, calling his attention to the goal. Then we reversed ourselves and, happily, easily found our way back to the starting point.*

Next we all had to make this round trip without Dave. There was nuthin' to it for me and Yankee, Edwin's dog—so our two teams got to the Library and back in record time. We were the last teams to do the lesson—and the only ones to ace the route in one try—so everybody went home to The Seeing Eye early. On the drive back, Dave told all the human partners this was "a valuable tool to put in 'memory,' especially for trips to places you will frequent in your daily lives at home."

Lloyd Burlingame

Kemp navigates the world-famous hubbub of Times Square

CHAPTER NINE

The Third Week of Training:
The New Team Confronts Manhattan's Big-league Challenges

The Fifteenth Day: Saturday, 11 November 2006

After breakfast we went on the day's first trip with Dave, Sally, and Gretel—to walk kind of a harder route to a big grocery store. We had to be real careful on the sidewalks, 'cause there were big cracks, some pieces were missing, and some weren't flat. There was lotsa stuff on the shelves, but moving through the aisles was easy. I showed how I can do

many things at the same time. (People call that "multitasking.")
I guided the Prof real well and thoroughly sniffed all the fruits
and vegetables at dog-nose height. We both easily remembered
the route back to the van—we did that with the patterning
techniques we learned yesterday. My Partner said he was proud
of me and I said the same of him by wagging my tail very fast.

After lunch we met Dave in the men's lounge to hear
him read the puppy raisers' reports on us dogs. Mine was
written by my main caregiver, Jimmy:

> *Our puppy-raiser family consists of Mom, Dad,
> and three children: 2 girls (17 and 19 years old) and a
> boy, 13 years old, who raised the puppy. The family
> and puppy experienced extended visits from our
> grandfather.*
>
> *We live in a two-story house in the suburbs, no
> fenced-in yard, in Pennsylvania.*
>
> *Two male cats were tolerated. Kemp spent lots
> of time with the family: club meetings, walks, vacations
> to the beach. Likes to ride in the car, and does well on
> long rides.*
>
> *He's playful, strong, happy, excited to see
> someone he knows, loyal, caring. Kemp likes hard
> bones and balls, and also likes to have someone play
> with him.*
>
> *Things we'll remember about our puppy are:
> his happy reactions to seeing someone he knows—
> wiggles his butt, likes to rest his head on a pillow on
> the floor, watches over you when you sleep or nap.*

My Partner told Dave he remembered hearing a report
kinda like that about you, Hickory, when you two were in
training. He said a family must be sad to part with such a
"beloved" friend. He said he found out for himself how
traumatic such a separation could be when it came time to part

from you when you retired. From the way he talked, I think "traumatic" means really sad.

Dave told the Prof that The Seeing Eye doesn't allow contact with the puppy-raiser families and their dogs after we go back to school for training. But if they stay out of sight, the families can watch "their" dogs working with their instructors around Morristown. (Once I had a peek at my family. They were standing on a lawn, across South Street from where My Partner and me were training with Dave. They all smiled and looked real happy to see me in action—but they didn't wave. So I played the game and kept my eyes straight ahead. I walked briskly forward but sent my love in code by wagging my big tail super-fast. I guess that was multitasking again—bein' a good guide dog and a loving family member.)

Dave was strict when he said, "After the team of dog and partner graduates, there is to be no direct contact between the dog's new partner and the puppy-raiser family." I figure this is so us dogs don't get confused about who's our real partner. But it's kinda sad. Hickory. Then the Prof told Dave about that time he and you met the Seeing Eye puppy raisers in New York. He said this young boy and his mom started crying when they saw you together on the street! Because they were happy to see you partnering so good.

After lunch Uncle Michael came with a copy of his book. It's "essays" named The Inner World of Abraham Lincoln, for Dave. The Prof says it's about our "sixteenth president," who Dave likes a lot. We walked the leisure path to the gazebo and found my sister Kalina. She was with her new partner—Julie from Louisiana—lying cozy by the bench where Julie sat. Kalina and I are "K"-litter mates, so our faces look a lot alike. But she's fifteen pounds lighter and two inches shorter than me. We had a bang-up lick-and-sniff session. I was so happy to learn that she really likes her partner. Uncle Michael took lots of pictures of us together.

The Sixteenth Day: Sunday, 12 November 2006

Whee! No real work today—our last Sunday in Morristown. After lunch we had visitors. Uncles Charlie and Sal, and my other aunts Renée and Camille. You were right, Hickory—I do like them a lot, and they were real impressed by the school grounds and building. We went to the warm Eustis Lounge, got settled in, and had a great time. I didn't park indoors this time. That was a big relief to the Prof—me, too.

After dinner one of the young vets led a special session on massaging us dogs. It was way cool to get my own from the Prof, after watching him have his back massaged so often. This was, like, the best class ever for all us pooches. I hope teacher Dave had an easy Sunday at home—maybe with a massage; he sure works . . . hmm . . . like a dog.

The Seventeenth Day: Monday, 13 November 2006

After breakfast, Training Director Pete Lang came to see us. (He's the one who matches up the right students with the right dogs. He's very busy, so it's a big deal to talk with him. But everybody—people and pooches—likes him. They call him Mr. Nice Guy.) Guess what, Hickory? He told My Partner we're going back to Manhattan on Wednesday. That's a day early—because I did so well in individual training, I don't need another day! I can't wait. We leave about 8:00 in the morning with Jennifer Thurman—she's been an instructor with Seeing Eye for four years. My Partner sent messages to Uncle Michael and the two Barbaras—Aunt and Cokorinos—to tell 'em we'll be home Wednesday.

We went to another Morristown department store—this one has an escalator. Now that I've met one, I'm not worried. They're cool—they're just stairs that move. (Why didn't somebody say so?) One goes up and one goes down and I got

My Partner on both with no trouble. This made him feel better—knowing my paws won't get stuck in the cracks. We sure look out for each other—like partners!

Pete Lang joined us at lunch. My friends under the table with me all agreed he's "dogs' best friend." At lunch he sounded real serious when he said the "bonding of dog and partner is the heart of the matter." (Later the Prof said this means "the heart of the deep connection between dog and person that allows the team to function." He seems to think adding big words is explaining.) At lunch he said that eight years ago he heard this "heart" thing over and over. But he couldn't understand what bonding really meant, and why The Seeing Eye made such a fuss about it. Then, Hickory, he sounded so grateful when he added that as he got closer to you, he "truly began to understand the importance of bonding."

I listened good to what Pete said next, even though now he was using too many big words: "It's so important for the dog partner to have both respect and affection for his human partner. This is what motivates him to do his miraculous job of guiding. 'Heart of the matter' certainly locates the process just where it belongs. It's about love being the center of *the* relationship."

I did get "miraculous"—and I was surprised to hear my job called that. Then I was very surprised to hear the Prof tell Pete something "miraculous" about you and me, Hickory. He said when he told you "goodbye," he figured his new dog probably would be okay. But he thought no other dog could come anywhere close to "inspiring the love and admiration" he had for you. Now he thinks maybe I can be as good as you! Gosh, I know that will be real hard—but I'm trying my darndest. The Old Prof's trust in me made my tail sit still.

When lunch was over, me and My Partner went into Morristown with Dave, Sally, and Gretel, to train with the metal detectors in the courthouse. 'Course, I'd already done the same thing—at those two airports last month—so I figured this trip would be easy. But when we got out of the van, the sidewalk was real uneven. Magoo tripped, fell, and landed on his bad left knee, but he did get up and hobbled on. I was surprised and I got worried because he seemed to hurt. I stayed at attention like I'm supposed to, but I gave his poor knee some healing licks later, when I was done working. Going through the detector thing was a lesson for the Old Prof more than for me. 'Course, he'd done it before, with you, Hickory, so except for his knee, we both did good.

The courthouse reminded me of a rabbit warren—except that rabbits plan better. The Prof calls it "the house of stairs," but that's only half the problem. It has all these narrow hallways full of worried humans, steps in the wrong places, and levels that change for no good reason. (Who built this thing?) My Partner "heeled" me going down all stairs, but used the harness going up.

Suddenly this ear-splitting, high noise started whining. Somebody set off an alarm thing. It went on and on and on—and it really hurt my ears. Then the Prof tripped on the stairs. He'd been limping ever since he fell outside. I stayed at my post on his left side, but I got worried again for the poor old guy. Later, in the van, My Partner told me the courthouse test reminded him of his old days in "boot camp" with its "dreaded obstacle course" exercise. That didn't sound good, but he smiled funny when he said it. He explained that remembering he passed that test made him feel better about the "obstacles" coming in Manhattan. (Uh-oh.) If we could survive the stumbling and the noise and the warren, we could survive just about anything.

The obstacle My Partner did want to try with me was called "revolving doors." They didn't have any at the courthouse, and the Prof asked Dave if we could for sure try one tomorrow. I don't know exactly what they are—except they don't like tails.

Gosh, tomorrow we move to New York! After breakfast me and My Partner had our "exit interview" with Director of Programs, Doug Roberts. (He's nice, even if he is important.) The Prof said he felt so good about the school that it seemed "beyond ungrateful to give negative criticism."

But we could tell Doug wanted to know about anything that could make the training better. So the Prof finally said he had one thing—"speaking as a senior citizen with a youthful spirit, but aging bones." (Like his knee, I guess.) It's the school's big new van. He liked its double doors, but he said there's no "grab-bar," like in the old van, to hold onto when he gets out. It's hard for him to make the big step down to the sidewalk.

My Partner said the old vans didn't have this problem. After his third fall, he got out real different—sitting on his rear end and swinging his legs down to the ground. He said he didn't know what I thought of all this. (He sure looked like a Magoo, Hickory—none of us dogs knew what he was doing.) Doug said other students told him about the same problem, so the school was figuring out how to add a grab-bar.

Then the Prof told Doug that Instructor Dave was a real "caring pro." And then he said something new—that I might be his last Seeing Eye dog. (Here we are, just starting out, and already he has me running around Virginia!) I didn't know where that came from, 'til he said that when I retire, in eight or ten years, he'll be in his early eighties. (I think that's old, even for people.) He figured The Seeing Eye might have some age limit for humans, like they do for us canines. Doug smiled right away and told the Prof a story. He said that not long ago he was very happy to help train a new Seeing Eye dog with a 95-year-old lady. The Prof lit up and joked (I hope it was a joke), "Now, let's see if I make it into my eighties."

My Partner remembered his first exit interview. He was

surprised back then, when Doug said, "Thank you for sticking with us." (Hickory, he means when the Prof and that German shepherd didn't get along so good, before you two were paired up.) After he left Doug's office that time, the Prof wrote a note (in real big letters like he does, so he can see them). It said, "No, no, it's I who must thank you and your team for sticking with me." He put it under Doug's door. I guess all of us are real glad that the people did stick with it.

After the meeting with Doug, we went across the hall to see if Director of Student Services, Judy Deuschle had time for a goodbye talk. She's still like the mom around here, Hickory. She does all kinds of stuff to help out the people; she's real kind to all of us. My Partner thanked her sincerely for all that. They talked about a lot—most important, your retirement, 'cause she'd been such a big help in finding you a good place. Judy was thrilled that it worked out so good in Virginia. They hugged and she said, "I'm so glad you got Kemp." I sure liked hearing that! But I think I'm a lucky dog to be hooked up with the Prof, so I thumped my great tail many times.

That was the best way to start off the biggest deal of all my training—the big test in Manhattan. I know My Partner was worried, but I was sooo ready to go! At 9:30 a.m. Dave drove us into New York City. (The Prof wanted a busy section of town, to test us "at the deep end of the pool." I hadn't had a good swim in a long time, so I was happy to hear this.) We got there in an hour and parked on top of the "Port Authority Bus Station Garage." That's at 40th Street and Eighth Avenue. I had trained there once before, so it was easy to find the elevator.

We went downstairs to take a subway train south to 23rd Street. The Prof said it was three years since he used the subway, so he had forgotten how noisy and dirty it was in the station. But I did this stuff a few weeks ago, with Trainer Jan, and it was all just the same to me now. We waited at one side while Dave bought two of those Metro cards. Several nice people asked if we needed help. I know My Partner feels this is one of the best things about partnering with a guide dog instead of using a cane. He says we dogs kind of invite people to be helpful. He looked touched when they offered help in this rough place.

I breezed through the turnstile (hah—the Prof looked surprised) and trotted right onto the train. It was real crowded, with all kinds of people and smells, but I just squeezed us three in. Everybody talked real loud, because the train made a whole lot of noise. I think the Prof was still worried about me, but I don't know why. I sat for a while, watching and smelling, then lay down. We got off easy—all the people got out of our way. (Two of 'em petted me as we passed, but I kept on going.) I liked my work, and I could tell the Prof felt good now about our trip. Then we climbed a lot of stairs up to 23rd Street.

It was almost lunchtime and people were pushing and shoving all over the sidewalks, rushing past each other in both directions. Many raced across the streets even when the cars were moving. And they didn't always cross at intersections, the way I was taught to. There really were a lot of people! The Prof sounded nervous when he told Dave, "Here we go, this is going to be Kemp's 'obstacle course' test." I took a deep breath and plowed ahead—first a block east and then back Uptown, to a place called "Penn Station." I tried to remember everything I'd learned on the streets in Morristown—but, gee, this was like three Morristowns all squished together and moving twice as fast. I was real proud of myself for getting through those ten blocks like they weren't a problem.

So, this Penn place was kinda like the bus station—and kinda like the train stations in Madison and Morristown. But lots bigger, and lots of the people ran around with those carts they call "luggage." (They don't "heel" so good.) Sometimes this big wuuffy voice yelled out commands, but nobody paid attention and I couldn't figure out the words. I had to work hard to focus on my job, what with all that action and noise and so many smells to sort out. We walked down the stairs to the main floor—I was careful to take it slow for the Prof. He didn't want to use the escalator 'cause he worried about my feet. That was nice. There were all kinds of restaurants (with all kinds of smells!), and Dave chose one. It was way bigger than the two restaurants we visited in Morristown. You'd really like it, Coach—not fancy, so the floor was great for sniffing and for finding stuff to eat. I got pretty comfortable under the table. It was one of those kinds with just one leg, in the middle. I had a good view of all the people passing by—lots of activity! The waiter brought me some water, and Dave gave me some little dog bone treats. Cool. Dave said I seemed to "adjust very well to just about any situation." (Yay.) Then out of nowhere the Prof said, "There's something magic about Kemp; he brings his own space and sunshine with him—his environment seems to adjust to him." (. . . Wow, Hickory.)

After lunch we walked back upstairs (up sure is easier than down), then back Uptown and up in the elevator to the Port Authority garage. Those last seven blocks were crazy. All these racks of clothes kept pushing into us on the sidewalk— people wheeled them around worse than the luggage.

It was still exciting back in the van—lots of other cars and people to look at, even in that long tunnel back to New Jersey. At the other end, My Partner gave me many pats and hugs and said I sure could handle New York. My tail thumped nonstop . . . till I slowed it down with a nap on the van floor. (Later the Prof said he'd heard small, happy whimpers and he wondered if I was having a happy doggy dream. I was!) We were back at the school in no time—that woke me up fast; I wanted to jump right out and under the dinner table to share the day's adventures with my friends . . . but it wasn't time yet. First we went straight to our room for some quiet time together. Like always, the Prof took off my harness right away, so I knew I was off duty. (He says our harness is like a man's "necktie"—you only wear it for business and you're glad it's gone when you're home relaxing.) My Partner suggested I take a nap while he sat down to type in his journal. I circled, pawed my mat into shape, and plopped down. I was still tired, but I couldn't sleep till I heard his report. I like hearing his computer talk while he writes:

> *Recalling the events of the last two and a half hours in the city, I am overcome by a tremendous feeling of relief that Kemp passed his "obstacle course" with an A+. Could it be that he has an edge in dealing with big-city challenges, even on mighty Hickory? Maybe so. He'd dealt successfully with crowds of people, heavy midday traffic, backfiring trucks, fire engine sirens, fast-moving Garment District clothes racks, daredevil bike riders, and the filth and roar of the subway. True, the litter-strewn sidewalks did occasionally tempt him to snag a bit of old bagel here, and a candy bar wrapper there—but those minor sins paled to insignificance compared to Kemp's self-assurance as a big-city guide dog. I can't wait to tell Jan, "Not only does he want to do it"; Kemp has proven that, indeed, he can do it.*
>
> *I was glad to have had Dave to myself for this test and lesson. After all, tomorrow Kemp and I will go back to Manhattan for good.*

I think he said that thing about Dave. I was so happy to hear My Partner's praise that I got all warm inside and dozed off before he finished . . . but I felt my tail still sweeping in content.

* * *

When I woke up, mostly we did packing, and we took thank-you cards to all our friends who helped us. Oh, and we gave tins of cookies to Head Chef Carl for the people in the kitchen.

Late in the afternoon my Partner and I walked the little way to what they call the Vincent A. Stabile Canine Health Center, for my final physical check-out. The vet gave him some notes. The Prof said they were "marvelously thorough," and he's going to take them to Doctor Lucas and Doctor Kutcher, my new vets in our neighborhood. (I'll tell them "hi" for you, Hickory.)

Then, at last, me and the Prof had our revolving-door training at the school. Geeze, I sure figured out fast why he was worried. The door started turning just as soon as we started to walk out of it, and cooped us up in this little glass wedge. It kept turning, too, so we had to move with it. My Partner grabbed my tail to get it out of the way of being squnched. When we got out on the other side, he told Dave that he stayed away from such "not-so-merry-go-round doors" with you, Hickory. The Prof expects to do the same with me, but he wanted to practice in case someday we can't choose. Once I got the hang of it, I liked doubling up—we both laughed a lot.

After the door, we gave Dave his Thanksgiving card and his presents. My Partner had given him a "4.00 grade-point average." (This is really good, right Coach?) Dave especially liked Uncle Michael's book about that Lincoln guy. Uncle Michael wrote Dave's name in it.

After dinner My Partner typed a few last notes in his Seeing Eye journal. It was such a full day that I was too awake to fall asleep, but I went to my mat and tried. I overheard the voice of Perfect Paul, the computer's mechanical reader, say what he typed:

> *All packed and ready for tomorrow's departure, I'm prompted to look back over highlights of the events of these past eighteen days. Kemp's problem areas of being distracted by other dogs, not*

Lloyd Burlingame

resting quietly when in "down" mode, and attempting to eat the furniture have all been solved. The indoor parking problem we will manage. My hunch is he has a small bladder and I'll give him extra times to relieve himself. I've managed to retrain my brain and mouth to not call Kemp by his predecessor's name . . . well, most of the time. I've mastered my pushy New Yorker's tendency of urging Kemp to rush across the street.

I've come to admire and trust Kemp. Knowing that Hickory in retirement is in the best possible new home has released me to open my heart to Kemp as well. He's a delightful companion. As he wrote Hickory, he's a Mickey Rooney – type of guy, full of high spirits and eager for adventure—and Kemp's not the least bit aquaphobic. He's lying by my bed now on his mat. Peering at close range at my boy, I must revise my first opinion of his looks. He's just as handsome as Hickory and, like him, Kemp is beautiful both outside and in.

I have the most wondrous feeling of being whole again and my spirit is rejuvenated. I am increasingly encouraged that the bond forming between us will grow even stronger. I well know how fortunate I am to have been blessed by The Seeing Eye with two such superb guide-companions. The great neurologist and humanist Oliver Sacks once called Hickory "inestimably precious." My heart tells me Kemp will soon be joining Hickory in that realm of high praise.

Wow!! I didn't understand all of that but I got the important part! It sure feels good to be almost in your league, Coach. . . . Now I really can't sleep!

The Nineteenth Day: Wednesday, 15 November 2006

My Partner was really happy this morning—he whistled while I ate my last (!) breakfast at the school and while I parked outside after. Then while he ate breakfast, all the other students and most everybody who worked at the school stopped to tell us goodbye. There was lots of hugging and laughing— and tail wagging with all my canine pals. Kalina and I nuzzled goodbye. Then the rest of the class went on their last day of training, and we got us and our stuff to the van. Doug, Judy, Pete (and, Coach, your Instructor Jeff) came outside to send us off with Instructor Jennifer. Then she drove us to Manhattan— and to my new home. I looked at everything on the way.

We stopped at a big white-brick building—and that was it! We were Home. There was a nice man named Steve, and two elevators . . . and a lot of great doggie smells! The elevator went up and then we got out in a long hallway, like at the school. The Prof had a key to one door . . . and when he opened it—there were Uncle Michael and Aunt Barbara!! She rushed to me, laughing and crying both . . . and then I saw the cats. Boy, Hickory, they didn't laugh or cry—they just disappeared. But I got your scent right off and that made it feel like home.

Jen, the Old Prof, and I went out right away, to see all the places I'll visit nearby. (Uncle Michael and Aunt Barbara stayed behind.) We walked over to Washington Square Park. On the way, I snuffed so many doggie messages on fire hydrants, lampposts, mail boxes . . . And at the park there were so many other dogs—all sizes and breeds I've never met before. The bummer was, I wasn't allowed to meet any of them! I thought Jen was nice, till she told My Partner to give me a leash correction when I tried to greet any other dog. That reminded me that I was in harness and on the job—and they weren't. So I focused hard on guiding the Prof.

After the Park, we walked five blocks in the other direction from our home. My Partner told Jen he used to teach at a school called New York University. Lots of the big buildings we passed were part of the school. One of them is the "Coles Sports Center," where My Partner has a trainer. (People have trainers, too, Coach.) It was like the exercise room at Seeing Eye, but lots bigger and full of more machines and equipment like we had there. In a smaller room where he does a lot of exercising, we met his trainer. Joel said I look a lot like you, Hickory, and that I'm friendly like you. I was glad he liked me, because he sure admires you.

Next we walked east to Broadway and turned north (that's Uptown, right?) toward home. I thought I was getting the hang of this "grid system"—but somebody made a mistake with Broadway, because it doesn't run straight north and south like the other wide streets. It's awful busy—full of little stores (but no pet shops with doggie bones), and the sidewalks are real crowded with people, especially young ones. My Partner told Jen that he was proud of me taking all of this "in my stride." At Waverly Place we turned into NYU's big Tisch School of the Arts building. We went up in the elevator to the third floor Design Department where the Prof was "chair" for 26 whole years. Out of a door came our other friend Barbara— her full name is "Departmental Administrative Director Cokorinos." We were real happy to see each other again—she came to The Seeing Eye. She didn't mind at all when I jumped up on her—she laughed. (But Jen sure didn't.)

I sooo learned stuff on this trip. New York is a lot bigger and taller than Morristown, and it has a lot more elevators. So far, though, I didn't see any escalators or revolving doors—no other problems, either. But on the way home, I was real surprised to hear subway noises underneath us! There was rumbling—I sure could feel that, too—and even announcements like the ones I heard on our subway trip the day before. They came up from big grates in the sidewalk that are hard to walk on. I think there are too many subways in New York.

Another thing different from Morristown is how fast everyone moves—walking, in cars and busses, on skate boards like kids had in my puppy-raiser town, on roller skates, scooters, and bicycles. That's hard to get used to—but the only real dangerous people are the ladies pushing babies in their little carts. They mow you down if you don't get out of their way! The Prof calls 'em "killer moms." I'm real careful around them, Coach.

From the school it was only three blocks Uptown to East Ninth Street—where we live. It was cool how much Jen taught us about big-city partnering in just two hours. This is called an "at home" visit. My Partner calls it a perfect final lesson from The Seeing Eye—our "transition" from school to a new life in the "real world."

In the apartment Uncle Michael and Aunt Barbara looked around to "puppy-proof" the place. At first I thought the Prof had a puppy to play with . . . but they meant me. Geeze, I'm old enough to guide the Prof around New York—I'm no puppy. They checked my two new big, comfy wicker beds and their tie-downs. One of them is near My Partner's desk, close to the kitchen with a good view. I like the beds, but I missed your smell, Hickory. Did you take your beds to Sunny Meadow? Jen and Aunt Barbara didn't find much, but the Prof seemed to like their help. I guess they want me to be safe and not get hurt on anything—especially something called "temptation" (which sounds pretty interesting).

I could tell My Partner was happy to be home and I tried to show him I was too.

First Jen, then Aunt Barbara and Uncle Michael left. It got real quiet. When I went to my kitchen bed for a snooze, Clemmie and Hugo finally showed up. They pretended I wasn't there and hopped onto the Time-Warmer cable box to cuddle and sleep. (They're no fun. I'd rather have a puppy.) The Prof went to his desktop computer and I heard Perfect Paul say his Seeing Eye Journal's last entry:

It had been a six-month-long haul from the first inkling Hickory wished to retire through the frustrating process of deciding to search for his new home, finding it, and returning to The Seeing Eye. Now it's highly likely Kemp will be the equal of my first dog, as both guide and companion. I discovered to my astonishment and delight, I have room in my heart for both of these splendid canines. Bonding with Kemp has gotten off to a strong start. Today we're beginning on a great adventure in loving partnership.

That sounds good, Coach. I'm glad my new best friend is My Partner. Starting our Great Adventure was exciting. And tomorrow is my second birthday! I sniff doggie bone treats in the air, and I hope those things in colored paper are major bones to gnaw on. Today was wonderful and tomorrow will be even better. With you and the Prof to teach me, there's nuthin' I can't do!

Lloyd Burlingame

PART THREE

Kemp at Work and Hickory at Play:
Viennas, Here We Come!

November 2006 – November 2007

Lloyd Burlingame

Mistress and Himself proudly present Hickory
for a blessing from the Bishop of Upperville

CHAPTER TEN

Thanksgiving to New Year's Eve

2006

20 November 2006: E-mail from Hickory to the Old Prof

Dear Dad,

    The photos of you and Kemp at The Seeing Eye were wonderful. They took me back to a time long ago. Knowing the exciting adventures awaiting Kemp gave my heart an extra beat. Don't mind his doggie socializing too much. He's only sniffing out the turf and the current turf-holders . . . I wager their time is short, given the new kid on the block!

Down here on the plantation, I do like being chauffeured. Just easing through the parking lot in our local mall makes my knees wobble, what with all the admiring glances in my direction. Himself drives slowly, revealing my best profile pleasantly framed in the window of the Porsche. This he has thoughtfully cracked, admitting enticing aromas of food stuff, to which I am very much alert.

At home Cheri, poor dear, is still smitten by my very presence. She sits and stares at me for what seems like hours. As I walk by her to my water bowl, she rolls belly up and squeals, pawing the air with all fours in a most unladylike fit. When Mistress throws toys for me to retrieve, little Cheri first scampers to keep up with my running and leaping, then sits to watch as I return. I don't understand this at all, so I try to ignore her, like a kindly uncle.

Now, Rusty is cut from another cloth. He is a slow learner and, I think, rather neurotic. Still, as a compassionate Labrador, I like the little guy; he's become a great source of entertainment. He has only recently understood: (1) I wag my tail all the time, (2) my tail is long, thick, and carries a punch, and (3) his head is in line with the plane of my tail. Lately he has developed a marvelous bob-and-weave.

Speaking of me: My neck chain, leash, and harness are no more than a wisp of memory! I now proudly wear a bright red collar with my name and telephone number woven into it. Outdoors, I run . . . not true . . . I *gallop* around the estate. When Himself returns from errands and I'm set free of the house, I canter to him and run back to Mistress, beginning a game of catch-me-if-you-can. They can't catch me unless I let them, and the game ends only when I do.

Indoors I know, of course, where the kitchen is and what goes on there. I think my ways have suggested to Mistress and Himself that perhaps I was sometimes given "extras" in my other life. Planting myself strategically underfoot to observe any food movement in my direction has not been successful here. Still, Thanksgiving rapidly approaches and my hopes are high.

Please continue to send photos of you and Kemp. We alumni of the wuuffing kind like to know how the new folk are performing.

166   Lloyd Burlingame

Hugs, wuuffs, and licks to all,
I am,
Hickory.

21 November 2006: E-mail from the Old Prof to Hickory

Dearly loved Hickory,

How grand to hear from you and to learn of the many joys of your new life now that you're released from carrying the burden of eight years as Mayor of Washington Square.

Perhaps you will remember our earliest days together, here on East Ninth Street? Days when, as per injunctions from The Seeing Eye masters, I had to keep you on your leash while moving around the apartment and on the long chain when in your beds in the living room and bedroom. Now young Kemp's undergoing that same treatment and, I am happy to say, approaches such partial confinement with good cheer and perky resignation. He has a horsey quality you never evinced, prancing in place with his huge Galileo Nylabone in his mouth. Kemp's rather in the Lipizzaner tradition and I have had some serious talks with him about species identity. He laughs this off in a charming Viennese manner.

Kemp went to the vet yesterday to have his identity chip inserted and to get a baseline checkup. Dr. Lucas remembered your newly adopted mom and dad's visit to her, with appreciative fondness. Everyone asked after your well-being and I was happy to report the good news of your contentment in Vienna. I've told them about the photos of you riding shotgun in the red pickup truck and driving the blue Porsche. You have proven that one *can* teach a mature canine new tricks.

Perhaps you will recall how your talent for eating just about anything was made known here early on, when you ingested your faux wicker bed. I have tried to remove such temptation by giving Kemp real wicker beds, like those I belatedly provided for you. His are sprayed liberally with Bitter Apple—yuck. Subsequently Kemp has turned instead to completing the work you so nobly began on your green "yard" carpet with the leaf patterns; he has made great inroads in true gourmand fashion. Even a freshly sprayed border of Bitter Apple availed nothing. The poor battered floor covering has had to be retired. I hope to find a replacement that will carry on the outdoor theme, without tempting Kemp to snack. ABC Carpet, here we come. I have such happy memories of the old rug; I will probably archive it since I can't bear to part with it. Many a good time we had romping on that bit of Indian textile, transported to our North American island.

What a time Kemp and I had training at The Seeing Eye. Everyone remembered you so fondly and rejoiced on hearing you had found your perfect new home and family. We had jolly visits with Jeff, Judy, Doug, Tom, and Karen. Remember Karen? She was in our class in '98, and here she was again eight years later. Back then her dog was Ruthie; I'm sure you recall her from your many visits under the dining table. Like you, she has completed a superb job as guide dog and now enjoys her well-deserved time-in-the-sun retirement.

Kemp and I fast-walk around the square two times early in the morning and will increase to four ere long. He is more interested in pigeons and squirrels than you were, adding to the distraction factors we're trying to correct. Yes, you're right, he is still a kid. Smart and well trained, but a youngster nonetheless, deserving understanding . . . if not indulgence.

We're going to Renée and Camille's with Charlie and Sal for Turkey Day. I've bought Kemp an obscenely huge and grotesque industrial-strength-plastic turkey drumstick. Gracie, their little doggie, is getting something more modest to suit her dainty jaws. Speaking of the fair sex, I hope you will be your old affectionate self with Cheri. She is nearly half your age and deserves sympathetic consideration. As for Rusty, I trust you are not thinking of bullying him with your larger size. Consider how small you must appear to your new dad's horse, yet I am sure Willy treats you kindly.

I am working hard on correcting my greatest fault with Kemp: I keep giving him commands that go something like this, "Hickory, left, Hickory . . . errrr, Kemp, forward." The other student-partners in our little group of five at TSE kept asking, when I honored you and dishonored Kemp, "Who?" Oops. It means you are still very much alive on my tongue as well as in my heart. I have so much to thank you for, especially teaching me the ropes of partnering. I know Kemp appreciates that I'm not a novice at working with guiding-eyes-with-a cold-wet-nose.

Well, dear Prince of Vienna, it is time for me to scrape my chin, water Kemp, and dash off to Coles for exercising. Everyone at the gym misses you. Trainer Joel sends you his best wishes, and Lenore her love.

Barbara has been wonderfully supportive (what else is new?) in helping with the great transition. She keeps a group of thirty friends posted on your doings and Kemp's, and shares the fabulous photos from your master and mistress, and those your Uncle Michael took on his recent visit. On Thanksgiving Camille will premiere her video treat showing your high-spirited working of the room at your gala farewell party last month. It was a pity only thirty of your closest friends could celebrate your graduation. What a blast!

I have so much to be grateful for in this world, and I am keenly aware of that, thanks to you, your new mom and dad, Kemp, Barbara, and uncles Michael, Charlie, and Sal.
Much love to you and your dear ones on Sunny Meadow Lane,
The Old Prof

P. S. Kemp sends cheery tail wags and the cats stretch lazily in feline greeting.

22 November 2006: E-mail from Hickory to Kemp

My Dear Kemp,

For eight years I walked where you walk now. The hand that held my harness then now holds yours. Your responsibilities today were once mine. The reward of my life each morning, each day, each night, was that hand. As you grow, so will it be with you. We have been blessed above all our mates. We got the Old Prof, and with him, the full bowl. You'll soon (if not already) forget that he walks upright, ignore his dry nose, and forgive his not having a real coat. They won't matter because you'll know the one truth that does matter: He's one of us!

I must leave you now—the Mixmaster hums. Upstairs Mistress is making good things for tomorrow's table. I'm responsible for keeping the place tidy while she goes about her tasks. I glue myself to her leg, keep a sharp eye, and vacuum things that pop from the table. I give 110 percent effort by anticipating bits and pieces getting too close to the edge, using my head-on-its-side grab technique.

So off I go—with best wishes to you, you most lucky dog, for your first Thanksgiving with the family.
Sending my best personal regards, licks, sniffs, and wuuffs to all.
Yours,
Coach

22 November 2006: E-mail from Kemp to Hickory

Dear Coach,

I really and truly thank you for guiding me. I've only been here on East Ninth Street for one week and I kinda see how things will go for me and My Partner.

Your portrait looks great—I see it from my bed. I have a red rubber toy or two like yours in the picture—not my all-time favorites. Better is the big new Galileo Nylabone I just got. That sucker will last for months. I hear you're real good at long bone-chewing sessions. The Prof told me you have two life-mottos: "To chew is to live," and "I eat, therefore I am." I bet you're living pretty well there.

My Partner's friends say I look a lot like you, Hickory. They even call me by your name—that's a compliment. Too bad Seeing Eye orders say I'm still not supposed to hang out much with them. I sure am missing out on Thanksgiving Day treats. I can't wait for Christmas, when it's okay to start romping.

How great that you run around without a harness, and ride around in cars and trucks. When people ask about you, the Prof tells them how happy he is that *you're* so happy in "Ol' Virginny." It's cool——he and his family keep on loving you, lots, but I think I'm getting to be much loved too. You're right—we're both lucky dogs. Best is, I think the Prof's pals think *they're* the lucky ones.

It's kinda chilly now, but the weekend will be brighter and warmer for Macy's Thanksgiving Day parade. I want to see that dog Snoopy—he flies!

Happy Thanksgiving, dear Coach—and to the rest of your new family,

Kemp

22 December 2006: E-mail from Kemp to Hickory

Hey, Coach.

Here's the news from East Ninth Street. The apartment's pretty. The Prof says this is how you like it at Christmas. That long pine thing (sometimes he calls it "garland" and sometimes he calls it "Judy") loops across the big window and a million white lights are twinkling. There's a spruce tree named Alberta behind the sofa—her lights are in lots of colors. My Partner hung fancy Christmas stockings on the long bookcase. I have one! It's quilted red satin and says "Kemp" -- *in fancy green writing*. Hugo and Clemmie have stockings, too, but they're just red velvet and probably full of catnip (gaggg).

Geeze, Morristown didn't prepare us for Broadway shoppers in Manhattan. They go crazy at this time of year—they don't care *who* they run into. But I'm holding my own. The Prof says you were pretty "assertive" when you had to be. That sounds like a good thing, so I hope to do the same.

Remember your "yard" rug from India, with the leafs on it? I followed your lead and did some artistic snacking along the edges—but the Prof likes *straight* edges better. He started calling me the "*Teppichfresser*." (That's German for "carpet chewer.") He said some important German guy used to eat *his* rug in a rage. (I was just hungry.) I guess he had a big temper, 'cause his name started with "Hit."

Anyway, one day your/our carpet was gone. I guess the Prof took it away, 'cause then he and Aunt Barbara and me went to ABC Carpet to find a new one. They looked at, like, *forty* of 'em, then finally put two side by side on the floor, and looked and talked and walked around 'em. The one I liked came from that India place, too. It had real pretty bright colors, but they kinda blended together. The other one had vines, like outdoors, but it was boring. I figured, this is gonna be *my* back yard, so I jumped into the middle of the pretty one to show them it was best. My Partner asked the French saleslady, "Have you ever sold a rug to a dog?" She shrugged her shoulders, slowly shook her head, and said, "Non." (I don't know why not.)

My rug fits the space just right, and Aunt Barbara says I look very handsome "posed on the field of rainbow colors." Yesterday I started nibbling on it. I got a stern "go to your place" command, so I trotted off to my bed in the bedroom, like I could care less. While I was snoozing, the sneaky carpet police double-sprayed the front and back with that awful Bitter Apple. Where's their Christmas spirit? If the rug costs too much money to eat, the Prof could throw a few Kibbles my way instead.

Trotting around the Square every morning is fun! In the gym they tie me down at the front desk and everyone asks, "How is Hickory doing?" Our pal tells them you're doing real good and having lotsa fun "transitioning from governing as the Mayor of Washington Square to reigning as the Prince of Vienna." (I almost understand all that—I'm getting used to the big words.) This good news makes all your friends very happy, and puts a big grin on My Partner's face.

On Christmas Eve, Aunt Barbara, Uncle Charlie, and Uncle Sal are here for supper, then aunts Renée and Camille come for dessert. Then on Christmas day Uncle Michael and Niece Jessie are here for dinner and present-opening. The Prof says some wonder if I'll be as good as you at unwrapping. I'll try. I'm practicing with my Nylabones—attacking 'em and really roughing 'em up. I think I'll be ready on time.

Lloyd Burlingame

Gosh, Hickory, everybody here wishes you a real happy Christmas in your new home. We both sure got awesome new families for presents. Thank you for giving me yours—and for all your advice. Big wuuff,
Kid Kemp

P.S. Merry Christmas, my dear countrified friend! Magoo

23 December 2006: E-mail from Hickory to Kemp

My Dear Kid,

I've been remiss in my correspondence and do apologize. Himself and Mistress spent a week in Spain. On returning, he flew to Colorado for a week of skiing. (That's like ice skating on long, thin boards; you won't see it in New York.) I could hardly get a bark out edgewise, without Himself to take dictation.

Tonight we loaded up in the car and Himself took the family—-Mistress, me, Cheri, and Rusty—to see the decorated homes. (Of course, I rode up front.) The lights on the houses are difficult to describe. Have you ever seen a toy-train village all lit up? Or pictures of a fairyland in your puppy family's books? That's a bit like it.

Back home I curled up in front of the fire, got a tummie rub, earned a treat, and took to snoring on Himself's foot. Good games followed: "try-pulling-it-out-of-my-mouth," "throw-it-farther," "clap-your-hands-and-watch-me-run," and "growl-grunt-and-grovel-for-a-treat." Life is good. In fact, I've begun to acquire a mild Virginian accent. Cheri says it's very becoming. Just this morning I caught myself slurping "watah" where once I sipped "water." Everything is casual in Virginia. I seldom make a sound here, because a simple eyelid lift usually does the trick.

Lately, Mistress argues I should be driving a Hummer, instead of "that wretched piece of 1995 Chevy junk" pickup truck Himself so loves. I'm not sure . . . I enjoy my cowboy hat and don't know how it would look in a Hummer.

Every day the delivery man loads me with gifts. The bell rings; I sing out and run to the front door. Mistress, Cheri, Rusty, and I give scary welcome to the bell ringer and crowd the door in anticipation. I can tell by the scent that I'm overwhelmed with good things from Dad and yourself. Himself does not allow any gifts to be opened until we are all gathered under the tree come Christmas morning. (Such an uninformed man.) I'm drooling in anticipation of Christmas morning. (Truth be told, I've already sampled some of my presents and eaten a hunk of my stocking. Excellent!)

Now Kemp, you're young and, I'm sure, also excited about the treats ahead for Christmas. But don't overlook your best presents. Aunt Barbara, Uncle Charlie, and Uncle Sal are a Christmas gift beyond all value—a gift that lasts year-round. Look to them for guidance. Love them as they love you and your Dad.

May your days be many in both good health and companionship.

I am,

Hickory

25 December 2006: E-mail from Kemp to Hickory

Hey, Coach!

Way cool that you were singled out at the "Blessing of the Animals" ceremony! Our Dad plans to share it with your New York friends and admirers.

Our Christmas was *real* merry. Aunt Barbara and the Prof liked talking to Himself and Mistress last night. He says there's "such good energy" at your new home and they "clearly think a lot" of you. (We do, too!)

I've already got a pack of new friends, and I'm having a good time in my new home on this little island between the East and Hudson Rivers. Today Uncle Michael and me did some major romping. He's fun—and he's coming back this weekend!

I got some awesome new bones for Christmas. All day I've been chewing with might and something the Prof calls "main." He says my young jaws are too strong for a couple of gifts, so I'm not allowed to play with 'em. But I *did* get to rip 'em open. I can't do that in one double head toss like you, but I'm workin' on it. Aunt Barbara gave our Dad a volume of photos of you, Mistress, Himself, Rusty, and Cheri. It's real cool, and he loves it, even though he has to have the photos described to him.

Last night it "rained cats and dogs." (Isn't that funny?) This morning when the Prof and I walked around the Square, he was real happy that I don't mind getting my paws wet. I guess you do, huh? He says you go around each and every wet spot to keep yours dry. I just plough straight through. But I forgot that takes *the Prof* straight through. So I accidentally took him through a deep pool of ice water, and soaked his shoes. That sure surprised him. He muttered, "Hickory would have never let that happen." I guess I've got more to learn about guiding and rain. I tried to apologize with lots of nuzzling and a face lick when we got home. His shoes may dry by New Year's Eve.
Happy New Year to you, Cheri, Rusty, Mistress, and Himself!!
Kid

Lloyd Burlingame

*On their Hudson River Park Walk, Kemp and the Old Prof
take a break at the North Cove Marina*

CHAPTER ELEVEN

Valentine's Day, Musher's Wax, and Easter Eggs

January – April 2007

15 January 2007: E-mail from Hickory to Kemp

Dear Kid,

. . . I'm taking voice lessons. Cheri has the most marvelous bark. And she uses it—greeting everyone with a sweet song that brings Himself and Mistress to her every time. I had no musical encouragement as a pup (and, of course, duets are frowned upon by the Old Prof—though he plays more than enough music to go around). So I've gotten by with a foggy wheeze whenever a noise of some sort was needed. But I have had nothing for the doorbell, birds and squirrels in the garden and trees, walkers, the garage door opening, delivery men . . . All of these bring Cheri to the front. As for Rusty, his range, I hate to admit, is remarkable: barks, whines, yelps, full voice, trembles . . . Cheri and Rusty in duet make eyes water and ears ring, but I was nothing in that vocal romance. I appealed to Cheri's mothering instincts, and right away she became *my* Coach. Already, just this morning, I let out a bellow that surprised even me and roused everyone out of bed. You should have seen the admiration in Cheri's eyes (and the envy and spite in Rusty's!). I got an early breakfast out of it, too. Himself remarked to Mistress that I sounded like the title character in *The Hound of the Baskervilles*, whom they must hold in high regard.

Himself and I took the truck up to the stables last Tuesday. Mistress had her book club in, so we were told to leave and not return until they were gone. I had my first nose-to-nose with Willie, Himself's hunter. (I have yet to see him or any other horse "hunt," but that's what they call him.) Not much conversation there. (Maybe not much at *all* there.) He's nice enough, but he stares too much and says very little. We do have one love in common: food. Hold out a treat for Willie and he comes on the trot.

Best wuuffs to you, Kid, and sweet dreams.

Coach

27 January 2007: E-mail from Kemp to Hickory

Hey, Coach,

My Partner's commands don't start with "Hickory" so much anymore! He always says he's sorry when they do, but I don't really mind. I still have to be ahead of him on a lot of things—like you were-—including directions. (He keeps saying one when he means the other.)

It *is* hard to *all the time* keep doing some of the stuff we learned at The Seeing Eye. Like being quiet. At Christmas, so much was happening, so fast, that I gave out a couple barks of joy. But nobody's asking *me* to be in a trio. *Hugo* has a lot to say—but it isn't very nice, and it sounds awful. He goes from a little snarling "neeyeeaaah" to an ear-splitting "Yowww!" And he doesn't want company. Clemmie just squints her big yellow eyes and shakes her head back and forth, like, "Silly boys." You're right—this place is always full of people singing on those machines. Some *quiet* would be nice sometimes. It's not bad right now—we're hearing this thing called *Das Rheingold.* I kinda like it. There's lots of clanking swords, stomping giants, and ladies who swim in . . . the Ocean! (Or someplace like it.) The Prof says that in the next part, called *Die Walkuere* (where do they get these names?), I'll hear barking dogs who belong to a guy named (see what I mean?) Hund-ing.

Aunt Barbara and My Partner are talking about a trip *across* the Ocean, next fall! Get this—it's to a place called Vienna. But not your Vienna, Hickory. This is in a whole different country, named Austria. They want to listen to music over there. (Seems to me we have enough *here*, but I'd like to sniff out the place.) Vienna music happens in a *Wiener Staatsoper*. (No luck, Coach—not wieners like hot dogs. It's just another opera house, with a funny name.) We're having trouble, though. The Prof asked a good friend over there—Frau Susie—to make sure the Wiener allows guide dogs. She just sent a E-mail. We're *not* allowed, because, "People don't pay to come to the opera to hear dogs bark!" You shoulda heard the Prof, Coach! He said, "Oh, yeah? I've been paying to go to that opera house for the last forty years and have heard a *lot* of barking—mostly from tenors on the stage!" If I can't get into the Wiener place, then I'll stay with Frau Susie. She lives real close, and I can play with her dog, Lumpi. (Which sounds better than the opera.) She says even nonworking dogs are welcomed in Austrian restaurants. That's a step forward.

There's not much space to romp here. But I put bones in every room and corner, and I'm real good at 24-7-365 chewing. The Prof says the apartment is like Henry VIII's dining hall. (He was some old king whose guests threw bones over their shoulders and didn't care where they fell.) Magoo can get a bit testy stumbling over a Kong here and a drumstick there. He's kinda spoiled 'cause you and I don't let him stumble outdoors.

This morning, did we have an adventure! When we went out for our 7:00 a.m. walk, Doorman Steve gave us a warning. He said that awful phony salt was over all the sidewalks. I'm glad the Prof's too smart to fall for the lie about this stuff not burning our paws. Right away we took the elevator back up to our apartment and he put that Musher's wax stuff all over my paws. Yuck. *Then*, when we went back down . . . turned out the sidewalks were sheets of ice! I wanted to get moving, but My Partner slowed us to a crawl. (Even then I was kinda unsteady.) We got to the grocery store, bagged the long walk around the Park, and made it home in one piece. (Well, in two pieces, I guess.)

One of the best times of the day is when the Prof puts his exercise mat in my yard. He gets into these real funny positions, and I can crawl under or walk on top of him. This makes him laugh a lot so I guess it's OK. It *al*most makes up for not being allowed to eat my own rug.

Well, the gods are about to cross over the Rainbow Bridge at the end of *Das Rheingold* (again). It's near 11:30 park time, so *we're* gonna cross over the street.
The Kid

14 February 2007: E-mail from Hickory to the Old Prof

Well, Dad, life is good.

I must say I'm delighted that Kemp has fitted the role once played by me. He's one lucky boy. . . . Though this East Coast snow storm must make him wonder what he's in for. (Surely curb food is harder to find!) For me, it's pure bliss. I have been romping in the stuff and running snow rings about Mistress. The white flies about, and I jump to bite each flake until I hear the call to the buffet.

Our end of the storm meant one glorious morning with all kinds of flakes falling from the sky, coating everything with the purest white snow. Having instructed Staff of my needs, I ventured forth for the day's first park. Imagine my surprise when what appeared to be a three-inch step was really a plunge into deep, soft snow. I abandoned the morning ritual for a good racing about. It was a few minutes before I remembered and addressed my main objective. The Staff seemed pleased with this conclusion and encouraged my retreat to the house.

Good hugs, wuuffs, and licks to all,

I am,

Hickory

16 February 2007: E-mail from Kemp to Hickory

Dear Coach,

Snow down there sounds lots more fun than snow up here. 'Course it's easier to move through on your own, too, without harness and human. My nose still isn't as good as yours at plowing a long, straight, football field – length furrow, but I'm working on it.

The Prof keeps putting the Musher's stuff on my paws before we go out. I don't like it, but it's that or get burned. We're not using the boots from Seeing Eye—yours are here, too, Coach. They don't stay on, so they're sittin' quietly way up on a shelf in the closet. (At least *they're* keeping dry.) Prof says doormen and porters in some buildings nearby are too lazy to shovel. So instead they still dump tons of that phony salt—even though lots of people complain. All us dogs on the block try to stay away from those bad sidewalks.

Early this morning, Doorman Steve got out the snow shovel and cleared a path across the street so we could jay walk safe to the other side for me to park. That was real nice of him—he's being a good friend to me, like he was to you. I hope it's OK with you, Coach—it's called the "Hickory/Kemp Trail" now. But nobody forgets you started it!

A dozen of the Prof's former students came over for dinner and drinks Tuesday night. You know lots of them—they were real glad you're doing well. But one said now it's sure easier to leave snacks on the coffee table. (I thought that was rude.) I sure don't mind a stolen snack or two, but I have more fun with my strong tail. It batted a home run that night. A wine glass sailed over the table and landed in the outfield near the stereo set-up. The cats lying there in the bleachers (on the Time-Warmer) jerked up and ran. Everyone was impressed—except for that rude guy. I guess I showed him that he'd better keep an eye out whether you're here or not.

You'd laugh to hear the Prof this week. He's sick in the throat with some long word. He can hardly talk, and I can hardly make out what he wants me to do. I just try to guess—like you told me. So far it's working out, but I miss hearing the commands.

So it's time to get mushed for the slush. Oh, I forgot to tell you what happened in our last snow storm. When we were in a drugstore, the man ahead of us in line asked the clerk, "Do you carry Musher's wax? I need it for my dog."

"*What* do you want for your dog?" asked the clerk.

"Musher's wax."

"You want *moustache wax* for your dog?" We don't carry anything like that. You should try a pet store."

I think of that every time the Prof puts Musher's wax on me. Some of the dogs at Seeing Eye could use that for their whiskers. It makes me laugh.

Take care of yourself, Coach. Our Dad sends his best regards to Herself and Himself. Me too—and to Cheri and Rusty. Dad says your E-mails "gladden" his heart.
Wuufff! with swishing tail wags,
Kid Kemp

20 February 2007: E-mail from Kemp to Hickory, and the Burkes

He still can't talk good, and I can't understand the commands he croaks out in a whisper. At his Dr. Zimmerman's, Jane told him I'd know what to do without commands. That gave me some good ideas.

Lloyd Burlingame

Like I could take us to the dog run and the pet store instead of the gym and the bank. Working with a near-mute partner could be fun!

How cool that you all want us to visit! The Prof says, "Southern hospitality is alive and well in Fairfax County." I think we have lots of time to plan our nose-to-nose reunion, though, 'cause he's talking about a summertime trip. I can't wait for all this snow to be gone, and to romp in your big yard.

A hearty wuuff to all—with very fast wags from my much-admired Louisville slugger of a tail,
Kid

23 March 2007: E-mail from Kemp to Mistress and Himself

Dear Mistress and Himself,

Wuuffs to you both, and to good ol' Hickory, Rusty, and Cheri.

We had sooooo much rain the other day. The Prof says it rained cats and dogs (that's a joke of his), and he called me "a very, very good dog"! Here, he wants to tell you about it:

Unable to find a taxi to bring us the mile-and-a-half home, I decided Kemp and I would just plow our way Downtown on foot, via crazily busy Broadway. We were going through a hyperactive commercial district and had to dodge "killer" pushcarts, aggressive umbrella-wielding pedestrians rushing for shelter, and hell-bent messengers on bikes. These moving objects, like dodge-'em fun-house cars, were only a few of the obstacles Kemp had to surmount.

Every other block had sawhorse barriers, forcing us to detour out onto traffic-snarled Broadway itself. Adding to the challenge of that zigzag pattern of movement was dodging around stationary objects, e.g., crates unloaded from trucks and ruined wrecks of abandoned umbrellas. Halfway home, in the middle of this mess, I thought my decision to hoof it was well beyond ill advised. Kemp didn't share my discouragement, however. "Hey, this is fun," he signaled, "I can do it— to heck with the pedestrians; full speed ahead!" I took heart and followed my intrepid guide dog's lead. Kemp got us home in record time. I was highly impressed.

(Hey, Coach, I wouldn't of told you that myself—but pretty cool, huh? It's real good to hear My Partner say such nice things, especially 'cause I'm tryin' to follow in your paw prints. Besides, I had lots of fun playing "dodge-'em.")

Happy spring to you all!

Kemp

28 March 2007: E-mail from Himself to the Old Prof

Hickory is in clover. He arises to suit his wont, speaks to us of his needs, gets immediate attention, returns at leisure, and droolingly awaits first treats. Speaking of drooling, he does it with the most carefree attitude imaginable. There is the downward-draining-puddling drool and the dribbling-spittle drool out the front of the mouth. The most wondrous of all (the one to observe from afar), is the fling drool, beginning as the downward-draining type, only to get wrapped around his muzzle and/or face as he simultaneously shakes his head in a fit to realign his skin.

Spring is early here this year, and Hickory can't get enough of it. That is, if "enough" is defined as thirty seconds of running and jumping (first from Lolly and then to me), collapsing on the warm driveway, slowly and mournfully rolling onto his side, and finally sleeping for ten minutes in the sun.

An inquisitive sniffing by Cheri awakens him, and the process repeats. Rusty's singing encourages things from a distance, and we all have a good time.

I read to Hickory excerpts from the journal Kemp and you are keeping—of course, highlighting those putting our old boy in a most favorable light. At those readings he focused half-lidded eyes upon me and gave a slight acknowledging nod. Not too much, you understand, but just enough to let me know I was reading truth and not to be overly surprised. When I slipped in a reading or two noting a favorable disposition to Kemp's accomplishments (walking in the wet, for

Lloyd Burlingame

example), I noticed the boy inevitably found an urgent need to lick himself.

Hickory is in seemingly great health and has taken us over—- that is, us as well as the house. We didn't appreciate just how inquisitive he was until we noticed that he simply couldn't bear to not be with Mistress when she went upstairs or into the basement. He needed to know about all things, big and small. His management of Cheri and Rusty has been a case study in applied psychology. They love the boy but can't figure out why.

As for the staff, i.e., Mistress and myself, it's a case of the *Masterpiece Theatre* epic *Upstairs, Downstairs*: The dogs get first-class service, and we live happily and pridefully serving. It's God's gift to all.

Hope all's well with you and that wonderful companion and new pal, Kemp.

Himself

Lloyd Burlingame

Kemp preparing to endure another performance at the
Metropolitan Opera at Lincoln Center to humor the Old Prof

CHAPTER TWELVE

After the Deluge, a Flood of Operas

Mid-April – Mid-July 2007

16 April 2007: E-mail from Kemp to Hickory

Hey, Coach,

    The Prof says, "April is supposed to be 'the cruelest month,' but thanks to yesterday's post-Easter Nor'easter, it's now the coldest and wettest—and the Big Apple is the Frozen Apple." He says if cleanliness is next to godliness (is it, Hickory?), I'm "near the gate of a mighty damp Heaven." I didn't get my spring bath a couple weeks ago because it was too cold. But since yesterday morning I've had *six* showers. I don't much mind rain and stuff . . . but, geeze, I've had enough.

However, getting toweled off after each dousing is more fun than a kennel of puppies. I grab one end of the towel and tug, and Magoo tries his blind-man's-best to dry me with other end. It's a kick. When I turn in circles the two of us get all tangled up. All this action slows down the rubdown, and the bathroom looks like a drying room in a laundry. (Hah, that's what it is.) The Prof says, "Thank the Good Lord and Noah himself, Hickory wasn't being put through this trial by deluge. It would have made him want to be the first one on the Ark."

The rain's s'posed to stop tonight, It's still real cold here, and the wind makes it worse. When we slogged to the gym today, the wind and cold and rain felt like a rotten day in January. Even the birds are quiet—but the tulips are hangin' in. If "April showers bring May flowers," like the Prof says, they oughta be awesome this year.
Hope it's dry down there. And warm. "Hey" to everyone,
Kid

P.S. The cats think we're nut jobs 'cause we keep going out in the rain. They're snug and dry on top of the new Time-Warmer cable box. That's cool with me . . . but they could stop sticking out those tiny pink tongues when I come home drowned and froze.

22 April 2007: E-mail from Kemp to Hickory

Hey, Coach,

We've had two big deals since I wrote. First—*no more rain!* Now it's *spring*. The sun's shinin' bright on all the Ninth Street tulips.

Second—I've seen the OPERA. This one's called *Il Trittico*. It's really three short ones, but together they're looonnnngggg. We listened to 'em at home a lot first. I guess where we sat at the Met is

Lloyd Burlingame

special. It's called a box, but it doesn't look like any box I ever saw, and the Prof's friend Doug Schmidt put us there. He's a "set designer" —he made all the stuff we looked at behind the curtain. Anyway, the Prof told me the box belongs to some guy named General Manager Gelb—that's why it's on the "ritzy parterre level." (I just keep listenin' to this stuff, like I understand it.) Then he leaned down to me and whispered, "Don't mess up!"

Two young-lady people sat in the front row, My Partner and Aunt Barbara sat in the second, and Ed Wittstein sat in the third. (He's a friend who worked with our Dad when *he* was a stage designer. Do you know him, Coach?) I got to stretch out in the aisle. All the people in the theatre chattered away, but they got quiet when the lights suddenly went out. I wondered what was up, but the people didn't care. Then the big curtain we were looking at went up and showed the stage. We saw this huge river named Seine with a big barge floating in it. Over that was a long bridge with people coming and going, and in the background was a whole city. It stayed black where we were, but the barge got lit up. People started doing barge-y things and singin' in Italian about how hard it was to work on the river. Nobody talked, but everybody onstage sang real loud at each another; maybe they're all hard of hearing.

In front of the river this deep pit was full of people named musicians, scraping, blowing, and banging away. Sometimes they played real soft and other times real, real loud. Some man in the middle waved his arms up, down, and back and forth, but nobody cared about him. I was so used to this racket at home, I took a snooze for a while and had an awesome doggie dream.

This first opera was called, "Il Tabarro," which means "the cloak." That's what the barge captain was wearing when he lit a match for his pipe. Then this young guy ran onto the barge, which was a bad idea for him. The pipe guy strangled him with his wife's clothesline, sat down, and hid the body under his cloak. The wife came upstairs, maybe lookin' for her clothesline. She snuggled up to her husband (another bad idea), he showed her the body, she screamed real loud, fainted, and everything went dark again.

Then everybody who was watching got real upset, started banging their hands together, and shouting "Bravo!" First I figured they were screaming for the power company and police. But then they seemed *happy(?)*, so I joined in, jumped up, and kissed the backs of the necks of the ladies in front of us. I wagged my tail like mad, whacking Ed's knees, jumped up on Aunt Barbara, and gave her face an extra-special kissy lick. This made her laugh, which was better than the barge lady's scream. Then the lights got fixed and came back on.

Aunt Barbara, My Partner, and me went outside to the big main Plaza and hung a left. We came to a great big pond where a guy with a hole in his tummy floated in the middle. His name is Henry Moore. We walked over to the Beaumont Theater, like you used to do. You're right—it's bad. The Prof must have been *really* young when he helped design it. I remembered what you told me about all the bad reviews it got. And what the Prof said on *your* first opera trip—when you headed right over to the Beaumont and parked on the wall: "That's the last straw. Thank you very much, we get the message." (I didn't even bother to pee on it.)

Then it was already time to go inside again. But on the way, I saw this *huge* rainstorm in the middle of the Plaza. The water shoots straight up! It was soooo cool. I wanted to jump in, but the Prof made it clear that would be a no-no—even if we *didn't* have to go back to the opera.

The lights went out *again*, and this time the barge was gone. When the curtain went up we saw a huge Italian church and a pretty herb garden. The musicians were back in their ditch, and a lot of bells were ringing in the church. There was not a single dog in Paris, so I figured there'd have to be a few in Italy. Instead, all these ladies wearin' the same black dresses brought in a donkey. The musicians pretended to "hee-haw." Give us a break. I went to sleep. The musicians woke me up when they got excited and played real loud. I stood up and my tail hit Ed's sore knee again (oops). One black-dress lady sang extra loud 'cause she was in trouble. She drank something that made her sick. I was afraid she'd throw up in the garden—I get hell for doin' that at home. Suddenly she fell to her knees looking at the

190   Lloyd Burlingame

church. There was this real bright light from high up, and over the church door this picture of a mother with her baby came to life. Awesome. The huge doors opened up and a little boy started walking to the sick lady. She was cheering up when the lights started going out and the curtain came down. But everybody in our box was *crying*. Maybe they didn't see the lady onstage get happy, so I tried to cheer them up. I kissed everybody (except Ed, 'cause of his knee). I got 'em laughing real hard—but they kept on crying all the same.

The lights came on again and people started standing up, now that they could see where they were going. Doug came to see us, and My Partner and Aunt Barbara said his sets were "magnificent." He was pleased, but seemed mostly interested in meeting me. (That was cool.) Aunt Barbara was taking photos of me, and I got compliments on being so quiet during the performance.

Then there was the *third* opera—named *Gianni Schicchi* after some guy who was in it. The lights went out again—I think they do this on purpose. When the curtain went away this time, Doug had put a big old-fashioned bedroom where the church used to be. The Prof said it was "in the Italian Renaissance style" (whatever) and belonged to a rich old man who had just died. He lived in Firenze, a city with two names. (The other one is Florence.) This opera had more energy, and the only bad thing that happened was this Gianni guy cheated a bunch of the dead man's relatives out of a lot of money and buildings that they wanted to cheat each *other* out of. This made the relatives real mad so they growled three times. It was like the kennel at The Seeing Eye on a really bad day. Way cool! When all the cheated relatives left, they stole everything in the room they could.

Last week Doug wrote the Prof that he hoped his sets wouldn't fall down. That was a joke—but guess what? After the angry relatives left, the big room started to sink! On top of the room we saw this big roof-terrace with a pool. Beside it sat Gianni Schicchi, in his undershorts, his daughter, and her fiancé. He asked us to clap for him. I don't know why, but everybody did . . . they went totally nuts. I joined in and kissed everyone, and all yelled and laughed and it was real fun.

That guy Pooch-eenie, who wrote the operas, is dog-gone good.

Next week some guy named Orfeo makes a trip through someplace called Hades to some other place called Elysian Fields. (Where do they get these names?)

Hope all's super-good with you, the poodles, and your people.

Woofff!!!

Kid

P.S. Hickory, dear friend, much love to you and your Sunny Meadow Lane pals. The Prof

24 April 2007: E-mail from Hickory to Kemp

My Dear Kid,

Your note about the rain brought back some very unpleasant days, indeed. I'm sure our Dad has told you that I am a most reluctant companion in the wet. But I must confess it was largely an act on my part. I enjoy the rain; it's the puddles that put me off, and the concentration required to steer Magoo around them. None of that responsibility down here. During the April storms (we had flooding in Virginia), I loped onto the back green, just did the necessary, and returned for a most generous rub—the best part of rain. You mentioned the bathroom and the towel game. Himself isn't onto it. I've spent forever trying to convince him that when he resorts to the bathroom, I'm to be there too. At first, when I took my position upon the bathmat directly in front of his shower, he inevitably stepped out—wringing wet with a towel over his head—and stumbled over me. He has improved . . . but without fancy paw work I'd be stepped on.

About that rising at 6:00 a.m., I'm afraid it's required for the working class. Not so for us retirees: I rise between 8:00 and 9:00. After a good bit of bumping about Himself's bed frame, I am escorted with Cherie and Rusty to the back grounds. A sniffing or two and our business done, it's off to the road to retrieve the morning paper. Then breakfast and a few hours of basking on the deck.

I'm flooded with joy when you write about the opera—joy

because I no longer must endure the screeching onstage and the "Bravissimos!" off. I couldn't get a decent act's sleep for all that racket. I am sorry you're trammeled with it now, but you'll find that our Dad does his poor inadequate best to make the experience tolerable. (He seems pathologically unable to consider not going at all. Too bad Hugo can't accompany him instead; that cat would be right at home with the yowling.)

Here in Sunny Meadow, music is kinder. I am most soothingly serenaded by robins, sparrows, blue jays, Baltimore orioles, and other feathered friends, as I drift off to nap in the sun. Only the crows, with their "caw, *caw*, CAW-ing," bring back my unhappy memories of the Met. You have my total sympathy and admiration for putting up with all that indoor cawing.

I agree that Lincoln Center's fountain is a temptation. Watch and listen. But Kemp, boy, remember: a lifted leg in that flowing water is truly bad—very bad—form.

Operas aside, I can tell as your letters progress that you're the dog for Dad. You seem to be off to a super start. As for myself, I've trained the Staff to suit me. I drool on the floor; the people wipe it up. I groan and roll over; they rub my tummy. I bring them my toy; they play. Himself sits to read and I sit by his side. He rubs me (and if Mistress is not near) slips me a biscuit. Cheri can't get enough of me and Rusty can't figure her out. All the grass, the smells, flowers, tree blossoms, and leaves poking out of tree branches are amazing. Why, all that's missing are curbside treats! On our truck rides, my spot is right up next to—and I mean *next to*—Himself. We drive to the shopping center, the cleaners, and the bird food store—everywhere. Sometimes we just go off sightseeing. I'm in good shape: 65 pounds, nails clipped, tight tummy, tail wagging (big time), and snoring every night in the master bedroom. Is there anything better?

I wish you equal joy in New York . . . and many wonderful years and adventures with our Dad.
Coach

Hey Coach,

Thanx lots for rooting for me. The Prof and me have been partnering for almost six months. I know he knows I'm a pro . . . but when I'm working he thinks I'm too friendly with my fellow canines. But I do work real hard to stay on the job when passing possible furry friends. It seems so rude to push on without a *little* sniff of greeting. How are you and Cheri and Rusty getting on? I guess you've been hanging out with them for six and a half months now. Mistress told the Prof that you're zoomin' around your big lawn like a pup. I do pretty well scampering here in the apartment, but I need a lot more zoom-room to practice my rodeo skills.

We were glad to hear that Himself and Mistress will have a new computer setup, so we can write easier and quicker. I hope it's not as much trouble as Magoo's new computer mess. We even had to get help from Stan. (He's our assistant super and computer whiz. Was he here when you were?) The Prof was trying to learn the new "selecting, downloading, and extracting techniques" he needed to get digital talking books from the Library of Congress. Geeze, did he swear! (Though it was sorta fun to see the air turn blue and smoke come out of his ears.)

My Partner took us over to NYU—to the opening of the "graduating student exhibition of the Tisch School of the Arts Design Department." Four hundred guests! Mostly show business professionals who came to meet the kids and see their work. When the Prof was in charge, he put on *26* of these. (We sure lucked out, Coach. One's enough for me—but the Prof sure enjoyed it. He looked like the grandfather in my puppy family when all the kids came for Christmas.) Everybody liked me—but I did mess up once. Magoo was talking for a long time to a big designer who used to be his student. I sat patiently by a fancy lettuce-green silk costume hanging on this thing shaped like a lady without a head. I was so bored, I started getting hungry. This real yummy-looking silk tassel was hanging down right by my nose, so I started to chew it. I was just about to swallow when the costume designer snatched it out of my mouth! I thought it was a spare—she had six more. I was already in the doghouse 'cause I got caught eating all the cats' food that morning, so I thought I was *really* gonna be in trouble. But the Prof was having fun, so he didn't mind much. I met lots and lots of new best friends and got high marks for behaving. I only leapt up to kiss people about twelve times in four hours.

Our Dad sends much love to all of you. Me, too—happy spring!

Kid Kemp—Lab about town

25 May 2007: E-mail from Hickory to the Old Prof

Dear Dad,

Where should I start? My digestive tract had been in fine order . . . until it wasn't. Perhaps the trouble started with my eating a few too-casually-placed peppermints. Next I ingested some thinly sliced prosciutto, snatched off the preparation table right under Mistress's nose. (I'd have enjoyed it more without the butcher paper that accompanied it—and perhaps caused the problem.) I gagged a bit in the ensuing tug-of-war before giving up considerable paper and a generous portion of prosciutto.

Mistress had me out of the house and in the garden in less time than you could say "Jack . . ." There I was with drool hanging down my face on the outside looking in. No help from Cheri and Rusty on the inside, either. She just wagged her tail and looked out; Rusty was looking for thumbs God hadn't given him so he could stick them in his ears and wag his paws at me. Ultimately time passed and Mistress let me in (with little welcome); I went to my place to crash for the night—-so I thought.

Morning came early, announced by a stomach rumbling to make women cry and strong men weep. Thankfully, it also woke the sleeping Staff. I was rushed outdoors—and none too soon. Once the barfing began there was no holding back. Even after bringing up the entire smorgasbord, I continued with dry heaving. When there was no more to give but strain and groans . . . I gave strain and groans. When it was all over—seemingly hours later—I was thankful for a garden-hose spraying required for admittance just to the garage. Himself said if I hadn't started to come around soon, we'd have been off to the vet's.

Things are back to normal, but now considerably more attention is paid to where I am in relation to bits of edibles. They shouldn't worry: I'm off the peppermints; they don't mix well with the meat course. Warn Kemp about that—or buy a garden hose.

My best licks, wags, and head-butts to all.

I am,

Hickory

28 May 2007: E-mail from the Old Prof to Hickory

Dear Hickory,

I was profoundly distressed and, later, greatly relieved to learn of your unfortunate experiment—mixing the mint with the meat—and its eventual happy outcome (so to speak). I sympathize with your ordeal and am delighted you're back to your old self—hungry, but wiser.

Let me remind you of a little preview of this peppermint adventure that occurred in our third week of training, almost nine years ago: Jeff had put us through our paces in downtown Morristown by going to a supermarket, a bank, and a department store. We concluded at a coffee shop, where we would have a chance to rest and to see how you did in a public eatery, as opposed to the school dining room. We were just getting seated at a table when you made a sudden mighty downward lunge. New at partnering, I didn't react until hearing Jeff bark, "He's got something. Get it out of his mouth!" I knelt down quickly, your leash in my left hand, my right tentatively exploring your tooth-filled mouth. I looked up at Jeff and shook my head, signaling I couldn't find anything. Jeff commanded, "Reach for his tail!" I thought, "What's he talking about? I've only got two hands; one in your mouth and the other on the leash. How in the world can I reach for your tail?"

"How?" I barked.

Lloyd Burlingame

"Not *out*side," he snapped, "reach *in*side toward his tail!"

"Aha," I thought, reaching deep into your maw without success.

"Deeper!"

I did as Jeff commanded . . . and way down, deep in your gullet, found a slimed disc-like object, held it up, and asked Jeff to identify it. He laughed: "It's a big peppermint patty, wrapped in cellophane."

I learned about being brave, "going for your tail" when necessary, and being wary of what you indiscriminately scarf down. Now dear old friend, you've gotten not only your peppermint and prosciutto, but also your comeuppance. What went around came around—and then back up. I'm glad your Staff has learned a lesson too. They will be more vigilantly monitoring what's available to snatch.

Aunt Barbara, Kemp, and I are happy to have a date set to visit you in a few months . . . I promise not to try to lure you back into harness. Rest assured, Dear Pal, your staying at your not-so-new home is a done deal.

Hugs and tummy pats,

The Old Tail-Reacher

9 July 2007: E-mail from Hickory to Kemp

Help, Kid!

I'm being stripped, I say stripped naked down here! Thank God it's not the dead of winter or I'd nearly freeze, what with these people wanting me bald.

So what if a bit of hair clouds my space when I find it necessary to rearrange my skin with a shake or two. I thought the situation had resolved itself when Himself bought a new vacuum cleaner. He runs the cursed thing every day, usually when I'm trying to nap. It must work because he gets a container-full of my hair each time. I think all went awry for me when I rubbed myself against Mistress as she and Himself were leaving for an evening out. She was wearing a black pants suit. In my opinion, you'd have had to look very hard to see the new hair that decorated her trouser legs. Nothing warranted the words I heard. In fifteen minutes they were pristine and she was on her way again. *I* thought the hair enhanced her outfit. It was mine, after all.

. . . Which leads to today's attack. The instrument of torture arrived in the post: the "FURminator." I should have expected it when I saw the advertisement on a turned-down page in a catalogue. It's a mean-looking, black, molded handle attached to a yellow crosspiece at the top. Bolted to that is a piece of fine-toothed, sharpened stainless steel ... the blade is so dangerous that it comes with a protective shield.

Mistress couldn't wait to get me outside to have a go. Holding my collar in a death grip with one hand, she wielded the FURminator on my coat with the other. Glory to God, I couldn't get away from her! I twisted. I tried to roll. I gagged, I backed up, I hopped about. I rolled my head, my eyes, and my tongue. I drooled quarts. She *would* not give up. She and that machine stole what must surely have been a pound of prime hair. I don't think that's the end of it either. As I write, the FURminator sits on the counter in the wet room—not in a drawer or stored away, but right handy to her reach. I bring this to your attention as a warning: Check the mail box for catalogues. Eat any with a cousin or cat on the front, and take a bite out of the postman who delivers them.

(This brutal shearing did yield one benefit: Mistress rewarded my eventual graceful submission with ice cream. Usually they only share that on special occasions.)

Give a good lick or two, and my best woof, to all.

Coach

Kemp sights his first mallards at a lake outside Vienna, Austria, and is immediately prepared for action

CHAPTER THIRTEEN

Reunion and Adventure in the Two Viennas

July – November 2007

11 July 2007: E-mail from Kemp to Hickory

Hey, Coach,

That was some scary story. But cool that you scored ice cream. (It's a good thing Dad can't *see* my shedding hairs. Do you think he knows about that machine? I don't want him to be around me with sharp tools.)

Remember Eva, the cleaning lady who didn't do much? She's gone and now we have Beautiful-Isabella-from-Cracow. She's real nice to me, but she spends too much time with the cats. I think she likes them as much as she likes me! When she hangs out with those two, I get 'em to move along with a couple of nudges and a low-growled "No loitering." After living with them all these years, you'd think the Prof would know better, but he seems to like them a lot—that's another thing about him I don't get. Sometimes they're OK—but they shed *so* bad. And Hugo's ho*wwwwwww*ling is *aw*ful. The other day Clementine ruined my nap with a real loud noise. She was sleeping on the Time-Warmer cable box . . . and somehow the stupid cat fell down behind the bookcase and dragged the box—and all the cables—after her. When Magoo finally figured out what crashed, he dashed to the rescue. (Hugo ran the other way.) Clemmie was wearing the cable box on her back and whining. We're lucky she didn't hurt herself and make us miss the evening news. Today she was up on the Time-Warmer again . . . stupid cat.

Guess what! The Prof and Aunt Barbara are talking about going to the Austria Vienna again. Turns out that *Wiener Staatsoper* is in a *place* named Wien, where they first made Wieners. (Better yet, they still do.) We'll be over there for ten days in October. And guess what again—*NO* opera for me!! While the Prof and Aunt Barbara listen to the barking tenors, I go to Frau Susie's for a play date with her sausage doggie, Lumpi.

There's a lot of talk about me riding in the "bulkhead" on Austrian Airlines. The Prof will ship my food, bones, and Wee-Wee Pads to the hotel over there, so it'll be homey. Do you think it'll be much like your Vienna, Coach? I did hear that it takes longer to fly there than it does to Washington. And I have to get a new sign over there. In German, "Do Not Pet Me/ I am Working," is, "*Streicheln mich, bitte nicht/ich bin im Dienst.*" "*Im Dienst*" means "in service." That sounds a little too much like the *Upstairs, Downstairs* Himself wrote about—with me Downstairs. But they really do welcome dogs in restaurants, and I want to see the Café Landtmann on the Ringstrasse— the Prof's favorite. The dogs of senators and actresses from the Burgtheater trot around the dining room and ask, "How are the green noodles today?" I want the wieners.

So we'll be in two Viennas in the fall—yours, in late September, then the other one three weeks later. I'll take notes and

Lloyd Burlingame

write you after Austria Vienna. I can't *wait* to see you on Sunny Meadow Lane.

Time to *im Dienst*. Gotta take the Prof to the gym. He chickened out on Tuesday 'cause the "real-feel" temperature was over one hundred. It's lots cooler today, so we leave soon.

I send you tail-wagging congratulations on your *Eiskrem* reward.

Wuufs and licks,

Kemp, der Wunderhund

P.S.: Dad sends much love.

29 September 2007: E-mail from Kemp to Hickory

Hey, Coach!

Saturday's visit with you and the Staff was awesome! I had so much fun, and Dad was *so* happy to see you again.

Before we drove to Vienna on Saturday, the Prof, Uncle Michael, and me walked down Brookville Road in Chevy Chase, from Aunt Susie and Uncle Eddie's house to the Brookville Market to get breakfast stuff. This five-year-old boy and his father walked toward us. For a while the kid stared at me. Then he piped up, "Daddy, why does that dog have a handle?" (Coach, did *you* ever think of a harness as a handle?) The father explained how it connects us guide dogs to our partners. It's cool that kids are curious about us and our people, and that their parents explain how we see for our partners.

When we finally got to Sunny Meadow Lane after lunch, I was real keyed up from waiting to see you again. When I did catch sight of you and Himself standing there in the middle of your big fenced-in lawn, my heart beat faster. You looked so happy and at home. I have lots more to learn from you, and maybe when I do learn it all, I can retire to a place like yours. It was really something, seeing you with no harness or leash, roaming free in your own meadow-y park.

Was I surprised when the Prof took off *my* harness and leash. I wasn't even thinking when I flew off that high porch. I loved my long dash back and forth—and leaping back onto the porch, ~~skidding~~ in on all four paws! That was funny when Himself yelled, "Faster than a speeding Labrador!" You sure cheered me on with those tail wags! I never had so much fun!

Rusty and Cherie are a kick, too—you really like her, don't you? And you sure keep a good watch on Mistress . . . especially when she goes into the kitchen. I think I like sports a lot more than you, but I do like to eat, too.

Oh, that's some bed you've got! The Prof says it's "a magnificent suede ottoman." I just sleep in an old wicker oval bed like the one you used to have in New York. I hope your new one gave him some ideas. (I wonder if it would fit in our apartment?)

Now I'm back in the Big Apple and spreading your good news to canine pals. Ruby—your "golden retriever Carole Lombard"—was glad to hear you're living it up Down South. When people ask our Dad how you're doing, he shows them that picture of you sailing through the air to the mailbox, only one foot on the ground. He calls you "The Flying Labrador" and says, "I hope to commission an opera with Hickory as hero, which should rival *Der Fliegende Holländer*. Though it must have more laughs." Then he laughed. (I don't get it.)

So, Best-Coach-*Ever*, thanx a million for an awesome afternoon. I know the Prof is so glad you're happy and he thinks the world of your Staff. I gave your good news to Aunt Barbara, Uncle Charlie, and Uncle Sal. They all send their best love to you and your whole family on Sunny Meadow Lane. It's totally right that "Hickory Sunshine" retires to there!

A great hug from our Dad and many licks on both your handsome ears from me,

Kid

13 October 2007: E-mail from Hickory to Kemp

My Dear Kid,

What an absolute pleasure to receive you here on the estate. I apologize for not previously advising our Dad that, thanks to my surrounding fence, you would be free to roam at will. I do so take it for granted these days. But he quickly appreciated the situation and happily acted on it. (Our alma mater graduates only the exceptionally well trained and most capable bipeds.) It was a joy to see you gamboling about the grounds.

I was delighted to learn that you enjoyed the visit and my friends. You certainly put a spark in the crowd. The Staff here is used to my being rather laid-back and had no appreciation of what sixty pounds of bounding Lab could do. Your astounding leaps off the top step were a revelation to all. Cheri was very much impressed.

About the bed, you really should have a word with the Prof. Wicker is out; lavish and overstuffed suede are in. Of course, I insisted on the king-size but even if you can only wangle a queen, you deserve it.

The Staff has picked up the photos of our time together and will post them tomorrow, with two copies to Aunt Barbara. Two of them feature our Dad (one with me and one alone in profile). I must say it's very difficult for me to look upon them and not choke up. My favorite is the one with you on the right, me on the left, and our Mutual Friend kneeling in the center. Controlling emotions is difficult when thinking of beautiful memories.

I trust your trip to "Austria Vienna" will be one you'll remember for all the right reasons. I'm pleased that you're going in my stead. (A word of caution: don't drink before the flight.)

Bone voyage!

Coach

19 October 2007: E-mail from Himself to the Old Prof

Dear Old Prof,

Lolly and I are celebrating Hickory's one-year anniversary with us! When we left you in New York a year ago, Hickory in the back of the car, you asked me to make a promise: If Hickory's living with us did not work out, I would return him to you. I knew in my heart that would never happen, but I reassured you, sensing your deep love for our boy and your pain at being parted from him. Well, Professor Magoo, that's one promise I did not need to honor, and we bless the day you shared Hickory with us.

We are all God's creations and to honor him is to honor all that He created. I believe that each has his role in life, but over time that role does change. Each of us is at one time the student, later the practitioner, later the teacher, and later still, the sage. So it is with all God's creatures.

Hickory makes me even surer of that belief. And he brings another dimension to his purpose: He brings people together through the power of innocence, forgiveness, loyalty, and love. And he does it by example. If only man could be so noble. Thank you for our dear four-legged friend and teacher, Hickory.

Jay and Lolly

31 October 2007: E-mail from Kemp to Hickory

Dear Coach,

Wuuff! We're back from Austria.

My Partner and Aunt Barbara sure put a lot into researching our trip—they really know how to worry a bone. There were lots of E-mails to and from Austrian Airlines, opera tickets reserved, and rooms booked in a little, friendly hotel (in what's called the "Seventh District"). The Prof got in touch with friends from when he lived in Wien, way back before you were born. (I finally figured it out—Wien and Vienna are the same place. Who knew?) He set up reunions with Frau Susie Riedl (I already told you that), Mike and Regina Busboom in Vienna (he's a good friend of the Prof's, an American who partners with a beautiful guide dog named Arla), and Linde and Raimund Brodner, who live outside the city, in a lovely place named Laxenburg.

They all took good care of me. Mike said he'd get my Eukanuba kibbles and, like I said, Frau Susie agreed to doggie-sit. The worst part was getting all these forms I needed to get into Austria. Lots of people helped. First I had a rabies shot (ugh) and Dr. Lucas and Dr. Kuhlmann examined me. He had this official stamp for the main form. Then all these forms went to JFK airport for *another* stamping.

Finally we packed my new Nylabone, brush, comb, diet bone treats, water bowl, and the new German sign. On 16 October I got a nice long walk in the early morning, before setting off—but not much to eat and drink. We left for JFK in the early afternoon, and got just the right seats on the plane (bulkhead, three seats across—the middle one was mine so I'd have room on the floor with my pals on each side). The airlines people were real nice to us. I was ready for a serious nap, so I made myself at home. Our flight attendant, Brigitte, gave me an apple-green blanket with a tomato-soup red border for my very own. I went into screen-saver mode and pretty much slept across the Atlantic. (The night was a lot shorter than we have in New York.)

Our new home was called the Savoy Hotel, on Lindengasse. ("Gasse" doesn't mean what you think—it's like a lane or alley.) The staff was real welcoming. But the Prof had a problem . . . then it got fixed. . . then it got unfixed. The tiny elevator had no raised buttons, so to help out our Dad, the hotel people put little raised rubber dots over the numbers for our floor and the lobby. That worked—but overnight the cleaning people took away the dots. So two desk clerks made a sign in German and English: "Do not remove 'buttons.' They are needed for a blind guest." That worked perfect.

Mike had delivered my food, and bowls for water and kibbles. At last I got breakfast! Then I went out to park for the first time on a cobblestone street. My Partner and Aunt Barbara said they were "trotting out their 'Baby Deutsch.'"

We set out to explore our neighborhood, then there was a lot of getting settled, then in the afternoon we visited the Prof's friend Frau Susie Riedl. She lives in a big apartment on Elisabethstrasse, near the opera house on the Ringstrasse. ("Strasse" means "street"—that's why there are so many of 'em.) I met Lumpi, and she showed me around the totally dog-friendly apartment. Frau Susie took to me, and I sure liked her and Lumpi.

That morning was sunny and bright, the air crisp and cool . . . and that was the last good weather for the whole trip. This was *supposed* to be the perfect time of year to visit Wien, but the next nine days were cold and windy—and sometimes it rained. I didn't mind much, since all us Labs thrive on wintry weather.

My Partner took Aunt Barbara and me to his favorite spots in the Kaiserstadt, Imperial City—like Karlskirche (Saint Charles' Church). Barbara went up in an elevator to look at the view and found a sign that said, "Schreien ist uncool" and "Screaming is uncool." Meanwhile, "Der Herr" Prof took me outside to a small patch of deep green grass. A nice Viennese man called this a "wiese" (a meadow). It was all grander than my usual park place. We walked the whole three miles around the Ringstrasse. That was lots of fun, but Magoo got us lost towards the end.

Things are different from New York: The city isn't laid out in a grid; the corners are wide arcs, and curbs are usually only about two inches high. This isn't easy for those of us trained in Morristown and now working in Manhattan for almost a year. Oh, and you know how in New York, they don't let bikes on the sidewalks? In Vienna, the sidewalks have bike lanes! The sidewalks are wider than ours, but the bikers speed down them like mad. We steer way clear of those lanes for dear life. The cyclists don't much care about the safety of lost tourists.

I was glad to see other dogs, but there weren't nearly as many as in New York. There *are* lots of signs curbing and putting a damper on dog behavior. Food stores don't allow us in, but all restaurants do. (Huh?) I was made really welcome at the Karlskirche, Stefansdom (Saint Stephan's Cathedral), and the Augustinerkirche (Church of the Augustine Friars). But not in Mariatreue (Faithful Saint Mary), Saint Michael's, and Saint Peter's. As a surly church worker tossed us out, My Partner asked in German, "God doesn't love dogs?" Answer: Guess not at Saint Peter's.

We were only turned down by two taxis. One driver was afraid I'd leave hair on his seat. The other said he was a Muslim, then added real quick that he was allergic to dogs. The Prof said he thought just one of those excuses was plenty.

Aunt Barbara was surprised to see no other dog-and-man team in all of Vienna—except our friend Mike Busboom and his new doggie partner, the beautiful Arla. We visited Mike and his wife, Regina, several times, in their big apartment. They need a big one, 'cause they have three daughters (twelve, fourteen, and sixteen), *and* three dogs: Arla (she's a super-frisky yellow Lab from San Rafael, California), a puppy named Akira, and a poodle, Fluffy. Arla and I raced around the apartment and circled the big round table while the bipeds drank coffee. My Partner called us the "Mariatreue Rodeo," because of that stupid church across the street. (The Prof says it's a "truly beautiful example of baroque architecture," but he wouldn't go in when they wouldn't let me.)

On one of the cold and rainy days, Aunt Barbara, the Prof, and I took a tram. (That's like a train.) People with disabilities get priority seating here, so I had plenty of room and got to look out the window. Mostly the inner city is beautiful, but some of the suburbs are kinda dull and dreary. We went to the huge Zentralfriedhof (Central Cemetery) to honor a lot of people who wrote all those operas we have to listen to. There were Beethoven and Schubert and Brahms and Gluck and Schoenberg and Johann Strauss . . . Jr. (As if "Sr." wasn't enough.) Magoo got us kinda lost, but finally we found the "sacred grove" and put our flowers on the graves of "the immortal composers." (Does "immortal" mean "boring," Coach?) There were some real tempting grass borders by the graves. But the Prof held me back. He actually hissed, "Don't you dare pee on Schubert's grave!" (Why would I park on Schubert? He put a *dog* in one of his songs.) A few days later we went to *another* cemetery—a long tram ride in the other direction—just to put a pot of heather on Gustav Mahler's grave. (Whatever.)

We were getting to know the old inner city pretty well, and we walked a lot on the Graben, Kohlmarkt, and Kärntner Strasse—all for pedestrians only. Aunt Barbara and My Partner did Christmas shopping at some of the terrific stores. (Coach, not *one* pet store in the whole historic first district.) We went to museums, *more* churches, the Staatsoper, and Musikvereinsaal. The city is full of statues—no Buddy or Fala—all these saints, emperors, composers, and generals. Near Frau Susie's are, says the Prof, "two imposing statues of a pair of literary geniuses, Schiller and Goethe." They keep staring at each other from across the ring . . . and they watch while we park in Schiller Park.

Aunt Barbara took photos of many signs around the city that forbid doggie activities. It was hard to understand why many pedestrians scowled at me and My Partner. Aunt Barbara noted this a lot. They just didn't get that we're a team and I'm his eyes. On the other paw, when we got inside and made friends, the Viennese were welcoming, helpful, and warm. Late in our trip we took the Busbooms and Arla to the Café Sacher in the old Sacher Hotel. (It's famous.) We met at lunchtime and the staff took really good care of us. We got a big round table with plenty of room underneath for Arla and me on the lush red carpet. We behaved like Labrador Angels. The people ate lots of *Sachertorte mit Schlag*. (That's chocolate cake with whipped cream.)

[Hickory, I just had to interrupt here: When three handsome, beaming waiters in tuxedos appeared with an elegant glass bowl of water for Arla and Kemp, I thought they might burst into song. The scene was so like a Viennese operetta. I swear, Kempy started thumping his tail in waltz time. Dad.]

Almost at the end of our visit, we went to the grounds of the Imperial Palace, the Hofburg. The big gates on the Ringstrasse (the Prof calls them "classical") led into a huge open space with huge statues of horses ridden by guys with long hair. It's called the "Heldenplatz" (Heroes Square). Aunt Barbara was amazed to see lots of tents, trucks, tanks—and soldiers with guns—in front of us. Our Dad wondered what in the world he had gotten us into. Aunt Barbara speaks good German, so she asked a policeman, who told her the next day was the Nationalfeiertag (National Day of Celebration). It's kinda like our Fourth of July and that's why they had all those soldiers and stuff. Our policeman was real friendly and excited about the holiday—he invited us to have our picture taken in a truck. The Prof was surprised, but he said yes. Wow, Coach—those trucks make your pickup in Sunny

Lloyd Burlingame

Meadow look like a *toy* truck! Somehow our Dad—even as old as he is—got himself up in one of the cabs. He saluted and I stood at attention on the cobblestones for picture taking. He reminded us he'd been in the US Army fifty (!) years ago. Now he looked like he was serving in the Austrian armed forces. It was all goofy. Magoo and Aunt Barbara loved it.

Okay, now this is *reallllllly* cool—the best part of my trip. We three took a streetcar halfway to Laxenburg to have lunch with those other friends I told you about—Raimund and Linde Brodner. The Prof says she's "a talented artist, intelligent teacher, and gracious hostess." We all enjoyed each other a lot. They said it was "sehr gemütlich," which means something like "warm and cozy." I got a lot of attention and felt most "zu Hause" (at home) under their dining table.

The day was (no surprise!) grey and misty. After lunch, Linde led us into this big hunting park. The people talked about history stuff that maybe you know, Coach: The park used to be part of a favorite "Imperial Hunting Palace" of an Empress named Maria Theresa. The palace had a flat roof where her daughter Marie Antoinette played with her brothers and sisters. We walked for about an hour through the mist. There were lovely groves of real old trees, wide-open meadows, and what Aunt Barbara called "charming summerhouses." I had a great time sniffing around.

Now, here's what I wanted to tell you about: Near the end of our long loop, we came close to the edge of a big lake. I heard bird sounds—sorta like a "honk." I never heard it before, but it made my insides all excited. We got to the very edge of the lake . . . and there they were! Ducks—mallards! I forgot all about being a trained guide dog and went into point position. I knew just what to do when I got the command to retrieve a water fowl . . . but nobody asked. So I was thinking I'd have to show Magoo how it works. I imagined myself leaping into the water, swimming out to retrieve an *Ente* ("duck" in German). I was in great form and really focused on that bird, when Old Prof Spoilsport barked out the "leave it command" and yanked me hard back from the reeds at the edge of the lake. I traveled four thousand miles to see my first duck . . . and *that* was my reward.

So—except for that letdown—ducks and trucks were the best parts of my trip.

Before it was time to come home, My Partner and Aunt Barbara went to *another* opera. (This one's called *Der Rosenkavalier*. Now that I've been over there I understand where all these funny names come from. I haven't met anyone named "Orpheo" yet, though.) I got to romp again near the Ringstrasse with my new best friend, Frau Susie. Her friend Erna came with her doggie, Fanny. So I got one more new Viennese dog friend. Frau Susie always praised my behavior by loudly saying, "Kemp is *perfect!*" (I know it's kinda tacky for me to say so— but she did repeat it at least four times.)

After sad good-byes to our dear friends, we left for the Flughafen Wien (Vienna Airport) with a cheery driver, Willi. When we passed the Parliament building, the humans made some jokes I didn't get: Willi said the building looked like a Greek temple and was "the greatest theatre on the Ring." The Prof said that was impressive, 'cause "the Ringstrasse is well known for the world-famous Staatsoper and the Burgtheater. Then he said our US Capitol was a "kinderspielplatz" (playground) for food fights. Then they laughed.

We got through security and customs real fast—a smart and charming young guy from Austrian Airlines helped. When we were on the plane (in the bulkhead again), poor Dad yelped and said no one had even asked to see all those papers he worked so hard to get so I could travel. Then he groaned, but he laughed too. After we took off, I curled up with my blanket from Brigitte, went into "screen-saver" mode, and dreamt about Arla.

. . . And then we were home.

I guess that's it for this E-mail, Coach. It's kind of the end of a big chapter for all of us—almost exactly a year ago I met you in your Sunny Meadow, and then met our Dad at Seeing Eye. And now we're a team. You helped me move from Morristown to Manhattan . . . and now I've seen Vienna! I couldn't have done it without you, Coach—- and I hope this E-mail makes you feel like you were there too. That would have been *fun*!

Just think: I'll be only three years old in two weeks—and with my D.C. and Vienna flights, I've already traveled more than 9,000 miles! This was a grand *"Abenteuer"* (adventure) and I can hardly wait to find out what's coming next! *Viele liebe Grüsse* (many loving greetings) to you all. I want to visit *your* Vienna again soon!

Love,

Kemp

1 November 2007: E-mail from the Old Prof to Hickory

My Dear Old Friend,

Kempy's E-mail of yesterday was a rich accounting of our wanderings across The Pond. I want you to know that visiting the two Viennas has been a memorable experience for me, too. But the greatest of all my adventures has been partnering with you and Kemp. You were with us, dear boy, in "Austria Vienna." Kemp and I could never have made that trip if *you* hadn't taught me how to make it during *our* years together.

You will remember how sad I was to have to cancel our flight to Vienna in October of 2001. I really thought I would find that we could live, at least half of the year, in that city so dear to my heart. This trip with Kemp proved bittersweet when I realized that wonderful city is not user-friendly for an old geezer partnering with a guide dog—it is not a place that we could call home. That was bitter, but sweetness followed when it became totally clear that New York is the perfect place for us to live. Gone are such lingering feelings as, "If only I could have retired to my dream city, Vienna . . ." I was thrilled when we returned home, where Seeing Eye dogs and their partners are totally mainstreamed and not greeted with scowls but—Barbara tells me—-with huge smiles.

Ten years ago, the Bad Samaritan incident convinced me that my hoped-for freedom of movement via the long white cane was a failure. My spirits plummeted when I considered the future: It seemed my mobility would be confined to my apartment and the immediate neighborhood. There would be no traveling to theatres, museums, and concert halls—much less to family in Connecticut and Washington. Certainly returning to Europe was totally out of the question.

Long pondering of this apparently insolvable problem led me finally to imagine that maybe—just maybe—a Seeing Eye dog might release me from so narrowly constricted a world. But I thought of this option without much hope or conviction; it was a "darkest before the dawn" time. I was little prepared for the wonderful new day that did dawn when, at The Seeing Eye, Tom quietly announced, "His name is Hickory" . . . and you, beloved friend, entered my life to turn black midnight into brilliant high noon. I could say that, in some unfathomable way since losing almost all my sight, I have never been happier in all my born days. A year ago, again at The Seeing Eye, Dave declared, "His name is Kemp" . . . and another bright day dawned.

When I look back on all of the traveling you and I did together, Hickory—and now that Kemp and I have flown to Europe together—I can but shake my head in happy amazement. You guys have been my guides and close companions; truly, "my cup runneth over." What you have done, Hickory, and what Kempy is doing, certainly answer my long-ago despairing question: "Can a Seeing Eye guide be the answer to my mobility challenges?" You *are* that answer, and much, much more.

I have been twice blessed by two most wonderful dogs. I understand bonding now, and I know that Pete Lang is right: at the heart of the matter is love. When I began these tales with you two, a human friend asked, "What is it?" I replied, "A love story." Our life together has been that, indeed.

THE END

Lloyd Burlingame

*An emotional moment when Hickory, Kemp and the Old Prof
are together in Vienna, Virginia*

Lloyd Burlingame

ACKNOWLEDGEMENTS

First and foremost I must express my eternal gratitude to The Seeing Eye in Morristown, New Jersey. Everyone there, from the President to local volunteers, is drawn to his or her vocation to serve, enriching immeasurably the lives of us visually challenged folks . The chief players are all part of the fabric of this book. I honor them all, but wish to single out a few 'saints' as concerns the dogs and this book in particular. Both Presidents, Ken Rosenthal and his successor James Kutsch have headed the school with sympathy, strength and dedication. Pete Lang, the legendary Director of Training, Doug Roberts, Director of Programs, and Judy Deuschle, Director of Student Services gave tremendous support to me and my dogs while in training and after when problems arose while working in New York City. They each have hearts as big as all outdoors. The actual instructors mentioned in the book are all superb but allow me to single out Jeff Mac Mullen, an inspired teacher who thinks 'dog' and is the model of a rigorous and supportive educator.

Rosemary Carroll, a talented, deeply committed and energetic Director of Development offered encouragement while at TSE, and now, retired from her post there, has been a huge booster of this book. Her excellent successor, Jean Thomas, has been equally enthusiastic and helpful. Both Jean and Rosemary read early versions of the ms and had valuable comments to help clarify and improve it. Teresa Davenport, now retired from TSE, has been a tower of strength and giver of great good energy to the project . Her encouragement and careful reading of the second version of this book is greatly appreciated. I owe special thanks to Dave Johnson who has admirably succeeded Doug Roberts and to Pauline Alexander, the big-hearted successor to Judy Deuschle. Chief Trainer, Walt Sutton has been generous of his time and expertise in answering questions of training needed for accuracy in the book.

Maryglenn McCombs' enthusiasm for this book, its canine protagonists and dogs in general has been an essential part of promoting this book with big-hearted generosity. Carol Gray has also contributed to 'the cause,' particularly in arranging a personal appearance of Kemp and his scribe at Manhattan's historic Cherry Lane Theatre.

Major supporters of The Seeing Eye are Lolly and Jay Burke, of Vienna , Virginia, who came into our lives by 'accident'. I thank a kindly providence for our seemingly 'chance' meeting. Later this turned into the best of friendships for me and, for Hickory in particular when they kindly and lovingly gave him a heaven-on-earth retirement home. It is Jay who acted so capably as Hickory's brilliant scribe and enabled Kemp and Hickory to write each other via e-mail!

There is an extra special category: Hickory and Kemp's 'aunts' and 'uncles'. Barbara Backer, a key player in the lives of the two dogs, came into my life as Hickory's friend. She has lavished love on both dogs over the years and is also a cherished friend of mine. An 'uncle' who has always been there for Hickory and Kemp is Charlie Cole, who is also a chief player in the narrative of the dogs' tales of Manhattan adventures. He too has shown loving devotion to both dogs and is my valued friend. Another 'uncle', my own most admirable brother Michael, has been a true friend of both dogs and is always welcomed by them since he is up for playing tug for long stretches of time. His fiancée, Lois MacDonald, has offered invaluable tips on the ways of Labs. 'Uncle' Michael and 'Aunt Barbara' have taken the majority of the photographs in the book. Our much beloved sister, Susie Coover, and her husband Ed, have been strong supporters of the whole adventure of training and living with guide dogs. Another dear friend in the 'aunt' category is Barbara Cokorinos, the matchless Administrative Director of the Design Department in NYU's Tisch School of the Arts. Among her thousand and one kindnesses to me was her dogged help in locating just the right new home in a dog-friendly

Manhattan building. She has always been there for me and for both dogs.

The apartment house on East Ninth St. has been and continues to be the best of all such dwelling places for both dogs and me. I am offered not only great assistance by my dogs but by members of the top notch building staff. Stan Salazar and Tony Grullon have been totally reliable helping solve all challenges offered me writing without sight with my 'talking word processor;' I owe what sanity I have left to them. James Cassidy is a prince of supers overseeing the maintaining of harmony in this canine filled building—a veritable peaceable kingdom...most of the time. Doorman extraordinaire Steve Elman, now retired, was a huge help getting me started bonding with Hickory and understanding what living and working with a dog in the big city entailed.

I salute Bob Keenan, an inspired teacher of computer techniques to the visually challenged. His patience and intuitive skills allowed me to make good friends with the new miracle of adaptive software used for the blind. His sense of humor lit up the most difficult learning sessions. Yayoi Tsuchitani and Piet Halberstadt have my true thanks for creative support, as does computer whiz, Christea Parent.

Another category might be called dear and close friends.

Agnes Beck, the distinguished librarian at the Andrew Heiskell Library for the Blind in Manhattan, has been a long-time and loyal friend. She has also read the very first draft of the book and made most insightful comments to move the writing process forward. The live-wire, straight shooting editor and publisher Pat MacKay has offered her long experience reading drafts of articles and books to help sharpen the focus on the core of the dogs' stories. She made me, the scribe/author, go way down deep to find the heart of the material and define it as a "love story." I thank her profusely for both tender and tough love.

In a class of her own in my life is my Braille teacher and close friend, Susan Niederman. It was she who, having patiently taught this old dog how to make friends with all those little raised dots, insisted I needed to improve my mobility situation. She was a true inspiration for me in the darkest days of struggling to cope with increasing sight loss.

Another saint, in this exalted category, is Janice Davis, whose splendid cover captures the spirit of the book exactly. Her work in bringing the book to publication is deeply appreciated. She is a distinguished alumna of 'my' design department at NYU and I take a avuncular pride in her accomplishment as an artist and now as an author.

Other close friends of many years, Stuart Vaughan and his wife, Anne, have been wonderfully supportive of the project. Anne has worked unstintingly to help improve the book. It was celebrated theatre director Stuart who suggested that the book would benefit from a preface written by a famous designer who could help the reader understand what sight loss would mean to a fellow artist.

Now, completely in a category of his own, in a box around his name comes a valentine of appreciation and affection to Tony Walton, a rare spirit and fabulously talented designer in the theatre and film. He has done me the greatest kindness and has brought forth the excellent introduction to the book. I am deeply in his debt.

In addition, in the spirit of "the last shall be first," comes the book's lavishly gifted line editor, Michele La Rue. She too is billed in a double box around her name! She has entered the world of thinking and feeling 'dog ' to bring Hickory and Kemp's thoughts and feelings to vivid life. The final version of this love story owes a great deal to her artistic sensibility and editorial expertise.

For Information about The Seeing Eye, please visit

www.seeingeye.org

Lloyd Burlingame

At home in Washington Square, Kemp and the Old Prof
Photo by Barbara Wertheim

ABOUT THE AUTHOR

Lloyd Burlingame, scenery, lighting and costume designer, educator, fine artist and author, designed his first summer stock set at age 12. At age 25 he designed his first Broadway musical (scenic and lighting design), Lionel Bart's *Lock Up Your Daughters,* an out of town flop. His first show Off Broadway, *Leave it to Jane,* a Jerome Kern musical (scenic design), was a hit and ran two plus years. His favorite Off Broadway production, *Moon on a Rainbow Shawl* (scenic design), was designed simultaneously with a season of plays for the Association of Producing Artists, brainchild of director/actor Ellis Rabb.

Burlingame designed scenery, lighting and costumes for five productions for APA. He then provided all three design functions on Broadway for *Philadelphia, Here I Come!* For producer David Merrick, he designed a total of thirteen plays on Broadway, as well as serving as chief scenic and lighting assistant on three major musicals for that same producer.

Mozart operas were the true love of his life, and he designed eight productions of that genius's works, the bulk of them for Maestro George Schick at the Manhattan School of Music's John Brownlee Opera Theatre. He also had the privilege of designing a combination of scenery, lights and/or costumes for major opera companies: new productions for divas Joan Sutherland in Boston, Leontyne Price in San Francisco, Beverly Sills, also in Boston and Martina Arroyo in Cincinnati.

Ten years into his New York career, opportunity knocked, offering the chance to redesign the NYU School of the Arts fledgling Design Department. With colleagues Oliver Smith and Fred Voelpel he created a school to nourish the individual talents of young designers by exposing them to a wide variety of design teachers -- all working professionals.

After more than twenty years of busily designing on Broadway, Off Broadway, regionally and in opera, he turned all the design skills he had learned into coping with the gradual loss of almost all of his vision. As his sight went 'down on dimmer', he turned to painting very large canvases and designing huge fabric collages, which had a major one man show at the Wadsworth Athaeneum in Hartford. It was 'touchable art' and the show was called "Once More with Feeling." Today three of these large fabric collages are on permanent display at the downtown Morristown, NJ, Student Center of The Seeing Eye, the guide dog school of which he, Hickory (his first guide dog) and Kemp (his present canine companion) are proud alumni

Burlingame continues to paint, doing so now with words. He has written two books, *Two Seeing Eye Dogs Take Manhattan! ...a love story* and his soon-to-be-released theatre memoir: *Sets, Lights and Lunacy: A Stage Designer's Adventures on Broadway and in Opera.* He has been the recipient of two Fulbright research grants for study abroad and has been awarded emeritus status as well as the "Distinguished Teaching Medal" by New York University. Alumni of the Design Department for Stage and Film from the 26 years Burlingame headed that school currently design nationally and internationally and have been recipients of major awards for design, including the Oscar, Tony and Emmy. He himself received the Robert L. B. Tobin Award for Sustained Excellence in Theatrical Design in 2012.

email: **lloyd@guidedogadventures.com**

Made in the USA
Charleston, SC
16 July 2012